The Beast Known as Terros

Dear Aunty Alison

Happy Birthday!

I hope you like my new book.

From
Haris

H. S. Harkan

Copyright © 2024 by – H. S. Harkan – All Rights Reserved.

It is not legal to reproduce, duplicate, or transmit any part of this document in either electronic means or printed format. Recording of this publication is strictly prohibited.

Contents

Prologue: Travellers from a World Yonder 6

Chapter 1: The Protector of the Jungle 24

Chapter 2: Space Pirates 35

Chapter 3: Cyborgs 50

Chapter 4: Stand-Off 59

Chapter 5: The Juggernaut 69

Chapter 6: A Fox Betrayal 82

Chapter 7: The Pirate Underling 89

Chapter 8: Worlds Above Worlds 93

Chapter 9: Shame and Glory 108

Chapter 10: A Hefty Target 115

Chapter 11: The Resistance 123

Chapter 12: A New Mission 143

Chapter 13: The Sniffer 159

Chapter 14: Bounty Hunter War 173

Chapter 15: The Mechanical Truth 193

Chapter 16: Rescue 204

Chapter 17: The Cogs of Disaster 217

Chapter 18: Convergence ... 225
Chapter 19: Construction ... 232
Chapter 20: Epidemic ... 251
Chapter 21: A Final Duel ... 272
Chapter 22: Sanctuary ... 283
Chapter 23: A Protoplasmic Endeavour ... 291
Epilogue: The Core ... 300

The Beast Known as Terros

12th July 18732

Dear Reader,

My time on Planet Guinthra was most… interesting, for lack of a better word. That is me being kind. In all honesty, my time on Guinthra was nothing less than torture, worse than my few weeks in the Federation Prison Colony. Terrifying creatures, malicious bounty hunters and maniacal robots populate the seemingly harmless landscape. And don't get me started on the hyper-intelligent penguins.

If you are seeing this message, know this. Do not go to Guinthra. Ever. From one human to another, trust me on this.

Yours,

Kaloro Eramund Secant V

Prologue: Travellers from a World Yonder

The trees of the emulsifying jungle rattled as large convoys drove across the muddy terrain. Branches were slapped to the side as metallic machinery ploughed through, their engines revving and disturbing the soothing chirps of nature. The harsh rain from above spat on the vehicles, washing the slick mud off the bonnets, while wipers were frantically trying to keep the windscreens clean.

The legion of cars and trucks was no greater than five in total, with one vehicle leading the charge whilst the others followed behind in single file. The one in front was big, with heavy, rugged wheels that made it tower above the others and it had a large exhaust pipe at the back where purple smoke was rushing out, bustling out of the car like factory fumes. The metal frame was barebones, a mix of different parts splatter-gunned together, held in piece by an array of nuts and bolts.

The cars that trailed behind all shared a similar rugged look, but that was where the similarities ended. Each was unique from the other, creating a spectrum of different colours and designs, including their engines, which all had different purrs – some quiet and mouse-like while others roared like thunder. When blurred together, the envoy of cars just created one loud crackle of sound that rumbled the ground and the surrounding foliage.

A few minutes later, the leading car was brought to a halt, and the ones behind braked suddenly. The leader's door opened and out jumped the driver, leaping onto the ground below. His brown and green clothes camouflaged him into the surrounding nature which would have made him be able to become invisible if not for his pale face that stood out. The man's hair was soon soaked by the rain and his boots became covered in thick mud. He trudged over to the back of his car and pulled open a flap.

"What seems to be the problem?" a soft voice came from the passenger seat of his vehicle. Out hopped a woman, looking of a similar age to the man.

"Something might have gotten stuck, Arnetta," the man in the green and brown said, his voice sunken and sombre.

"This place gives me the creeps," called a voice from another vehicle, which was a short and stubby racecar that had been haphazardly sprayed red and blue, but now had multiple chips in the paint and scratches throughout it.

"Once I fix this, we will be on our way," the leader said, wiping the blend of sweat and rain from his face. "Arnetta, pass me the wrench."

His wife, a woman with a tattered coat and ghostly pale skin, opened up a toolbox, pulling out the relevant piece of equipment. "Do you think it could be the fuel?" she asked, pointing at the purple crystal stuck into the engine, glowing dimly.

"I doubt it," her husband said. "This crystal should last us another day at least."

"Perhaps we got scammed by that crocodile at the outpost?"

"Oi boss!" shouted someone from two vehicles back, his voice loud and cheery. "What's the problem?"

The leader started fiddling around with the mechanics, twisting the odd screw and straightening out some tubes.

"How bad is it, Rett?" Arnetta asked, looking at the insides of the machine.

The leader, Rett, winced as a green liquid squirted out and onto his face. "I found the problem," he growled. "And it is worse than I thought. Go and call Rig. This will take him a few hours at least."

When the sun had set and the jungle was a dark and ominous field, the crew were sitting around a fire, trying to warm up. They were all soaked from the day's rain and covered in mud. Rig, a mechanic with a rustic prosthetic arm was fixing the engine. It appeared that a branch had gotten stuck inside it and had torn a few pipes. He had been working on fixing it all day and now into the night.

"You think the rumours are true?" a fat and round man said as he placed his stubby fingers over the fire to warm himself. "I 'eard that this jungle is full of mystical creatures – like man eating bats and two-headed trolls."

The Beast Known as Terros

"Don't believe that nonsense, Johnny," the leader said. "We have been stationed here for five hours and we have not seen any life apart from insects and snakes."

"Your funeral, Rett," Johnny chuckled heartily.

"But you raise a good point," Rett added. "This place could be dangerous, and it is our duty to get out of here as soon as possible."

"I say we ditch your car and keep driving," a stick-thin man said, wearing a leather jacket and a red balaclava. "We still have four cars and should have enough space for you and Arnetta."

"No," Rett said simply. "That vehicle has kept us alive on this planet for years now, built to survive the harsh deserts and the immense jungles. We would not be alive without it."

"It is falling apart," the man in the balaclava said. "It is a monster-truck, yet it got put out of action by a twig. A twig!" he laughed.

"I am not abandoning my car," Rett hissed.

"Maybe we should," Arnetta said soothingly. "I know that vehicle has a lot of sentimental value, but perhaps it is time we left it to the elements. It has become a hindrance these last few months." She gave her husband a soft look, that seemed to break through his rough exterior.

"Ugh," Rett came again. "If Rig has not finished by the morning, then we will abandon it," he said slowly. He then turned around. "Did you hear that Rig?"

There was no response, followed by some light rustling.

"Rig?" Rett asked again, a moment later.

The mechanic said nothing.

In fact, when Arnetta raised her lantern, the whole crew saw that Rig was missing, no longer under the car.

Some more rustling followed.

"He is probably urinating in the bushes," someone said. "Give him some peace."

The rustling got louder, echoing through the jungle.

"Sounds like a right big one," another laughed hysterically. "You okay Rig?" he called out. "You must'a drank too much," he chuckled.

Eerie silence followed.

"Something ain't right." Rett said, jumping onto his feet. "Pass the gun," he called out to one of his comrades.

"Boss, you overreacting a bit much?" someone asked.

"Just hand over the gun!" Rett snapped as he snatched the weapon away. He looked at the mechanical wonder in his hand, a plasma rifle, able to shoot rounds that could vaporise another being. "Stay by the fire. All of you," he said, glaring. "I will investigate." Rett ran off, into the shrubbery, and explored for danger, maintaining a firm grip of his weapon as he ducked under trees and pushed away at leaves. He took a glance and saw that there was no signs of Rig. His tools were still on the ground, surrounded by a multitude of different metal parts. Rett raised his weapon and gingerly stepped forward. "Rig?" he whispered.

A shaking of the trees occurred. Initially, Rett assumed this was just the wind. When it happened again, he almost jumped. "That you, Rig?" The man noticed a shadow bulge through the bushes. It could have just been a wild animal, but he knew better that to not assume the best. Standing his ground, the leader of the human group marched forward.

"Aargh!" came a shout, causing Rett to jump. The sound appeared to be coming from the campfire.

The Beast Known as Terros

"Oh no," Rett cried, realising that he should not have abandoned his crew. The man charged forward sprinting back to where he had just come from. "No, no, no," he was saying as he knew that he had taken away his people's main weapon. "Arnetta!" he called out.

The man's eyes widened as he saw something unexpected. Dark shadows were descending from the skies, swooping down and grabbing his men. They had large wings that spread out and impressive beaks that looked like they could bite through metal. They also had arms and legs – making them bipedal and wore uniform that was black and grey in colour. The flock of bird people were flying down and attacking his men, who were desperately trying to wade off the beasts with swords and arrows.

"Rett!" Arnetta shrieked as a creature grabbed her arms by its talons and levitated her off the ground. She frantically tried to shake it off, but the animal was persistent, cawing loudly and wailing out a shrill cry.

Without hesitation, Rett cocked his rifle and aimed at the bird, forcefully pulling the trigger as a red blast zoomed out and hit it. The man then leapt forward, to help his wife as she tumbled to the ground.

Arnetta pushed her hair out of her eyes and hugged her husband. "Thank you," she said.

"No time for that," Rett said, preparing the blaster once more and firing at another bird. "Everyone get to the cars!" he yelled as he started shooting the animals, one at a time, hoping to make a dent on their dozens of numbers.

Some of his men had pried themselves free, while others were being taken into the sky and flown off into the black night. Rett tried to save as many as he could, but his aim was not the best, and any bird he missed would have the getaway.

"No!" he growled as he missed yet again. "To the cars!" he bellowed out, firing at another bird.

"What about you?" Arnetta cried.

"I am going to save as many of my men as I can, dying if it comes to it," Rett said, taking a deep breath and shooting again.

"Rett?" Arnetta asked.

"Go," Rett said. "Take the group and drive as far away from here as possible. Keep driving until you find other humans like us. There has to be some out there." Rett paused. "Now go!" he demanded.

Arnetta slipped off into the darkness, a tear of hers trailing behind.

"No regrets," Rett whispered, firing again and again, taking out bird after bird. He quickly realised that the numbers seemed to be self-replacing. *Why are they after us?* he thought. His initial assumption was that they were going to be eaten, but that would not explain why they were being flown away. There had to be an ulterior motive.

"Stop resisting, human!" a bird squawked, landing next to Rett and resting the shimmering snout of a gun to the temple of his head. "Move and you die."

Thoughts raced through Rett's head. He needed to act fast if he did not want to end up abducted or dead. But before he could do anything, he felt a sharp sensation as an electric pulse rippled around his body, numbing all his muscles as he slumped to the ground. As he fell, he saw that a bird had shot him with some sort of electric rifle. It did not hurt, but it had immobilized him entirely and made him feel like mush.

A second later, a bird had picked him up off the ground.

"No!" Rett shouted, his toes tingling as he gained vertical distance from where he just was. He wanted to shake free but knew he could do nothing. Instead, all he could feel were the sharp talons gripping his skin tightly. He firmly believed that this was it, closing his eyes and accepting his fate.

"Pathetic human," the humanoid bird cawed as it flapped its great wings into a powerful thrust.

Rett then heard a faint roar. It appeared to be the rumble of a car, but the man knew the purrs of every single one of the vehicles in his crew. He had memorised every nook and cranny of each truck and car, and so knew that the noise was not one of his.

The roar came again, louder this time, followed by some heavy puffing and a faint clatter of metal.

"What?" Rett's captor shrieked as he witnessed a dark mass from within the jungle pounce out and defeat birds.

Rett was suddenly dropped as the bird holding him darted forwards, speeding towards the dark calamity. The human leader was unable to make out what this being was, hearing only muffles and loud grunts.

"RARRR!" bellowed out a sound that pained Rett's ears. As he thumped to the ground, he could vaguely see a hulking figure beat up each of the flying people one at a time. From the darkness he could make out large teeth, an immensely wide frame and a long, snake-like tail.

When laser-fire began, aimed at the newcomer, the being leapt to the side, faintly roaring as he ran around, picking off each and every one of the birds. He was barehanded and yet refused to pick up a weapon from the ground.

Despite the ferocity of this beast, it did not once kill a bird, let alone draw any blood, opting solely for heavy blows in an attempt to knock them out.

Rett noticed his own fingers begin to tingle. Sensation had returned to his body and he bolted upright, immediately picking up his plasma rifle. He held it and helped the beast take out the last few birds.

When they were all gone, he suddenly remembered Arnetta. He did not hear any engines start, so assumed that they had been unsuccessful in their escape.

Suddenly the large being stepped out of the shadows, revealing himself. His pale white fur was striking in its majesty, seeming to be almost royal in nature. He walked on two legs and stood slightly taller than Rett. The beast had a long white, bushy mane and the features of his face were feline, with sharp green eyes, a short snout and thin whiskers. He did not wear a shirt, revealing a dense array of muscles. The only garments he wore, were a pair of black trousers.

In the distance there was a faint crash and one of the being's ears twitched and it jumped forwards with immense speed and power, heading towards the vehicles.

Rett followed behind, hoping to catch some action. He saw that the birds were once more swooping down, attacking the cars and the people inside. However, in a matter of seconds, the mysterious beast had jumped from vehicle to vehicle and had tossed the animals to the side like they were paper. Rett was simply amazed at this extraordinary feat of power. When all the birds were down, the beast gave out a massive roar, causing the remaining conscious animals to fly off into the distance, scared to ever return again.

The strong being leapt off the car and in front of Rett.

"Thank you," the human leader said.

The beast gave him one look, before jumping back into the jungle, never to be seen again.

"What was that?" Arnetta asked, hobbling over to Rett.

The man's eyes widened when he saw the talon scratches on his wife's arms. "Are you okay?" he asked, checking for any blood.

"I am fine," Arnetta nodded. "Not so sure about the rest of the crew though."

Rett looked at the remainder of his people, in the dozens a few moments ago; now no more than a handful. "No," he mumbled with great sorrow. "How did I allow this to happen?"

"We have to keep going," Arnetta sighed. "We must find sanctuary."

"No," Rett said. "We will keep driving till we get to the human kingdom. Then we will get reinforcements and more weapons, before returning for our men and rescuing them. I am leaving *nobody* behind."

"They were probably eaten," one of the crew members said. "They will be long dead by now."

"That is where you are wrong," Rett snapped. "Those birds were not carnivores. They were very meticulous in capturing each of us, as if they did not want us to be in 'damaged condition.' When they tried to take me, they used a non-lethal canon, only causing paralysis. They are smuggling us for reasons unknown and I intend to get to the bottom of it."

"What about that lion-man?" someone else said. "What if he comes after us? We should hunt him before he kills us all in our sleep."

"He is our friend," Rett replied. "Not sure why, but he seems to have our back." The leader of the group paused. "Now then, let us finish our journey. Afterwards, we will rescue our friends, guns blazing."

Miraculously, after a few days of driving through the jungle, the cohort of human travellers had stumbled upon a lone building, no greater than four stories high, surrounded by large trees that wrapped around it. The structure was very much decrepit, with moss spluttering out of the walls, which was certainly unsurprising for a building in the jungle

Rett was enamoured by the sight of this and was filled with great joy. He hoped this was the sanctuary that him and his people so desperately desired. *There is still hope,* he thought, cautiously stepping out of his vehicle and holding his rifle firmly, anticipating the worst.

"Welcome!" a well-spoken voice boomed, that had enunciated every last consonant to perfection.

"A man?" Rett asked, his voice moderately elated. He had most certainly not expected to see another human – let alone one that was so well dressed, wearing a white formal suit and tie, with a black ponytail. Behind him were many more dressed just as impeccably.

"How was your journey, brave traveller?" the leading man asked.

"Forget about us. What is this place?"

"You made it to the human kingdom, here on Planet Guinthra. I take it you have not seen others of your kind in quite some time?"

"No," Rett smiled, putting his gun down. "We have been on the road for a few years now. There were rumours of a major human civilisation on this planet, but we thought they were just myth."

"Well, I guess those rumours are true," the well-dressed man said. "You have made it to the outskirts. Stay here for the night and tomorrow we will take you to the Megalopolis where you will meet the last sanctuary of men."

"What's going on?" Arnetta asked, walking over from her vehicle, rubbing her sleep-filled eyes. When she saw there were other humans, a great smile appeared on her face.

"We found the human kingdom!" Rett laughed, unable to contain his joy. "We finally found it!" He then turned to the man he was speaking to. "This is my wife, Arnetta."

"Pleasure to meet you, Madam," he said, bowing his head. "I awfully hope you enjoy your stay here."

"We shall not be staying long," Rett sighed, realising that the situation was too good to be true. "We needed somewhere to rest and re-equip weaponry, for most of my men were taken by strange bird creatures. We intend to rescue them."

"I am most sorry," the man in the suit said. "But your companions are as good as dead."

"What?" Arnetta asked.

"It brings me no joy to say this, but many travellers come here from the jungle. Every time people come, they are ambushed by those wicked Tizi birds. But when we located the nest, we discovered that all the captured humans were devoured and dead. There is no saving your friends."

Rett noticed a tear roll down Arnetta's face.

"I am terribly sorry to be the bearer of bad news."

"I understand," Rett finally said. "At least we made it here. The fallen would be happy for us."

"Exactly," the suited man said. "My name is Cornelius Dalrethian. I pray you all come in." A large smile grew onto his face like a sapling. "Leave your vehicles out here. They will be washed and serviced."

"Everyone!" Rett called out to his people. "It is safe to come out!"

As each traveller came out, they would smile one by one upon seeing another human, fully in flesh.

"I have one ask," Cornelius said quaintly. "I must request that you all hand in your weapons. It is a big demand, but it is for the safety of the other inhabitants of this sanctuary. They often get intimidated by newcomers.

"I understand," Rett said, handing over his plasma rifle. "Everyone, these are good people," he said to his men. "They will take us to a civilisation of humans, the one we have been searching for all this time. Hand in your weapons and they will accept us with open arms."

The travellers did not hesitate. Rett had done more than enough over the years to earn their trust.

"Thank you," Cornelius replied as his underlings collected all the weapons. "Now then, follow me inside. You will all be showered and dressed for the banquet tonight."

"Banquet?" Rett asked.

"Of course," Cornelius replied. "You must all be famished. We always hold parties for newcomers to help them settle in and meet the other inhabitants."

A great smile beamed on Rett's face. He only wished that the rest of his comrades had survived this long to see what he was now experiencing. So many of his friends and family had fallen during the years of voyaging. Now he had made it, but were their sacrifices worth it? He then pondered over what foods they would be given, for he had become so accustomed to tinned beans, dried fruit and more, that he had forgotten what flavour was like.

"Now then," Cornelius said. "Follow on behind me."

Rett nodded and gestured for his crew to follow, into the tower, where they would finally be reunited with their species. There was an aura of excitement as he could see how his crew were elated by the dozens of other humans; men and women all dressed smartly and standing in aisles for them to pass through.

As Rett entered the building, the dank marshes of the jungle could no longer be smelt, replaced with fine perfumes and squeaky-clean surfaces. Everything inside felt very old fashioned, with a large hall that had checked black and white marble tiles. There was an ornate fireplace that cackled calmly and the whole mansion was also filled with servants, wearing suits and offering trays of delicacies to the newcomers.

"Now then," Cornelius said. "Each of you will get ready and dressed for tonight's banquet. It shall be a night to remember. Then, each of you shall be assigned an ensuite bedroom for tonight. And then finally tomorrow we will go out to the inner city. The glorious Megalopolis"

"Are there enough rooms for that?" Rett asked.

"We have eighty-seven bedrooms and seventy-one bathrooms," Cornelius charmed. "I think we should have *more* than enough."

An hour later, Rett watched in awe as a tap was gushing out water. It was so clean and pure that it was transparent to look through. And then when he closed the tap, the water stopped coming. It was a luxury he had long forgotten. The man stood in a bathroom, laced with ornaments and shiny surfaces to the point where he could not believe that he was in a jungle just a few hours ago. The mansion that he had stumbled upon was so perfect in every way. Rett could not help himself but put his hands in the steaming hot water and leave them there as he revelled in the sensation.

The shower he had was one of pure bliss. As the water from the jet sprinkled over him, he felt great joy and was refreshed as dark mud and water descended from him. He scrubbed hard at all the hardened dirt and washed away any lice that had manifested on him. When all that was done, he took a razor and glided it across his face, removing his uneven and ingrown stubble.

When Rett put on a robe and stepped into his bedroom, a servant said, "My, you look wonderful, sir." The worker was holding a white shirt and a black tuxedo. "You are to wear this to the banquet tonight," he smiled.

Rett did as was asked, putting on a suit for the first time in years, and his first ever clean one that had not been passed down to him after being used by a multitude of different people of all sizes.

The banqueting hall was immense, with large red curtains and hundreds of small tables. Rett noticed a live orchestra was playing at the back, with shiny instruments, pumping out melodies of joy. There were many people seated at tables, much from his own crew. However, there were others that he did not recognise, so he assumed they were from different travelling groups who had also arrived at the tower that day.

The Beast Known as Terros

Rett almost laughed when he saw some of his gang wearing suits and having brushed hair. These were some of the most hardened smugglers and riders and now they were dressed like royal aristocrats.

One of them, Johnny, broke into hysterical laughter. "Oi everyone!" he called to his comrades. "Look at the boss! He looks like a right posh man now." The gang started laughing.

"Without your beard, you look like some boy, not our leader," someone chuckled.

Rett decided to play along with the amusements. "Fair play," he said, taking a seat. "Where is Arnetta? I have not seen her since we got in."

"We not seen Madam either," Johnny replied. "She is probably still getting ready."

"No, here she is," came another, pointing at the entrance.

Rett swivelled his head and almost fell backwards.

"You good, boss?" someone whispered to him. "You lookin' a bit pale."

"I..." Rett tried speaking as he looked at his wife in awe – now wearing a magnificent ball-gown that glimmered in colour.

"Are you okay, Rett?" Arnetta asked, walking over as her high heels hit the ground with a clack at each and every step. She walked cautiously, trying not to trip over.

"Of course," Rett said, smiling and standing up.

"You look official," she grinned.

"Forget about me," Rett said. "You are..."

"Everybody welcome!" Cornelius bellowed out from the stage. He held a microphone in his hand, echoing his voice throughout the hall. "Thank you for coming to the royal event. Before we bring out your food, I want all of you to put your hands on the table. It is part of a ritual we all do here."

Rett looked at Arnetta, confused. But they both decided to do it, placing their palms flat onto the tables.

A long line of servants then marched into the room, all in unison, with each arm and leg moving as if part of some hive mind.

"Good," Cornelius said. "Now take a minute to be grateful for being here. Be happy that your days of jungle food and survival are over. Relish in the fact that you will be transferred to a superior world and your sadness and despair will be shed."

As the man said this, a flap opened on the table and within the blink of an eye, a metal glove had crawled out and enveloped Rett's hands, pinning them to the surface. He frantically looked around and saw that this had happened to everyone. "What?" he cried, trying to yank his hands free from the metal machine, but it only seemed to grip him back tighter.

"What is happening, Rett?" Arnetta called out, also trying to break free.

"What is happening is that you *all* let your guard down," Cornelius cackled, walking over.

The servants then touched the faces of all the guests, one by one and their mouths became covered with metal, robotic gags, the likes of which Rett had never seen before.

"Stop this!" the leader of the gang cried out as the servants started covering the mouths of each of his friends, one by one. When they got to Arnetta, she aggressively shook her head side to side, trying to avoid them. Unfortunately, one servant yanked her hair back, holding her still, while another slapped the gag on. Once everyone was gagged, some sort of mechanism activated and they all suddenly went unconscious, slumping in their seats as their eyes closed.

"No!" Rett yelled, pulling at his hands more and more, as he saw the servants get close to him. He had a small pistol in his pocket that he had almost forgotten about – one that he had snuck in through the entrance. Somehow he wrenched one hand free, before pulling out his gun and blasting the servants around him. They fell back, their chests smoking.

Cornelius shouted, "What are you doing?" as he ran over.

Rett tried to pry is other hand free, but it was not budging. So, he was forced to use his left hand to shoot at Cornelius. He pressed the trigger multiple times until it would shoot no more, leaving Cornelius a mangled mess of flesh.

The man in the white suit did not stop walking. "That was unwise," he growled, a glow of light peeking through where his eye was. There was silver underneath his skin, pure metal.

"No!" Rett called out, as he watched the servants he had shot crawl back up. "You are not human. You are…"

"Machines," Cornelius said, his voice much more hoarse and creaky now, filled with coarse static. "Who knew that after escaping my birds that you would still walk into this trap?" the man laughed. "You humans are all so dumb."

Rett tried to act, but a large force hit him on the back of the head, instantly ending his consciousness.

Chapter 1: The Protector of the Jungle

The jungle of the planet Guinthra had a life of its own. Not in a sentient way, but rather as an entity – a connected mind some would describe it as. Legends from millennia ago claimed that there were great beings that duelled on Guinthra – sentinels of life and destruction. When the great Gehrios was slain in battle, it is said that his corpse formed the very jungle. Of course there was no scientific proof or evidence of this tale as it was seen solely as a myth and a child's bedtime story.

Within the jungle, there was a natural food chain where the weak would be eaten by the strong. Then the strong would fend the jungle from attackers, allowing the weak to renumerate themselves. Like clockwork, this would happen on repeat every day, over and over, maintaining a perfect equilibrium.

From behind a great tree emerged the beast known only as Terros – a Gedrul, which was a humanoid beast species native to Guinthra. He glanced at the great tyre tracks across the ground and growled ever so slightly. For reasons he was not willing to admit, he hated humans. And so, he felt a great distaste seeing them pass through his lands. When he had seen the Tizi tribe, a group of flying mercenaries attacking, he knew he had no choice but to act. As much as he hated mankind, there was nothing worse than having armed mercenaries flying through your home turf and potentially endangering your own kind.

One of the vehicles that the humans drove - a large truck with immense wheels and a rustic exterior, had been left amongst nature, appearing to be an eyesore within the landscape of peace and beauty.

Terros looked around for any other life before pulling the, already open, door of the truck. He slipped in and examined what was around. In a small compartment there was a small stuffed toy – a bear that was missing its menacing visage and was smiling for reasons unknown. He then fished out a flask from under a seat. Taking off the lid, he took one sniff from his snout and almost recoiled from the foul stench. It was an alcoholic substance, something the humans would often drink to make themselves feel high and mighty – not that they ever were. Terros poured the liquid out the window and into the soil below.

Snooping around further, the beast found a small metal locket. When he opened it, he saw that there was a photo, devoid of colours, printed poorly, but still visible. There was a man and a woman, a happy couple with the sun behind them. He recognised the man to be the one he had saved from the mercenaries. He seemed much happier in the photo. The woman had to be his wife or soulmate of some kind.

Terros put the locket down and continued searching for anything of interest. In the boot of the car, he found a leather jacket, not made from actual animal, evident from the texture, but still looked impressive. It was black in colour and had some human words written on the back. The beast tried to put it on, but his large arms would not fit through the narrow sleeves. So, he decided to gnaw the sleeves off before slipping the new jacket on. The animal gave himself a nod of approval as he looked at his reflection through the muddied wing-mirror.

Having found nothing else of interest, he decided to abandon the vehicle for he would get no benefit from the metal parts, so left it to nature. The beast knew that scavengers would have torn the vehicle apart by the end of the week – something he could most certainly guarantee.

Terros then strolled off, slipping back into the mighty jungle and becoming one with nature's hivemind once more. The trees were markers to him for he knew where each one was situated and so, if need be, could find his way home blindfolded, relying solely on the scents and textures of each plant.

The rustling vegetation had a quiet and musing tune, one that filled Terros with joy as he made his way back home, leaving the truck behind to gather cobwebs and moss.

Eventually he popped out of the bushes and appeared in an open, majestic enclave, filled with many small huts and a great waterfall, gushing benevolence in the distance and singing a melody over the world. The beast then walked over to the huts, adjusting his jacket as he did so.

"You missed dinner," an aged voice said that was almost entirely smooth but had hints of raspiness. The speaker, someone with white fur and a human physique having large green eyes and a smaller snout than Terros, while also having softer curves to her shape.

Terros looked at the old Gedrul, wearing a purple shawl.

"Ancient Nan cooked some fresh antelope and you were not here. I would have left you some but…"

Terros said nothing.

The elder then walked over to Terros, using her snout to sniff him for any wrongdoings. "What are you wearing? It smells human."

He nodded.

"You killed some humans and took their clothes?" the woman asked. "You would not do that, would you?"

The male beast once again said nothing.

"And why is your mane so messy?" she asked, pulling a twig out of his dense fur. "I cannot keep brushing it forever." She then noticed a small red cut on his arm. "What happened here?" she demanded.

Terros shook his head.

"Terros Tarthanian Mrilmus, I demand you to tell me what happened!" she snapped. "Did you get into a fight with some humans? Why were they passing through this part of the jungle? Unless you went to the forbidden tower? You *know* you are not allowed there."

The beast bit his tongue hard.

"I can't with you," the female Gedrul sighed. "This vow of silence needs to end soon, else you are going to give your Aunt Tirra a stroke." She then dusted off his leather jacket. "It does suit you though. Not suitable for someone of royal blood, but still rather fashionable. Now then, come inside. Let me see what food I can muster up for you."

Terros smiled and followed his Aunt Tirra inside.

The hut was relatively big, with walls made of logs. Inside there was a thin, red carpet that covered the floor, with some pots and pans in the corner.

"Terros!" a group of children called out in unison, small cubs with only a few sparse hairs and shorts stubby arms with legs that could not have been more impractical for hunting.

"What's he wearing, Mother?" one of them asked.

"Human clothes, from the looks of it," the old lady said. "Let your cousin rest," she added. "He has had quite the adventure today."

Terros smiled at the cubs before following his aunt into the kitchen. He was famished, having only eaten the odd mushroom while out on his adventure. Now he just wanted to eat something and then sleep once and for all.

"You know, if you are going to be chief someday, you need to start behaving," she said. "You cannot keep getting into these dumb adventures. Humans are a dangerous species and if you are not careful, you can end up tangled in their affairs – a series of endless civil wars, robotic uprisings, galactic conquests and more."

Terros knew his aunt was right. So, at night, while he lay restlessly in his bed, he could not stop thinking about the humans he had seen that day, and the mercenaries that came after them. Ever since 'The Great Purge', many years ago, he had not seen another human being. But on that day, for some reason, they seemed friendly, compared to their usual warmongering selves.

During the night, Terros woke up doused in a sweat. He took in a deep breath and then wondered what had awoken him. Taking a glance outside, he could see that the entire village had been lit up with lanterns and there were people, wearing night robes and staring at the black sky.

The beast got out of bed and slipped into some trousers. He then walked through the hallway to the exit.

"What's going on, Terros?" a small cub asked him, shaking the hem of his trousers.

The male Gedrul simply put a finger to his lips and headed outside. He did not want his aunt to be disturbed by all the commotion.

As soon as he went outside, he was hit by a bitter cold, causing him to regret not putting a gown on.

"Over here, Terros," an old female called out.

The beast did as was asked and stood next to her and his eyes followed where she was pointing in the sky. There, in the distance, was a small circle with a bright flash coming from it, like a star, but bigger.

"Any idea what it could be?" someone asked Terros.

The beast simply shrugged and kept on looking at the faraway object, now getting bigger by the second as its glare got brighter.

By now, the entire village had left their huts and were gathered to watch the strange commotion above, first hand. A light humming began which in turn filled everyone with hysteria.

"Do something, Terros," someone asked.

He turned to look at who had just spoken and then merely shrugged. There was nothing he could do.

Another person screamed, resulting in the following events; like a contagious disease, they all started screaming, wailing out in hysteria. Young cubs were clinging to Terros' legs as the beast stared up. He felt no fear; at least on his own behalf, for everyone else he did tremble a bit.

Looking at the object in detail, he realised what it was. From the large mass to the sound of its thrusters, it had to be a spacecraft.

"Are they coming to kill us?" someone cried.

"Will they abduct us and take us to a planet of slime?"

Terros looked around, wanting to console everyone. He was the last male alive, not including the small cubs. The females, elderly and cubs all relied on him to help, especially since he was supposed to be the chief. He opened his mouth to speak, to warn everyone that everything was going to be okay. When he realised that he could not make false promises, he stopped himself in his endeavours.

"We are doomed!" came a sob.

The beast knew he had to act. The village was relying on him - their sole protector, and so it would be insufficient to have no answers. He had read books on space, about the vast world of different planets and galaxies, about the Galactic Federation and the feared 78th Battalion. He thought that humans were the problem, but now it seemed like he was about to meet some aliens, for the shape of this craft was not of human design since it lacked the bland and sophisticated architecture of man. Had the humans alerted their location to others? Questions were pulsing through Terros' mind, and he was getting increasingly worried.

The Beast Known as Terros

The spaceship, a large galactic convoy that was made of nonuniform angles, with a large point at the front, had now blocked one of the two moons as it hovered high above, with four great thrusters on each corner keeping it upright. The vast amount of jet that it had was blowing downwards on the village, disturbing the peaceful grass and pushing everyone back.

"Terros!" Aunt Tirra roared out, running up to the young beast. "Invaders!" she called, trying to catch her breath.

A large flap of the ship folded open and out flew smaller spaceships, looking like transport crates due to their boxy appearance. Many more of these flew out, in the dozens, swarming like insects and soon there were enough to populate an entire kingdom.

The winds and the lights were getting more intense, as the once stout and solid trees were blustering in the wind, their leaves and branches being torn off. The crates were now getting close to the ground.

"Terros," Aunt Tirra came again. "You *must* leave. The females and I will protect the cubs but *you* need to find help. These are pirate ships - they will ransack this land and destroy everything. We need backup!"

Terros looked at her blankly, pondering what she had just said. He could not just abandon his people in their time of need.

"Run, Terros!" Tirra shouted, grabbing him by the shoulders. "You are the last adult male in this village. You must…"

Before she could finish, one of the boxes, the size of a skyscraper on its side, had landed. It opened up a second later, as ten trucks drove out of it, huge vehicles that had tyres that tore through the ground.

"The Pirate King claims this land!" someone shouted as a massive tanker ploughed through the village hall, flattening it instantly and blasting shards of wood everywhere.

"Go now!" Tirra shouted, pushing Terros back.

The beast turned to see that many more crates had landed and his once peaceful village was now populated with trucks, hovercrafts and much more. His initial idea was to fight back, to take them all on, but he knew that would be suicide. And so, he swallowed his pride and ran off into the jungle, hoping to find what he needed. For a second he thought about the human kingdom, going to the Forbidden Tower and requesting their help. He dismissed that idea immediately, acknowledging the absurdity of trusting such a species.

My people, Terros thought, knowing he had a duty. And now he had abandoned it, leaving them all to die as he paced through the jungle.

"Make way for the Pirate King!" boomed a voice from a speaker that rippled and echoed through the landscape, shaking the trees.

"The Pirate King!" came a chant.

The car, Terros thought, remembering the truck he had seen earlier that day. If he could get it to work, then he could drive fast and hopefully find some backup. The young Gedrul had not travelled much outside of his kingdom, so what he would find was up in the air.

The truck was where Terros had left it, gathering moss in the shrubs. The beast dashed over to it, but as he did, discovered something. There was someone or something underneath it, rustling about and tinkering with metal.

"RARRR!" Terros growled, hoping to scare it off.

The being, a cloaked someone, then stealthily sped away from under the machine and raised its arms.

Terros roared again – loud enough to petrify it, but not loud enough to alert everyone to his location.

"Wait!" the cloaked one said, pulling off his hood to reveal bright orange fur. He had large white ears and a narrow nose. From under his cloak emerged a large, bushy tail. "Please do not kill me!"

Terros shoved the fox to the side and jumped into the car, sitting in the driver's seat. He then looked around for an 'on' button so he could start moving. There were so many buttons and switches that the beast quickly got confused.

"I take it you have never driven one of these before," the fox said, pointing at a lever. "Pull that and then put your right foot on the pedal and start driving," he stated.

Terros could not care what the bipedal animal had to say. However, his advice was correct since when he pulled the lever, the whole car jittered to life. The beast then slammed his foot onto the pedal, but nothing happened.

"That's the brake pedal," the fox said.

Angrily, Terros roared at the orange creature, hoping to scare him off. The pirates had just landed and would find him within minutes.

"Only trying to help," the orange animal sighed, raising his hands above his head.

Terros then tried the other pedal and once more nothing happened.

"The engine needs fixing," the fox came again. "You interrupted me before I could finish."

Terros looked out his window, into the night sky, where the spaceship still resided. He pondered how long it would take to get going and if he could outrun the pirates.

"I'll be quick," the fox said. "Just give me a few minutes."

Terros reluctantly let the animal get to work, while he looked around vigorously for any sort of pirate threat. From where he was, he could no longer hear the megaphone, but could still feel the distant purrs of the trucks.

"And we are done," the fox said, minutes later.

As Terros was getting ready to step into the car, the animal stopped him.

"I suggest you let *me* drive," he said. "You will probably crash into a tree."

This annoyed Terros, for he knew he could not trust this sly fox. In the end, he decided to let him drive, opting to sit in the passenger seat; but if the orange creature stepped out of line, then he would be on the breakfast menu in the morning.

"Name's Gides," the fox said, once the truck started moving. "How about you?"

"Terros," the beast let out, his voice deep and gruff.

"So, you *can* talk," the fox smiled as the two of them raced off into the distance.

Chapter 2: Space Pirates

The truck that once belonged to Rett and Arnetta was now being driven by Gides the Fox and Terros the Beast, who ploughed through the immense jungle, looking for sanctuary.

Terros was growing increasingly worried by the minute, for his remaining family were at the mercy of intergalactic pirates and he felt ashamed for having abandoned them.

"So, Terros, tell me about yourself," the fox asked.

The beast said nothing, only looking to the jungle surroundings with an intense stare.

There was a sudden jolt as a branch smacked into the windscreen and the side of the vehicle scraped a tree trunk.

"I am not the best driver," Gides laughed. "You know, I wanted to be a pilot, and fly a spaceship. But when the Federation Academy came to our kingdom to access the applicants, they said I was too reckless and unsteady. Maybe they were right, but from my point of view, they missed out on a great pilot. What about you? You got a tragic backstory?"

Terros said nothing.

"It must have been harrowing," the fox laughed. "A vow of silence – I like it."

Terros wanted to say something, but did not see its worth. So, he decided to sit and listen to the fox ramble on.

Sometime later, the fox stopped talking and looked out his window. "Rabbits!" he shouted.

Terros looked at the orange creature and wondered what he meant.

"Oh, that just means damn. One would shout 'rabbits' if they see or experience something bad. Like right now."

The white beast looked at Gides, now even more confused.

"What I am trying to say is look behind us."

A second later, Terros was looking out his window to see that a motorbike was right outside his door, its rider a purple reptilian creature with large eyes and short, stubby wings. It had a black hat on, with a skull and crossbones printed on.

"Turn yourself in!" the pirate yelled with a gravelly voice that sounded like coal being dragged across a slab of steel.

The beast ignored it and opened his door, smacking it into the rider and knocking him off his bike. He then fell off and disappeared into the tall grass.

"Nice one!" Gides called out. "But I highly doubt there was just one."

The fox was correct, for mere moments later there was a loud rumbled as a new vehicle was brought into the scene – a large green truck with massive exhaust snouts on the bonnet, leaving a massive trail of fumes. The frame was all spiked with ivory teeth. Driving it was another purple pirate – this one with an eyepatch and a sinister grin.

"Hold on!" Gides called out as the pirate truck got closer and closer, until the bumpers of the two vehicles were kissing. From within the vehicle crawled some dragons, holding blasters.

"Can you deal with those?" the fox asked.

Terros nodded, jumping onto the top of his car. He could feel the wind rushing against him as his mane blew back.

"Hand yourself in," snarled a pirate. "The Pirate King requests your presence."

The beast was puzzled at this. How did this so-called king know who he was? And why was he wanted? He jumped over onto the spiked truck, careful not to sink his feet into any teeth.

"You know, your village is filled with a bunch of weaklings," a pirate cackled. "It was so fun watching them get tortured."

Within the blink of an eye, Terros had picked up that pirate and chucked him off the side of the moving vehicle and into a tree. He then roared and prepared to take out the other snivelling creature.

"Unwise," the other hissed, shooting his gun.

The beast known as Terros dodged out the way, grabbing the gun and then kicked the pirate into the jungle. Now wielding a pistol, he shot the driver of the truck, causing his body to slump down and release the pedal, making them slow down and come to a halt. As this happened, Gides decelerated, giving Terros an opportunity to jump to safety.

"Great work, Terros!" Gides smiled. "Now get ready to fight off more of them. We just need to survive a few more minutes before we can get to my people. Then we will be ready to take them all on."

Their journey did not go much further. Immediately, they stopped as a large blockade of trucks became apparent, blocking the path. Gides had slammed the breaks, almost hurling Terros into the opposition. The beast held onto the truck tightly as the fox quickly changed direction and started driving.

The many trucks then started following behind, some of them with large gun turrets on the top, chain-gunning hundreds of bullets at their car by the second.

Terros jumped back into the vehicle to shield himself.

"The tyres should be able to handle the fire," Gides said, exasperated. "But we are going to have to take a longer route to get to my people."

A second later, a massive metallic weapon bust through the back window of the car. The harpoon hooked on and started slowing down the truck.

"Could you remove that?" Gides asked.

When the beast tried to release it, another one hooked on, followed by a spray of bullets. And then the hooks kept on coming, a new one latching onto the car every second.

Gides was slamming the acceleration as hard as he could, but the vehicle had now been brought to a complete halt. "I guess this is it," The fox sighed as armed pirates surrounded the vehicle.

Terros roared, preparing for battle.

"No," Gides mumbled. "We have no chance of winning this. Just hand yourself in and we will come up with a new strategy."

The Beast Known as Terros

"Gedrul!" screamed a purple dragon. "You are to be brought upon the Pirate King." They then grabbed him and completely surrounded him in chains, before knocking him out with something Terros would never come to remember.

Terros ran around in circles, his short stubby legs going as fast as they could, while he panted relentlessly.

"Try and keep up!" someone shouted to him, a small cub, slightly larger than him.

"Okay Rufus!" Terros smiled. He sped up and hit his friend on the back. "Tag!" he called out.

"Fair play," Rufus replied, swapping direction and chasing after his friend.

This went on for a while until Terros was exhausted and collapsed in the tall grass, smiling.

"Terros!" a voice called out.

The cub did not want to get up, enjoying the relaxing breeze.

"Hey, your mum is calling," Rufus said. "Better be quick."

"Fine," Terros sighed, getting up and running to his hut.

There, a tall being stood, wearing white robes with a thin mane. "Up to shenanigans again?" Mella asked Terros, pulling a twig from behind his ear. "Are you ready to go?" she asked.

"Go where?" the cub asked scratching his ear.

"Hunting!" a loud, heavy voice came, as a large male Gedrul walked out of the hut – a great being with an immense mane, large muscles and a purple cape. Upon his head was a ringlet made of leaves and twigs. "It's not every day that the chief gives a hunting lesson. You are lucky you are his son," he said with a hearty chuckle.

"Let's go then!" Terros laughed. "Last one there is a…"

"Slow down, Son," Chief Durros said. "Hunting has an art to it. A slow and methodical approach is best." He then stepped forwards and kissed his wife.

"Have fun, boys!" Mella called out, waving to the father and son as they disappeared into the dense world of trees.

In the depths of the jungle, Terros was running. The antelope he was after was pacing through the lands, constantly changing directions and sprinting as fast as possible.

"Come back here!" Terros called out, trying to go faster, but his body would disallow it. The beast then rethought his strategy and jumped upwards, grabbing onto a vine, using it to propel him forwards and onto the back of the creature. "Time for the kill!" he smiled, pulling the dagger from his belt. When he tried to make the slit at the throat, the antelope kicked its front legs up and threw the Gedrul cub off.

Terros rolled through the mud and grinded to a halt. Now his meal was too far away to catch up with.

"No!" he growled, trying to get back up. But then he collapsed out of exhaustion.

"Quite the spectacle," his father said. "A decent attempt, boy," he added. "Now back onto your feet and keep going."

"But I cannot keep up with it, sir," Terros replied. "How am I supposed to catch up?"

"You are a smart cub, my son," the being said. "There will be times in your life when you are forced to adapt to the situation and do what you can to take out your superior opponent."

"I suppose you are right," Terros sighed, jumping back onto his tiny feet.

Something then pricked into Terros' vision - a bright pink flower hidden amongst the green foliage. Without even realising, he found himself entranced by it, creeping over and staring at the wondrous petals. He went to go and smell it but his father stomped on his tail, preventing him from moving any further.

"What are you doing?" Durros asked. "That is the Jyko flower. One sniff of it and you are dead."

"Dead?" Terros asked, wondering how such a little thing could kill someone.

Terros' father then put his finger up to his lip as the sound of faint rustling could be heard. Terros nodded, backing away from the pink flower and listening out for anything with his tiny ears.

"Why have *you* come along?" a squirming and scratchy voice said. "The Pale King said nothing about hiring bounty hunters."

"I want to prove myself," the other voice replied, one very dark and deep in sound. "I hear these Gedruls are some of the strongest beings out there. What better way to prove myself than to fight the chief."

Durros ducked, fading into the trees, and pulled Terros with him.

Terros tried to speak but his dad covered his mouth. "It will be okay," he mouthed. "Run home. I will deal with these lot."

Terros found himself nodding.

"Keep an eye out!" one of the people called out, walking out into the open so that Terros could see who it was – a cream coloured being with a brown mane. His features were very skinny and he seemed oddly tall. *Is that a human?* he thought.

"Go," Durros whispered faintly, pushing Terros away from the ambushers.

The cub then started to stealthily run, careful to not make any noise. His steps were rhythmic and methodical, blending into the vegetation. All until a loose root caught him and he tripped, his face thudding on the floor.

"I found you!" a human shouted without hesitation – this one wearing a silver helmet that covered his face and had a long black cape. "You are not the chief," he said, walking over to Terros and picking him up by the tail. "Where is your father?" he asked.

"Bring him in," the cream-coloured one said. "Boys, cuff him," he added as some more humans emerged from the bushes, carrying metal chains. Terros gulped, knowing he had landed in serious trouble.

"Leave him!" Durros roared, stepping out from the bushes and bellowing out. His face was one of pure rage and his claws were now bared. He was much taller than any of the humans and could have made quick work of them if he so desired.

"There he is," the helmeted one said, pushing his cape behind him. "Time for some real fun." He did not get very far, for Durros picked him up and threw him to the side until he smacked into a tree.

"Hand over my son!" the beast roared out, storming forwards.

Terros could see how much the humans were shaking. But despite being so scared, they stood their ground against the Gedrul who was twice their height. They all pointed silver devices at him with long snouts. When they pressed buttons, small flashes of light occurred and small pelts hit Durros.

The chief roared, mowing through the humans and tossing them to the side. In the matter of seconds, he had finished them and then picked up Terros. "Back to the village," he said, panting.

"No!" the helmeted one called out, now with a large crack on his helm. "I have waited too long for this fight." He charged forwards and leapt at Durros, throwing metallic disks at him that stuck to his skin. He then pressed a button and Durros started screaming out as bolts of lightning forked around him.

The chief then plucked them off, one by one and clapped his hands hard, making a loud sound. He gripped the man hard, by the cape and swung him around.

But the man tore off his cape and pulled free of the attack. "Too long have I waited," he came again, pulling a silver snout from his pocket and aiming it at Terros' father. He pressed the button multiple times and the great beast was hit with red light that seemed to burn at his flesh.

Durros stormed forwards, taking long, heavy steps, but seemed to slow down with each one. "No more!" he yelled, grabbing the silver snout and crushing it with his hands. "Look away, Son!" he growled as he grabbed the hand of the man.

Terros did as was asked, turning away and looking at the green shrubs. As he did so, he heard a loud scream, and so he covered his ears as well.

"All is done," Durros said, patting Terros on the back. His angry visage had gone, but there was red paint all over his chest. It stunk as well.

"Let's go, Dad," Terros said.

"Get him!" a human called out and suddenly a large red net burst into the air and surrounded Durros, catching him and tangling him. The beast roared, but in a matter of seconds he was immobilised. His previous fight had tired him out too much. Then a cannister was thrown at him that spat out thick, emulsifying purple smoke that filled the air and made him fall asleep instantly.

Terros covered his mouth so it would not hurt him.

"What do we do with the cub?" one of the cream-coloured people asked.

"Leave him," another said. "The Pale King wants only the chief for now."

"So be it," they said, grabbing the net around Durros and dragging him away.

"Dad!" Terros cried out, chasing after them – but was shot with some red feather thing that pierced his skin. It was sharp, and seconds later he was fast asleep.

The beast known as Terros awoke to a loud and chaotic zone. As his eyes opened, his ears were ringing in agony. He was back in his adult body and the memory of the past stung.

"Sing for me!" someone clamoured, his voice gravelly and grotesque.

This was followed by violent cheering.

"SING!" the same person cried. Then in unison, the crowds started chanting.

The Beast Known as Terros

Of Whim and Want,
To sing and song,
We tell thineselves upfront,
And t'was the mango bong.
For Quinth and Quenth,
To whither and thither,
Flence thee flock.
And if this all goes well,
Then we'll all be drinkin' rum,
Hey!

Terros forced himself to wake up, wrenching open an eyelid.

"Sing my children!" a loud voice came. "Sing for the Pirate King!"

Oh hey ho, merry ho,
We are pirates through and through.
We drink rum and we all know,
That singing is a what we do.

Terros saw hundreds of purple beings fluttering with tiny wings, all chanting while holding large churns of a bright blue liquid that was frothing and writhing at the top. The pirates then began the next verse.

We all love the Pirate King,
He makes us so filthy rich.
That is why, we do sing,
Else we'll end up in a ditch!

We sing high, we sing low

He shows us what to do and say,
For he roared us up from dough,
And we love him oh so every day.

"Beautiful!" called a voice so loud that it could have made Terros' ears bleed. He turned his head to see that there was a giant shadow being cast over him.

"It looks like our guest is waking up!" jeered the thunderous voice.

The many pirates then started cackling intensely, all out of tune, creating a rustic orchestra of agony.

"My my – the last of the male Gedruls. Tis a pity that you must die. For whim and want is what I say, and a sentence I shall bestow to your dismay."

Terros finally looked up at a colossal structure hovering above the ground – a great stone and metal object with a large backrest and two sides to rest one's arms. And atop this mighty throne was a being with intense oceanic-blue skin, plated with scales and wrinkles. A dragon, like the rest, but this one was gigantic, large enough to swallow a kingdom whole, whose head almost touched the clouds.

"Greetings boy, for you know who I am. Some say my rhymes do annoy, but as for that, I could not give a damn. For I am the Pirate King, and when they hear it they shall sing."

We all love the Pirate King,
He makes us so filthy rich,
That is why, we do sing,
Else we'll end up in a ditch!

The Beast Known as Terros

When they finished singing, the pirates broke into hysterical laughter, filling the fields with echoes of fear.

Terros finally stood up. He could see that Gides was to his right, wrapped up in chains as well.

"Let us go!" Gides called out.

Terros yanked at his chains to no avail.

"Mwah hah hah!" boomed the Pirate King, stooping his neck down to reveal his face with a great red scar and a milky eye. His ears were fanned and withered while his teeth were numerous, yellow and caked in moss. "You have quite the planet, beast," the dragon bellowed. "I will stop rhyming, just for this minute. This jungle here, shall be my domicile - stretching on for every mile. Oops, I seem to have rhymed again. Whatsoever shall I do then?" The Pirate King then burst into laughter, shaking the grass and trees with every cackle. When the pirates joined in, the combined noise created a howl of energy that could have been heard anywhere in the world.

Terros was fuming – for the destruction of his village was now being played for laughs.

"I have made many a money in my days," the Pirate King said. "Ever since I were a wee lad, I have been scamming, wheeling and dealing to fulfil my greed. Yet as I ruined the lives of more and more, it donned on me that I enjoyed it. I would bathe in piles of gold and do so much more. And so when I found out that there is a special flower, exclusive to this world, that can make the most splendiferous hallucinogens, I knew I had to come here. The Jyko Flower, in its purest form is lethal. But when extracted properly, you get Rotu, the finest hallucinogen out there. This jungle shall be my humble farm, where I grow this Jyko and sell Rotu on the intergalactic trade.

Then I will be rich enough to coat a planet in gold. Oh it would be so marvellous."

The beast tried to hack at his chains, but they did not budge.

"In a rush are we, animal?" the dragon hissed. "I will have you know that your entire village is at my mercy, including your precious Aunt Tirra and her freaky looking cubs. Now you had better listen before I have your family cooked and put in sandwiches for my people."

"What do you want with me?" Gides then called out.

"Fox fox fox fox fox," the Pirate King said. "You are an interesting fellow. My spies tell me that your sister was picked over you when the Federation Academy came to your city. They took her over you – a smart and witty creature with a little too much ambition. OUCH! I have kept you alive to pilot my warships – someone like you would have oh so much potential. Then who knows, you might reunite with your sister in the stars, but on opposite factions. Would be quite the reunion if I do say so myself."

"How do you know that?" the fox asked, his eyes widening.

"Hey ho, what is this? There is nothing I do miss. I like to know everything about everyone and now you belong to me. But I know you intend to betray hence you will see. Send you to a place I shall where they will turn you to a bot. Then escape from me you shall not."

"No!" Gides called out, desperately trying to wriggle free.

"And so it ends," the dragon bellowed. "You will both be sold off and I will become immensely rich."

Two pirates then walked over and picked up Gides. Then four came to pick up Terros, and even that many struggled to lift him.

"Goodbye Terros. And so, you will be sold as well. Tis a shame you could never fight on my side. We could have made a could team you and I. Lest the humans have sent a bid for you – one I cannot resist. To them I send you." The Pirate King paused. "And as for your people, I have many plans with them."

At the mention of humans, Terros' heart sunk inside. He was filled with rage, but the chains were on so tightly that he could not even wriggle if he wanted to.

The Pirate King then spoke once more. "You know, I might make Gedrul-dragon hybrids. That could be a lot of fun!" he cackled hysterically as Terros was taken away from his view.

Terros and Gides were dragged to a large convoy, where they were put into a compartment at the back, surrounded by half a dozen pirates who were all smoking pipes with one hand and holding blasters in the other. There was a thick stench of sweat, ash and rotting flesh. Terros had accepted his fate and stared at the ground as the vehicle started to move, driving off forever.

Chapter 3: Cyborgs

When Rett opened his eyes after a long sleep, reality sunk back in for him. His memories started pouring back in and his surroundings became apparent. When he saw that he was in a plain white room, feeling like infinity, he wanted to cry out in anger. He looked to the side and it was as if his brain was taking extra-long to process everything. "No more," he mumbled.

In the distance of the white void, a door slid open, revealing the outside world. Through the gap in reality walked a man with a bright red suit and long black hair.

"Cornelius," Rett growled, remembering the one who had betrayed him – the robot. Despite this, the being's mannerisms were completely human and his face had been repaired after being blasted. Rett stood up and rushed over to the man, throwing a punch. Somehow, he completely missed, as if his eyes were lagging behind, and the man tumbled to the ground in confusion. *What?* he wondered.

The Beast Known as Terros

"Good to see you again, Rett," Cornelius replied. "My scientists tell me you have put up quite the resistance. Their thought experiments have not worked on you, which is *most* impressive."

"You…" Rett said, feeling exhausted. "Betrayed me," he gasped.

"That I did," Cornelius said, bending down beside Rett.

"Megalopolis?" Rett asked.

"Does not exist," Cornelius replied. "There are no humans on this planet. Not a *single* one. The place you have been looking for, The Gigafactory I call it, is populated entirely with machines and enslaved cyborg animals."

"No," Rett cried. All this time he had been scouring Guinthra for this sanctuary – but had it been made up?

"No indeed," smiled Cornelius. "Anyway, I shall be on my way. I just wanted to check on you."

Rett looked at him, his vision clouding. "Wait!" he shouted. "Where are my people? Where is Arnetta?" he took a moment to catch his breath. "If you have harmed her, I will…"

"No need," Cornelius replied. He then touched a few things on his watch, before bringing it up to his face to talk into. "Send in Subject 83," he said. "Your wife is quite alright," the man said as a door opened and in walked Arnetta.

She had a wide smile on her face and was wearing simple white clothes, free of any wrinkles or creases. Her hair was in a very neat braid – one far too complex for her to have done herself – which made Rett twinge in suspicion.

"Arnetta!" Rett smiled, wanting to get up and hug her, but his body refuted him. Her skin was oddly pale, but he ignored it, just being happy to see her.

"Hello Rett," she grinned. "How have you been?"

Her mannerisms seemed normal despite their far from normal situation. She did not seem drugged or experimented on like he had been.

"I…" Rett tried to get out, his vision all over the place and jumbled up.

"Arnetta has been very well-behaved during her time here," Cornelius said, stroking her head.

"What is that supposed to mean?" Rett asked.

"She did not put up as much fuss as you did," Cornelius said. "And now that we are finished with her, she is most happy. Isn't that right, Subject 83."

"Yes," Arnetta nodded. "The pain stopped once I ceased to resist."

"What?" Rett asked, forcing himself to stand up as his legs felt like jelly. "What did you do to her?" Rett's head started to heat up as anger thrust his heart into overdrive.

"Nothing bad," Arnetta replied. "I was broken, and they fixed me."

"Good girl," Cornelius said, stroking his scrawny and sleezy hand against her hair again as if she were some pet.

Rett scrunched up a fist and got ready to attack.

"Your whole crew was complicit," Cornelius added. "You were the only one that put up a fuss."

Rett tried to punch, but his arm was not working.

"We may not have gotten into your mind, but we have put in a program that stops you from attacking me," Cornelius grinned maniacally. He then turned to Arnetta.

"Go and put your uniform on. We have a special shipment on its way to us. A Gedrul and a fox."

"Yes, sir," Arnetta nodded before marching off.

"Arnetta!" Rett called out.

She turned around and looked at him. "Do not resist, my love. Let them turn you and then we can be together again." After saying that, she disappeared into the void.

"You!" Rett shouted, now blinded by rage. They had brainwashed his wife and had turned her into a chivalrous puppy. And what of the rest of his men? Had they done the same? "Fix her!" he screamed, bellowing out his rage as his face turned a fiery red and saliva burst out his mouth.

"No," Cornelius said. "She is *perfect*." He then clapped his hands and the doors opened again. This time two beings wearing white pristine lab coats walked in. They had rounded facial features and black fur. "These hyper-intelligent apes will break your mind," Cornelius said. "Then you will be mine."

Rett looked around for something to grab and use as a weapon. His window was getting shorter as the apes approached. One of them had a sharp metallic contraption in his hands and it made him scared. Rett tried moving, but one forcefully grabbed him, wrenching his mouth open. Then the other dropped a large pink pill down his throat. The man tried to gag it out, but it slithered down his gullet and all of a sudden he felt drowsy.

"Get to work, boys," Cornelius said as one of the apes prepared a sharp device. "Some Rotu extract, courtesy of the Pirate King, ought to fix you."

Rett woke up on a bed, a breathing machine on his mouth, while he was surrounded by a dozen or so apes in lab coats.

His breaths were short, sharp and heavy and his whole body ached relentlessly.

"Subdue him!" an ape called out. "But before they could do anything," Rett was up, having picked up a piece of machinery and hurled it at them. "How dare you put me through something like that!" He had just experienced the strangest of dreams that was so weird and loopy that he could not even think about it without having a migraine.

Terrified, the monkeys all ran off, leaving him to be by himself.

"What was that?" Rett asked himself as he suddenly felt queasy and threw up on the floor, a large purple puddle of goo. "What did they do to me?" he asked himself as his stomach twisted and churned. He then remembered Arnetta. "I must save her," he said, stumbling out of the room.

"You know," came a voice, thin and raspy, from another room. "We can easily get out of here. These monkeys may be mathematical geniuses, but they lack any sort of common sense."

There was then a large growl as if from a great beast.

"Trust me, Terros, it should be easy. If we can throw them a banana then we will have a window to escape. Then we can go to my people and convince them to rescue *your* people from the Pirate King. Easy."

There was a growl again.

"Hmm, my plan does seem to have flaws in it. Like how do we get out of this cell? And where do we get the banana from?"

Rett stumbled out of the lab, dragging his legs behind him. After every few steps, he would stop and catch his breath before moving again, slithering like a slug and his brain operating like a mashed potato.

Now in the hallway, Rett could see that there was a stretch of cells, all with transparent doors and small holes for air to get in. There were buttons on the sides of them, all red and blue. Rett went to the cell with the two people talking. He could see that one was a fox with orange fur and the other was…

"You?" Rett asked, looking at the white beast – the same one that had saved his life from the flying creatures days before, but what felt like months. "How did you end up here?"

The beast roared back at him, as if blaming him for his current predicament.

"Terros here is rather cranky," the fox said. "Name's Gides by the way. Gides the Fox."

"Am I still dreaming?" Rett asked himself, looking at the animal that was beaming.

"Say, brother," the fox said. "You look like poo. Not just the ordinary sort, but the one after a spicy meal."

"Life's not looking so good. They turned my wife into a puppet," Rett said, stumbling onto the door of the cell. "How do I open this and let you out?"

"How can we trust you? I take it you are like the rest of the humans here."

Terros nodded, standing up.

"Terros trusts you," Gides said. "Well then, I guess you are a good guy. Try pressing one of those buttons. One of them ought to open this cage."

Rett started smacking random buttons, trying to release the door's lock. Eventually he got to one that opened it up, freeing the two prisoners.

"Let's create some havoc!" Gides said, getting excited.

"Wait," Rett said. "The man with the ponytail – the leader. He is mine," he growled.

The beast known as Terros nodded.

"Let's make some noise!" Gides called out.

"No," Rett hissed. "We need to find my wife and then escape. The rest of my crew is here, but we will have to come back for them another time."

Gides then pointed at a bulbous, robotic-looking eye in the top right corner of the room. "They are watching us," he said. "We need to leave now, then."

"I cannot leave her," Rett mumbled. "They have turned her into a... I need to free her."

"Then the female is as good as dead," Terros said, his voice thick and deep.

"That's the second time I have heard you speak," Gides chuckled.

"What do you mean she is as good as dead?" Rett asked, squaring off against the large beast. "They have probably hypnotised her. If I can break the spell, then she will go back to normal."

Terros simply shook his head, exhaling deeply.

"What do you mean?" Rett shouted, grabbing the beast by his jacket - one that looked just like his own. "What are you not telling me?"

"Enough of this," the fox said. "We need to go."

"I am not going until this animal tells me what has happened to my wife. Tell me!" he shouted.

"Keep it down," Gides replied. "We need to go."

"TELL ME!" Rett yelled.

The Beast Known as Terros

Terros raised a fist before thrusting it into Rett's face, hitting him with an incredible amount of force. The human flew backwards, before falling into a black void.

When Rett awoke next, he was outside, under the gentle breeze of day. He was slumped over the shoulder of a large being, with white fur right up in his face. They were moving - running rather fast.

Rett looked to his left to see a humanoid fox sprinting, smiling while doing so. He held a large plasma rifle and had a satchel strapped on. "What just happened?" he asked, his vision becoming clearer.

"He's back," Gides laughed. "You missed all the fun. Terros took on a panda robot and destroyed it with his bare hands. Anyway, we have escaped."

"Where are we going?" Rett asked, seeing them get closer to the jungle he had only escaped from days earlier.

"We are going to see my people. They will provide us shelter and can give you the weapons needed to save your folk. Then hopefully we can all work together to save Terros'…"

"STOP!" screeched a voice.

The three of them turned to see that behind them was Cornelius, looking dishevelled. To his right was a woman standing tall, wearing a white uniform that had golden epaulets. Her hair was in a sleek, militaristic bun and her face was devoid of any emotions.

"The three of you, come back or General 83 will kill you."

When Rett looked back at the woman, his heart sank. "Arnetta?" he asked, only just recognising her under the imperial visage.

"I warned you before," Rett's former wife spat. "Join us or we will dispose of you."

"What have they done to you?" Rett asked, walking over to them.

"What are you doing?" Gides hissed, seeing Rett walk towards the danger.

"Hand yourselves in or die!" Arnetta screamed.

"It is a shame it came down to this," Cornelius said, scratching his nose. "887562431!" he called out.

Rett suddenly stopped moving as his body completely froze in place.

"It worked," Cornelius smiled. He gestured to Arnetta. "Shoot the fox, then immobilize the Gedrul. It is time for our prize."

Chapter 4: Stand-Off

Terros gulped as he saw what had just happened. Rett's face was now pale and statue still. Arnetta's gun was pointed at Gides. Cornelius to Terros.

"Rett, what are you doing?" Gides asked, his voice risen.

"I cannot resist," Rett grumbled.

"Those apes never fail to impress me," Cornelius laughed. "Your mind may not be mine, but your body certainly is," the man cackled.

"Terros, we have landed ourselves in quite the situation," Gides sighed. "I guess every man, or animal, for himself," he said as he shot his blaster at Arnetta, missing.

Meanwhile Terros smashed Cornelius to the side, took a shot from Arnetta, before picking her up and tossing her away. The beast then winced as he saw that his left shoulder was smoking, his jacket burnt from where it had been hit. He placed his hand on the wound, hoping to soothe it.

Terros then ran over to Cornelius, to finish the man off once and for all. The human lay in a pile of mud, his suit torn and his face blackened. The beast punched his face over and over.

"Stop!" Cornelius spat. "I have alerted the pirates to your location. Run before they get here!" he laughed.

Rett, having broken free of his spell, hobbled over to where Cornelius was. "I will finish him off," he growled, taking the plasma rifle. "You lot go. I need to find out how to break this spell and free my wife. Then I need to rescue my men."

Gides and Terros looked at one another for a second.

"I guess so," the fox replied. "But before I go," he added, spitting a massive globule onto Cornelius' face. "I just wanted to do that!" he laughed.

Terros then stomped on the suited man's legs, crunching his robotic skeleton and preventing him from walking. The beast then laughed – a deep and echoing chuckle.

Cornelius shouted. "887…"

He did not finish as Rett kicked the machine across the face. "You dare try to control me again!"

When a shadow was cast over the area by a fleet of black flying shapes, Terros knew that it was time to go.

The fighter jets then started swooping down, like birds, and opening fire, with great gatling guns that spread across the ground with ferocious intensity.

"Run!" Gides shouted, diving into the thicket of the jungle and hiding to the side of a log, using it as a shield.

Terros did the same, bursting into the jungle and using a tree as shelter. As he lay down, with his ear pressed to the earth, he could feel a small vibration. Wanting to curse out loud, the beast growled and pondered what to do next. It would only be a matter of minutes before the pirate trucks would arrive and have them surrounded. He needed to think of something quickly.

Gides and Terros glanced from behind the bushes to see what Rett was doing. The human fished out a small device from Cornelius' blazer pocket.

"Hello, this is Cornelius," Rett said in an overly dramatic voice. "The animal miscreants have fled north, towards the Kraim Desert." He then put the machine down.

The jets changed direction and swooped away, far into the distance. As for the trucks, they drove past Terros, dozens in number and massive in size, clattering the jungle each second. The vehicles went past them and disappeared northwards, meaning somehow, they had escaped.

"Good thinking, human," Gides said to Rett when they reunited.

"You monsters!" Cornelius spat. "You dire creatures!" he came again.

"Does he have an 'off' switch?" Gides asked.

"Not yet," Rett said. "I need him to show me where my people are and how to break the mind-control."

Cornelius burst out laughing. "Your friends are gone – off to the Gigafactory where they will be put to work forever!" He continued to laugh. "You are never getting in there. The security will fry you in seconds."

"That is why you are going to take me there," Rett smiled. "How far is it?"

"A week's drive," the suited man cackled. "But like I said, *you* are not getting in."

"Remove his head," Rett sighed. "He doesn't need his body to survive."

Terros did not hesitate and walked over to the machine, before plucking his head off, tearing the metal under his skin and snapping wires in half.

"Unhand me!" Cornelius screamed – now just a head.

Rett then grabbed the machine by his hair and held him in his palm. He then walked over to Arnetta's unconscious body. "I will save you, my love."

"You think you can save her?" Cornelius screeched. "You have no…"

"Speak again and I will remove your ability to see," Rett hissed back at him. "You will be a sightless, floating head for the rest of your existence!" He then turned his attention to Terros. "Please could you carry Arnetta inside," he said. "Help me load up a truck so I can go to the Gigafactory." He then walked over to the entrance of the building, raising Cornelius' head to the eye-scanner, causing the doors to open.

"I guess this is where we say goodbye," Gides said, outside a truck that was almost perfectly shiny. In the passenger seat, Arnetta was resting, her hands cuffed in case she woke up still controlled.

Rett was wearing black tactical gear with many pouches and pockets, as well as having an array of guns loaded in the back of his truck.

Terros and Gides had taken their fair share of weapons as well – for it would have been a shame to not take advantage of a human outpost.

"Thank you for your help," Rett said smiling as much as he physically could – more like a frown. In his right hand was still Cornelius, who had a permanent scowl on his face and had not said a single word since Rett had threatened him.

"Anytime," Gides said. "Once we have sorted things out with the Pirate King, we will be sure to come and give you a helping hand."

Terros nodded.

"Anyway, I shall be going," he said, stepping into his car and taking another look at Arnetta.

"Goodbye," Gides spoke, while Terros waved.

The human then drove off, leaving the two animals behind.

Terros smiled, unaware that he could ever be acquaintances with a human.

"Back to saving your village," Gides sighed. "The Pirate King must have learnt about what has transpired here by now. Let's get to my people. They can help us."

Terros looked at the vehicle they were going to travel in – a black, heavy truck, with large exhausts and a metal frame at the front to plough through enemies. The beast then had an idea and gave a long stare at the fox.

"What is it?" the fox asked, almost jumping back.

"Sister," Terros mumbled, barely audible.

"My sister?" Gides replied, raising his brows. "Oh, you heard about what happened to my sister. You know she is part of the 15th Battalion."

Terros nodded.

"You are wondering if she can help us?" the fox asked. "If the Federation can send forces to defeat the pirates?"

The beast nodded.

"It is a long story. But we cannot. I can explain in the car."

When they were driving, Gides started to speak. "So you see, my family is a bit odd. My parents were politicians within my kingdom, and they had four children. My sister first, then the twins, then little old me." The fox gave out a small chuckle. "My sister was 'perfect' in the eyes of my parents – top of her classes, smartest person at the institute, an ultra-perfectionist and much more. Then the twins, Garlo and Grimlo were athletic beasts, with multiple scholarships from the top academies. And then there was me." Gides tried to give a smile, but Terros could see that he was failing.

"I know I may look like a smart guy, but in reality, I am not. When I was young, our region had a little political unrest so my parents became fully involved in the running of the country and I would not see them for days at a time, sometimes even weeks. The twins were at boarding school, so I would just be left with Grella, my strict sister. And then when my parents died in an accident, Grella had full control over me. She knew I was not at the top of my classes, so would make me work day and night in order to get smarter. So, I would often go to school sleep-deprived and had a habit of falling asleep in class. My grades never improved and she would punish me for it – not allowing me to eat from time to time. She would often call me a failure and more.

"Every ten years, the Federation would come to my city. The greatest honour would be to pass their entrance test and leave with them off-world. When they tested my siblings and I, my sister and the twins were successful. I still remember them all wearing their purple armour the next day and getting onto the spaceship. My teacher said, 'I wish you were more like your sister'. That day I left home and never looked back.

"They wanted me to be like Grella – a horrible person who was filled with pride and looked down on everyone else. I have not spoken to my sister, and if I did ask her for help, she would laugh at me."

Terros could not relate to the story, being an only child. Yet the emotion that Gides expressed was clear, and almost made the beast feel sorry for him.

"That is my story," Gides said. "Sorry for just dumping it on you. It is just that…" Gides did not get a chance to finish, as a large object smacked onto the windscreen of the car, flying upwards from the collision.

The beast got out of the truck, confused as to what had occurred.

"What was that?" Gides pondered aloud.

"AARGH!" came a loud grunt.

Terros sniffed, looking to see that there were smidgens of purple blood nested on the front of the truck. He tried scouting the source.

"Ow!" came the same grunting voice, as a skinny being emerged from the bushes. "Ow! Ow! Ow!" he squealed, standing upright and then cracking his own neck. "Quite the hit," he grumbled, standing out in the open.

As soon as Gides saw that it was a purple scaled dragon with a black hat and a leather jacket, the fox had already pulled the blaster from his pocket and had shot three times. Red bolts of light zoomed through the sky at the pirate.

"Hey!" the dragon called out, two shots missing and one going through his hat. "This leather is expensive," he hissed, looking at how it was smoking. "Not all animal skin can absorb blaster fire."

Gides cocked his pistol and prepared for another barrage.

The beast barred his arm in front of the weapon, growling. He wanted to see what the pirate had to say, if anything, and how they could leverage him. Killing him would be a waste.

"It is not polite to shoot someone without greeting them first," the pirate said. "Especially since you just ran me over."

"What are you doing Terros?" Gides asked. "Let me kill this worm."

"Terros?" the pirate asked, his scaled eyebrows raising. "Huh," he added, looking at the beast. "The Pirate King wants me to bring you both in. That is why I got dispatched in this part of the jungle. This horrible sector filled with snakes, moths and more. I could not even get a good night's sleep without leeches appearing on my legs."

The beast slowly walked over to the pirate; a being far too pathetic to put up a fight.

"You going to kill me?" the pirate asked. "Well, I quit."

Terros stopped in his tracks.

"You heard me right. I quit being a pirate."

The Gedrul looked back at the fox, who shrugged in response.

"I am fed up of doing errands for the Pirate King. I only just got promoted from my position of toilet cleaner on his warship. You should see how much poo comes out of these pirates. But this promotion sucks. I was promised the Golden Rum someday, but once again, I am stuck doing endless labour. So, I quit."

Terros picked up the being by the neck, squeezing tightly.

The pirate squirmed, wriggled and writhed. "I am telling the truth!" he cried out, removing the blaster from his belt and dropping it to the ground. "I resign from being a pirate."

Terros dropped the pirate into a swamp of mud, trying not to chuckle as the creature splattered around.

"You're sparing me?" the dragon asked, wiping himself clean.

Gides sighed, realising he could not argue with the Gedrul. "You are going to tell us how to beat the Pirate King," he hissed.

"Easy," the dragon said. "My name is Zemu Zarillian, by the way. And if you want to kill the Pirate King, then my entire race of dragons will attack and kill you, as well as the other pirate factions from across the galaxy. If you want your land back, you will need to challenge the Pirate King in one-on-one combat. Should you win, then by tradition of our clan, you will take control of the dragon pirate crew, all our land and our motherships. Then you can rid us from this world. Easy."

"Do you take us for fools?" came Gides. "The Pirate King is the size of a mountain, maybe two. How are we supposed to duel him and win?"

"You asked how to get your village back. That is the only way."

Terros was getting frustrated. From what he was gathering, it seemed like his home was gone forever, his people sentenced to permanent imprisonment. Unless he could beat the king somehow, but that was worse than an impossibility. The only way he could win was by enlisting the help of someone else to defeat the being, but finding someone of that size was also not feasible.

"We should kill you," Gides said, pulling his blaster up to Zemu's head, getting ready to make the shot.

Terros barred the fox, looked at the dragon and nodded at him, gesturing to the car.

"You want him to join us?" Gides asked, flabbergasted.

The beast nodded.

"My, oh my," the fox sighed. "Come along then," he said to the pirate. "If you try to kill us though, I am sure Terros will tear you apart."

"Thank you so much," Zemu laughed. "You will not regret this. I can teach you everything about my people, their weaknesses and all. You will not regret this decision."

The three of them then got into the truck, Gides the Fox driving, Terros the Beast beside him and Zemu the Pirate sitting in the back.

Gides revved up the engine and the squad blasted off into the jungle, preparing for their next adventure.

Chapter 5: The Juggernaut

Terros could see the sweat dripping from Gides' head. The beast honed in on the sounds of the fox's breaths - short and sharp. They had been travelling for a full day now and his home kingdom was not too far away.

The whole time they had been voyaging, Zemu had been quiet, watching the surroundings out of his window in awe, as if he were a child. He may have been a child in fact, for Terros had never asked him his age, and dragons could have aged differently to other beings. That would explain his overly skinny limbs and tiny wings.

"So," Gides said at last. "It is time to meet my people. If we could get an audience with the Elder, then that would be perfect."

"The Elder?" Zemu asked.

"The Elder Fox is our ruler and the wisest among us. If anyone can help or advise us, it would be him."

Terros noticed the trees disappear, now replaced with large huts with small children running around. It was far bigger than Terros' village for there were actual buildings present, no taller than two stories. There were markets, tailors, grooming stores and much more. This was a functioning society, a civilisation of fox people.

They did not get very far until they were barred by two foxes, standing in front of some wooden gates that halted the road. They wore visors and heavy armour, with the only parts of their body showing being their ears and their tails.

"State your business," one said, walking up to the car.

"We are here to see the Elder," Gides replied.

"Why?" the officer asked, looking into the truck to see Terros and Zemu. "Who are these two? Why have you brought a pirate and a hairy freak to our peaceful city?"

Terros let that statement slide.

"Zemu here is an underling of the Pirate King. I have arrested him and want the Elder's advice on what to do with him."

"You have done enough," the other guard said. "We will take him off you and deal with him accordingly."

"Actually no," Gides said. "I want to take him to the Elder personally."

"No problem," the guard replied, pulling a small contraption from his belt which looked like binoculars with two circles to look through. "We just need to take your identity and then we can let you in."

"Identity?" Gides asked, his hands visibly shaking.

Terros was confused. Why would Gides not want to be identified?

"There's no need," Gides laughed. "I am clearly a fox. Why do I need to be checked?"

"Just in case," the official said, holding the machine up to Gides' face. "You never know what synthetic robot might be trying to infiltrate our ranks."

A red laser scanned the fox's face. The guard then looked back at his device. "That's strange?" he queered, raising his brows. "Gides, it says. Your name is showing up in red," he said, clicking a few more buttons. His eyes widened and then he pulled a small pistol from his belt. "Criminal," he said, "convicted felon, manipulator and so much more."

"Let's go!" Gides shouted, slamming the acceleration pedal and tearing through the barriers.

Terros' head whipped back and he shut his eyes as chunks of wood flew up into the air.

"Criminal!" Zemu laughed. "That is what I like to hear."

"Shut up, *Pirate*," Gides hissed. "The things I have done are child's play when compared to the atrocities your kind have committed. Now hold on; we need to get to the Elder."

"Why would the Elder help a criminal like you?" Zemu asked.

Terros looked at the being he thought was his friend. The fox had told him his life-story, but had left out the most critical part – that he was a criminal. Then again, it did not surprise him, considering that he met Gides trying to steal parts from a car. No wonder he had looked so nervous driving in.

"The Elder was friends with my parents, before they died. He even came to my house to pay respects to my sister and I. He will help us – I have no doubt about it."

As they blasted through the main city, Terros could hear blaring sirens and loud engines hallowing as small aircrafts had been dispatched, simmering through the air and following them tightly behind.

On the sides of the road, foxes of all shapes and sizes could be seen – some small, some tall, a few were plump and there was the odd one in the shape of an upside-down triangle with large broad shoulders and a narrow, almost haggard core. The foxes were wearing business suits, ties, glasses and much more, resembling the humans.

The citizens all watched in awe as the crew blasted through the streets, followed by vehicles.

Terros saw that the children were not scared but rather had their mouths wide open and had large grins, ecstatic at what was playing before their eyes. It must have been a rare feat to catch a high-speed chase.

"Stop, or we will be forced to open fire!" called a megaphone from one of the vehicles behind.

"This is so much fun," Zemu cackled, hysterically watching as everything unfolded. He then leaned forward, putting his head between Terros and Gides. "Any chance you could go faster?"

Terros put his palm on the pirate's face and pushed him back into his seat.

"Faster?" Gides asked. "I don't want to lose control and run over innocents."

"Well how much further to this Elder?" Zemu asked. "I am starving."

"How has this got anything to do with your hunger levels?" Gides grumbled, trying to maintain complete focus on the road as they zipped around corners.

"He is the leader of this place. So, he should have access to vast amounts of food," the pirate dragon laughed. "Ain't I right Terros?"

The beast did not respond.

"We are going to the Elder to request support – *not* to steal his refrigerator!" Gides shouted.

"Watch us get food," Zemu laughed. "The pirates had me on a diet of canned frogs for months. I cannot wait for some *real* food!"

"Keep dreaming," Gides said, pushing the accelerator further, pulling everyone back into their seats tightly.

Their sense of escape was disrupted when there was a loud clank on the back window.

Terros and Zemu both looked around in unison to see that the glass was cracked as laser blasts were constantly hitting it.

"That's not good," the pirate said. "I will get on the roof canon and fight back."

"Wait," Gides said. "Once we get into the forest then you can jump onto the back. I don't want you hitting any civilians."

"Fair enough," Zemu laughed. "The other pirates say I am as blind as a Kilinth."

"Get ready!" Gides shouted. "We should be in the forest very soon."

Terros noticed the buildings in the distance slowly disappear, now replaced with tall trees.

"The Elder lives in a forest at the centre of this city." Gides then pointed at a green button next to the gear stick. "Terros, press that."

The beast did so, causing a mechanical whir to occur as the roof of the truck opened up, creating a gap just big enough for Zemu to slide through. On the ceiling, a black box opened, revealing a large canon with two handles to aim it.

"Now!" Gides yelled with a smile as Zemu leapt through the ceiling and onto the roof where he took control of the gun, firing dozens of shots per second, causing the truck to rattle with noise and vibrate with life.

They were passing through trees and tall grass, ploughing through nature and kicking up mud. Unlike Terros' home, this area of vegetation was very dull in colour with only greens and browns and nothing else that popped out.

There was a large explosion behind them, as Zemu was successful and a police vehicle erupted into flames.

"I underestimated that pirate," Gides said.

Terros nodded, watching as the dragon destroyed everything that followed them.

"Now keep your eyes peeled," the fox said. "The Elder lives in a wooden hut out here. We do not want to drive into it and run him over by accident."

The beast raised his arm, pointing a claw at a small house in the distance, almost invisible by the fact that it was blended in with the nearby trees and very small – underwhelming for the residence of such an important being.

Gides slammed the breaks, causing the vehicle to screech to a stop as the three of them were dragged and

The Beast Known as Terros

lurched forwards. Grass was massacred and mud was vomited into the air as they skidded to a halt.

"This is it," the fox said, stepping out.

Terros did so as well, happy to step onto solid floor.

The pirate was the last to touch grass, struggling to stand still as his head rocked side to side. "That… was… so… much… fun," he said, stopping after each word to take a breath.

"Let's see this old man," Gides said, pushing open the wooden door that was unlocked for some reason. There was no light on the other side, so when Gides went through, he was swallowed by the darkness.

Terros followed, stepping cautiously, walking into the darkness and wincing at each creak as he moved.

"Is there any light to this place?" Zemu asked, looking around.

"Can't you breathe fire or something?" Gides whispered back.

"I wish," the dragon replied.

"Grand Elder?" Gides called out. "Are you there?"

Unsurprisingly there was no response, only the darkness whispering back in silence.

"Grand El…" Gides did not get a chance to finish as the ground beneath the three of them felt uneasy and it opened up, causing them to be swallowed by the light.

They fell for a second, before striking hard ground, a painful instance.

Terros' eyes were blurry at first as the lights gnawed at his vision. He slowly got back onto his feet, trying to silence the constant, gnarly ringing of his ears.

The three of them were surrounded by foxes, in armour and with visors down. Even their tails were covered in plated armour. They held laser rifles which were all aimed on them.

"How dare you disturb me!" shouted a harsh, rustic voice that was a menace to the ears. There was a pause with the only sound being the pumping of a balloon inflating, followed by some cogs whirring. The being came into sight, a cloaked individual with the head of a fox, but his mouth was covered by a metal box that had pipes strewn out of it that wrapped around his body and fed into his chest.

Is this the Elder? Terros thought, gazing at the newcomer, whose entire body was rattling with each and every breath.

"Elder?" Gides asked, his voice overly high.

"State your business," the walking pile of nuts and bolts replied. "Else I shall have the three of you shot."

"What happened to you?" Zemu asked, visibly shocked by the appearance of the leader.

The Elder raised his arm, a metal skeleton with sharp, elongated fingers. He then pulled back his hood, revealing his scarred and wrinkled face, with one eye permanently closed and the other barely open, but with a techno monocle over it, having a bold red lens. "How old do you think I am?" the ancient fox replied, his voice mechanical, perhaps amplified by the box he spoke out of.

"One hundred," Zemu replied. "If so, you look good for your age."

There was a sequence of metallic crunching and clattering that could have very much been the sound of laughter.

"I am called the Elder for a reason," the old fox said, before breathing for a few seconds. "Eight-hundred and sixty-four long years it has been."

Terros was shocked by that. He widened his eyes and looked in amazement at the beyond ancient being. It was a miracle he was still standing after all the centuries, despite his robotic implants.

"Now then, state your business… or I will kill you," the wheezing fox said.

Gides opened his mouth to talk, but before he could utter anything, there was the sound of static coming from the helmets of one of the soldiers.

"Thank you for letting us know," the soldier replied after the static had finished. He then turned his attention to the Elder. "This is Gides Formon. He and his crew broke into our city and killed multiple officers. Shall we execute?"

"Gides Formon," mumbled the mechanical being. Gingerly, he raised his hand and pressed a button on his monocle, causing his eye to cartoonishly enlarge. He stood statue still and stared at Gides for a minute. "Gides Formon," he said again.

"Yes," Gides replied. "I apologise for breaking in, but you see I am here to request urgent…"

"Gides Formon," the Elder said for the third time. "I… know… you," he spoke very slowly.

"Yes, you do," Gides replied.

"Yes. Your parents, Rinard and Lisandra were close acquaintances of mine." He paused for a considerable amount of time. "They were politicians, were they not?"

"Yes," Gides said.

"My condolences for their death," he croaked. "You... are like family... to me."

Terros looked at Gides, confused.

"Lower your weapons," the Elder said. "Prepare a feast for my three friends here." He wheezed for a moment. "I would like to hear their proposition."

The soldiers all did as was told, lowering their guns and then exiting the room, leaving Terros, Gides and Zemu alone with the ancient being.

"Told you we would get food," Zemu whispered to Terros.

The beast could not help but smile.

"All this talk has tired me out," the Elder said. "So, you will speak to my... son... on my... behalf."

Entering the room was a very tall fox, one that towered over everyone. He wore sunglasses that covered his eyes, and his ears were oddly large and fanned. His jacket was overly baggy with sleeves that went past his hands entirely.

"My son... Frecto," the Elder said.

"Take a seat, Father," the newcomer said, his voice very deep. He helped the old man to a chair.

The ancient animal crumpled his face as he winced in pain, sitting down on his chair.

"You are tall," Gides said. "How comes I have never heard of you?"

"My primary duty is protecting my father," Frecto replied. "Knowledge of my existence would put my primary objective at jeopardy."

"What's on the menu?" Zemu asked, speaking out of turn.

"Six-arms will prepare something. Should be done in five minutes," Frecto said.

"Six-arms?" Gides asked.

Frecto immediately responded. "The chef was so good at his craft that he implanted four extra arms so that he would not need anyone else to help him in the kitchen. He also has two extra brains – one for each pair of arms. If you see him, his tall head is covered by a tower of a hat. He has been providing food for the cabinet for years now."

"So many wonders to this place; things that my parents never told me," Gides added.

"What is your proposition?" Frecto suddenly asked without warning.

"Well," Zemu replied.

"Let me answer this," Gides said. "Terros' village was raided by pirates like Zemu here. They have taken his people hostage and are mining his home for Jyko, a special hallucinogenic flower. We need reinforcements so we can go back to his kingdom and free his people."

"I thought... the Gedruls... were all extinct," the Elder said. "Who are... you?" he asked, pointing his shaking skeletal finger at Terros.

"He does not speak," Gides said. "Well, he does *rarely*, but he is on a vow of silence."

"Why?" the Elder asked.

"Because..." Gides replied, looking at the beast. "Because..." the fox then furrowed his brows. "In all honesty I do not know."

"Gedruls like him go for a high price," Frecto said. "Besides, why should we help him? What is in it for us?"

"The reputation of our people," Gides said. "Those Gedruls need our help, so we should provide it. It is the right thing to do."

"How would you know about the right thing to do, Gides Formon?" Frecto snapped. "I have read your file – you have quite the history. Shame your sister was picked for the academy and not you."

"Wait," the Elder said. "His parents were good people. We must treat him… nicely."

"Apologies, Father," Frecto said, bowing his head. He then turned his attention to Zemu. "What is your story, pirate? Have you betrayed your own people?"

"I no longer want to be a pirate," Zemu stated simply. "It is not the lifestyle I desire anymore."

"No help," the Elder came suddenly. "We give no help," he wheezed.

"My father says that we do not have the numbers to spare. The Pirate King's army is too vast for us to take on. So we will not help."

"You must!" Gides shouted. "We are foxes. We help people."

"That is what your parents believed," the Elder said. "Before the crash."

"Politics is a nasty game," Frecto said. "Look what it has done to my father. The technology for his parts is so old that we cannot update it to modern cyber. He is barely alive, but still holds strong due to his duty to this country. Only the brutal survive politics. It was a shame we had to rid your parents from the game."

"What?" Gides asked, his eyes wide and red.

Terros clenched his fists, knowing what was about to occur.

"Pirate King is my friend," the Elder said.

"The Pirate King funded my father's rise to power centuries ago. We have made many transactions with him across the years. When your parents discovered our dirty secrets, we had to silence them – like we will to you now."

"My son is Frecto," the Elder said. "But his codename is the Juggernaut."

As soon as the Elder had said this, Frecto had torn off his jacket, revealing his body was mechanised entirely, with sleek metal parts that glowed red. He then grew in size as his body transformed, turning him into a large, fearsome robot.

"Enjoy, my son," the Elder said as soldiers came into the room and escorted him out.

Chapter 6: A Fox Betrayal

The old and withered Elder croaked hard. "Frecto, my son. Execute these scum."

The machine took off its sunglasses, revealing two purple eyes, with a menacing glint. The being, once known as Frecto, but now was called the Juggernaut, stared at Gides. He stood at twice the height of Terros and looked to have as much weight as the three of the crew members combined, plus some.

"I take it there is no food," Zemu sighed, pulling a blaster from the side of his boot, before firing at the mechanical boulder of a being.

The Juggernaut did not even flinch, instead stepping forward with large, emphatic steps.

Terros spent some time trying to figure out the optimal way to win this skirmish. He knew there was not much he could do, and so hoped that his claws and teeth would be able to tear away at the shell. The beast jumped onto the back of the Juggernaut and he then slashed his hands at his head.

The orange fur of the machine tore off, revealing a metal head underneath. This was not a fox, but rather a robot in entirety. Did that mean that the Elder never had a son?

The beast continued to hack at the metal exoskeleton but came to no success as the tips of his fingers begun to sting and there was not even a scratch on the enemy.

The Juggernaut raised an arm, picking Terros up by his jacket and then tossed him across the room without any sort of difficulty.

Sliding against the floor, Terros growled, his skin stinging all the while.

"How do we beat him?" Gides asked, panting.

"He cannot be beaten," the voice of the Elder echoed through the room, using speakers that were rustled with static. "He was engineered by the smartest beings on this world. In the skies of above, in the Paradise Haven, where the penguins lie. They forge the greatest machines, my son being one of them?"

Penguins? Machines? Terros thought.

The Juggernaut then stopped as one of his hands sunk into his arm, moulding into a large laser canon. For a second he stood there, analysing everyone around, while the seams in his arm started to glow a molten orange and got brighter by the second. There was a loud hum as the room started to reverberate.

A beam of laser pounced through the room, tearing through the air.

Terros leapt to the side, feeling a gush of heat that made him grunt. When the beam hit the wall, the metal surroundings instantly started to melt, as silver started to rain down like goo.

The Juggernaut started to rotate, the beam moving with him, as he tried to hit Gides and Zemu.

Both of them were fast enough to dodge.

The blast stopped and the robot's arm started to smoke relentlessly.

Terros gazed at the mechanical brute, trying to compute a way to destroy it. There was none; for its shell was far too hot to touch and it had no moral compass – only opting for death and destruction, something that could not be bargained with.

Zemu on the other hand, saw that there was now a gaping hole in the wall where the being had just shot. With a smile, the dragon walked over to it, gesturing for his friends to follow. "Let's ditch the tin can!" he called out, jumping through. However, as he touched it, there was a blue glow as a holographic wall formed, translucent in appearance, that shocked Zemu upon touch. The being shook vigorously before being hurled back onto the floor, his whole body steaming.

"No!" Gides yelled out, fumbling to go and help his team member. As he got close, the Juggernaut swatted him with an arm and into the holo-wall, shocking him for a second. "AARGH!" he screamed as he fell to the floor, smoking as well.

"You cannot win," the Elder said through the speakers. "There will be no… escape."

The Juggernaut then pointed his canon at Terros, preparing to fire. The arm started to glow orange once more and the humming began.

"I guess this is it," Gides said to Zemu, his voice weak and raspy.

"Well, I had fun," Zemu croaked in response. "Beats working for those pirates any day."

"You are a good person," Gides added. "I may not have trusted you earlier, but I do now."

"That means a lot," Zemu said. "I think you and Terros are my first ever friends."

While the pirate and the fox were having a cringe-worthy heart to heart, Terros had already figured out how to beat the robot. He figured that if the walls of the room were made of a tough metal and the laser could melt through it, then surely the beam could eat into the robot.

The Juggernaut continued to charge his blast and Terros just stood still, anticipating the attack.

"What are you doing, Terros?" Gides shouted out.

The beast ignored his friend. A second before the canon shot out, he dashed forwards, ducking under the arm and pushed it upwards before the robot could even comprehend. Then the orange beam tore out and blasted through its head, instantly incinerating it.

Terros panted as the being stopped moving, its head now gone. It then fell backwards, completed dilapidated of power.

"He did it!" Zemu called out.

Rather than celebrate the victory, Terros carefully watched as a small hatch on the chest opened and there was some mumbled coughing from within. The beast tore open the machine and pulled out who was inside – a tall and skinny fox with lanky limbs and squinted red eyes.

"Let me go!" the fox screeched.

"Frecto, I presume," Gides said, standing up.

"I surrender!" the skinny fox shouted.

Rather than give in to the pleading, the beast held the pilot of the machine by the neck before ramming its face into the holo-wall.

"AARGH!" the fox screamed as he was shocked and rippled with energy.

"Elder!" Gides boomed. "Turn off this wall or your son loses his face."

"Always so pathetic," the speaker replied. "I gave my sole heir the best piece of technology… yet *still* he failed me."

"Switch it off, Father!" Frecto screamed as he continued to be shocked.

The wall instantly disappeared and the gaping beyond was revealed.

"Let's go," Gides said. "Keep hold of him," he added to Terros as they all stepped out of the room.

Unsurprisingly, as they did so, they were surrounded by soldiers, all aiming their rifles at them.

"Drop my son and get back into your cage," the Elder spat, emerging from behind his fox army.

Gides looked at the ancient being and then at Terros before he started to hiss. He breathed heavily at first, trying to hold back, but then his laughter burst out and he could not help but bend over and howl out. He chuckled so loudly and hysterically that he could not stop.

"What is it?" the Elder growled.

Gides slowly stopped laughing. "You said that Frecto is your sole heir, meaning that if he dies, then you lose your bloodline. All it takes is for my friend Terros to squeeze his clawed paw and your *only* son dies. Your body is in hardly enough shape to produce another, which means, *we* have the bargaining power. So, I suggest you all lower your weapons and let us walk out of here alive, else your son bites the dust."

"I am sorry," Frecto sobbed. "I..."

"Close your mouth!" the Elder hissed. "You have brought great shame on me today." He then paused for a few moments to allow himself to breathe heavily. "Lower your weapons," he said softly.

His soldiers followed.

"Good," Gides smiled. "Now you will let us go back to our car and only *then* will your son be returned to you."

"Fine," the Elder said. The soldiers then all backed off.

The trio of unlikely friends took Frecto and went up some stairs until they were back in the forest of which they had come from. Gides sat in the front seat, Zemu in the back. Terros was left outside, holding the hostage.

Once the engine started, Gides spoke to the beast. "Give him back now, and then jump in."

The Elder put out an arm, urging for his son to be returned and Terros did so, shoving the lanky fox towards him. And then, before he got into the truck, he walked up to the mechanical, ancient fox who was barely standing.

"Die!" Terros growled as he slashed one of his claws across, cutting one of the pipes coming out of the fox. Then before anything could happen, he jumped into the vehicle.

"What did you do?" Gides shouted out as the Elder fell to the floor, his body shaking. Gides then smiled and spat out a massive globule, so that his saliva hit the face of the fox who had killed his parents. After that, he slammed the acceleration pedal and the car roared to life, blasting them off into the distance.

From the car, Terros watched as the Elder continued to writhe, while brown juices squirted out from his severed breathing tube. He shook vehemently, until the last of his energy was gone and then he lay there, lifeless. The surrounding foxes tried to help, attempting to reconnect his pipes, but their efforts were futile.

"Nice one Terros," Zemu laughed. "You showed that metal retard who the real boss is."

"Now they are going to come chasing after us," Gides sighed.

"Not if I do this," Zemu laughed, jumping onto the top of the car where the canon was. He pressed a button and a large ball shot out, hurtling through the air before hitting the hut in the distance.

"AFTER THEM!" Frecto cried out, pointing at the car that was fleeing.

A second later, the ball erupted into flames as energy shot out in all directions and the small hut was obliterated, exploded and scorched. Shards of metal and wood sprayed in all directions and the destruction was immense.

None of the soldiers perished, wearing their heavy armour. But Frecto stood no chance.

"I guess that's one way to make an exit," Gides said with a smile. He then looked at the sky, seeing the Pirate King's spaceship as a distant dot. "What happens now?" he asked.

Chapter 7: The Pirate Underling

"Next!" boomed a loud voice that echoed through the land and sent the trees shuddering.

"Yes, Your Majesty," a small and squeaky voice said, as he pushed a large, round and metallic sphere across the ground, huffing and puffing all the while until it got onto a platform. Having finished his task, he smiled. Next he pulled a lever, and then the platform began to rise, taking the silver ball up with it.

A large hand reached from above and picked up the shimmering object when it was high enough.

"Third time's a charm," the Pirate King muttered, closing one eye and then hurling the ball across the massive field. The object spun and twirled before smacking into a small hut, instantly obliterating it. "Bullseye!" he called out. "Next!" he immediately added, waiting for his next ball.

"Yes, Your Majesty," an underling said, rolling another one onto the platform with great heft.

After picking up the next ball and hurling it at another hut, the king let out a large yawn, one large enough to create a vacuum and suck everything in.

"Is everything okay, Your Majesty?" the underling called out, using a megaphone so the king could hear him.

"I am bored!" the colossal being announced. "There are no stakes to this game."

"What should I do?" the small pirate said hesitantly.

"Take one of the Gedruls and stand her atop a hut. That way, if I make the shot, the game would be more fun."

"But you would kill her?"

"So…" the Pirate King cackled. "Go and fetch me one else I will use *you* as a target." The Pirate King then yawned again. "And please hurry," he said, looking at his fingernails in detail.

As this was said and the underling got to work, another one loaded up a large animal – a wide elephant, onto the platform. The Pirate King then picked it up and swallowed it in one go. It tooted his horn as it was lifted and then stopped after the first bite.

"Sirrah!" a pirate called out, standing bolt upright.

The Pirate King looked down, at the small dot in the distance.

"News, Your Majesty," he said, trying not to run out of breath. "The Elder fox is dead. So is his son," he added, panting.

"What?" the Pirate King replied. "That old, rusty man had a son?"

"Yes, he, erm, was killed. The beast known as Terros was seen on site."

"What?" the Pirate King said, louder and more angrily this time.

"Him and his fox friend got away. But now they have a new companion. A dragon - erm, one of ours. I think his name was Zemu."

"A prisoner?" the massive entity asked.

"Yes, sirrah. They took one of ours," the small one said. "I, erm, what do I do?"

"You have done enough," the Pirate King replied with a great sigh as he slumped in his floating seat. "Stand on that platform will you."

"Yes, sirrah," the underling said, standing on the metal disc.

"Now pull the lever there," the King growled.

"Yes," the underling said as he was slowly raised upwards.

A second later, the Pirate King had grabbed the tiny being and held him upwards, before swinging his arm back and hurling him through the air. He smiled as one of the huts was hit. "Bingo!" he chuckled.

"Sirrah!" another pirate said.

"*What* is it?" hissed the king.

"You just killed your second in command," the underling said.

"Did I?" the Pirate King asked in an overly dramatic and high-pitched voice. "I merely transferred the rank."

"To whom?" the underling pondered.

"To you!" the Pirate King chuckled.

"Am I?" the underling asked, standing at attention. "I am!" he clamoured. "I am the second in command!" he then realised that he needed to tame his excitement. "What would Your Majesty have me do?" he asked humbly.

"Find Terros!" the Pirate King growled. "Put a bounty of ten million Bonku on his head! I will not have that vile Gedrul defy me! He took one of my own. Now *that* is a cardinal sin."

"Yes," the new second in command said, walking off.

"WAIT!" the Pirate King exclaimed, his voice levitating the nearby grass and mud and almost deafening the underling.

"What is it, sirrah?" he replied, dazed.

"Sing my name before you go. Cheer me up if you so will."

"Of course," the underling replied, recomposing himself.

We all love the Pirate King,
He makes us so filthy rich.
That is why, we do sing,
Else we'll end up in a ditch!

The Pirate King smiled. "Good. Now leave me."

As this was said, another underling stood by his throne with a megaphone in hand. "Sirrah, I have strapped one of the Gedruls to a hut. Enjoy your next game," he said.

"Splendid!" boomed the Pirate King.

Chapter 8: Worlds Above Worlds

"Where to next, captain?" Zemu asked, putting his legs up and lying down at the back of the truck.

"Captain?" Gides the Fox replied, half confused and half smiling. "What makes me the captain?"

"Well, it sure ain't me," the pirate replied. "And Terros doesn't talk, so it has to be you."

"Captain Gides!" the fox cried, sitting bolt upright. "I like the sound of that." He then turned his head to look at the beast, looking unamused as always. "Cheer up old boy," he said.

Their journey was a combination of bumping up and down, followed by some sloshing through puddles and the odd skidding here and there.

There was a great issue with their plan – a glaring fault that gnawed away at everything. None of them knew where to go. They were just driving aimlessly through the jungle to find something of interest.

The beast known as Terros wanted to do something to help his people that were suffering, but there was nothing. He needed an army to defeat such a maniacal being as the Pirate King, but masses of infantry did not just grow on trees. His other option was to combat the Pirate King, one on one, and the victor would take control of the intergalactic pirate crew. But duelling a colossal being was no easy task and Terros would need some sort of superpower or strength enhancement to do even that.

"Paradise Haven," Terros mumbled, an idea forming in his mind. He needed to beat the Pirate King in one-on-one combat but was too weak and small to do it. If he could build a suit like the Juggernaut then he would have a chance against the extraterrestrial lizard and the so-called penguins could build that.

When Terros was a cub, he had heard the odd story about the Paradise Haven – an ultra-technological society in a floating island, somewhere on Planet Guinthra. The penguins had discovered the secret to invisibility so cloaked their entire kingdom.

"Where's that?" Gides asked.

Zemu and Terros both shrugged.

"Any hints?" Gides pondered. "This place could be anywhere, and we do not have a map. Zemu?" he asked.

"Why me?"

"Well, you are the only one who has been to space so maybe…"

"What?" Zemu asked. "I used to clean toilets. Do you think I know this planet?"

"Maybe you found a map once?"

"You seriously over-estimate the intelligence of space dragons."

"You never know – one might have…"

Terros gave a hard stare at Gides the Fox, wishing for the being to silence himself.

"Well, what plan do *you* have Terros? You barely even speak and have not told us why we want to visit the penguins. How will they help us?"

"Robot suit," Terros growled, not wanting to talk too much. "Use to fight Pirate King."

"That is smart!" Zemu squealed in excitement. "I would pay good money to watch a giant robot kill my old master."

"Why would the penguins help us?" the fox asked. "*Assuming* we find them."

Terros could not answer that question. Based on their confrontation with the Elder, it seemed that nobody cared about their cause.

"Here is an idea," Zemu let out. "I know I have my fair share of bonkers statements but…"

"I do not like where this is going," Gides sighed.

"What we need to do is infiltrate a pirate miniship. They have maps in them and infrared scanning devices. We can use that to discover this island and then fly there."

"You know…" Gides said. "That is not the worst idea you have come up with."

"Gides, you can fly right?" Zemu asked.

"Sure," the fox replied. "I have done enough simulators – the real thing should not be *too* bad."

"That is settled," the pirate said. "I should have my clearance card in one of these pockets. We can get to a miniship and take control of it with relative ease." The dragon leaned forwards. "What do you think, Terros?" he asked.

The beast nodded.

"Okay, so let us find a minishp," Zemu replied. "They usually are not too hard to break into, just need to lure one onto us and jump in from above. Remove the pilot politely and then once in I can use my card to access the database. Easy."

"Huh," Gides replied, impressed that the purple scaled creature was able to conjure up such a good plan. "That is settled then. How do we lure one?"

The beast pointed at himself.

"Bait," Zemu replied. "That does work." The pirate then pulled a small mechanical device from his pocket, opening it up and stretching out the antenna. "I will make a call."

"Wait, you have had that this whole time?" Gides asked. "They could have been tracking you with it. You just gave away our…"

"I took the tracker out," Zemu smiled. "I am not *that* dumb."

Gides shrugged. Once again, Zemu had proven that he was adept.

"Here goes," he said, pressing a few buttons.

"Hello…" came a static voice through the device.

"Ren Giflum!" Zemu replied. "I have found something interesting. Could you send a minishp to investigate? One should be enough."

"What have you found?" the speaker said, his voice rough and crinkly.

"Erm…" Zemu said. "The… the Gedrul, Terros. I have him apprehended."

"Okay, I am sending in a full legion…"

"No, no, no!" Zemu cried. "The beast is chained up. Only send one ship."

"The Pirate King has listed Terros as a top priority. Do not worry, soldier, I am sending in one hundred ships."

"Just one!" Zemu called back. "We just need one."

The beast was getting worried. If an entire legion were to come, then there was no chance out of this.

"It is okay, soldier, I have already…"

"No!" Zemu called back.

"Good job, soldier. What is your location? Your tracker does not seem to be working."

"Abort!" Gides hissed. "We cannot take on an entire legion…"

"What is your location, soldier?" the voice asked.

"I… erm…" Zemu stuttered. "Trees?" he replied, unconfidently. "We are surrounded by trees."

Terros was fed up. He reached over and grabbed the phone, turning it off and ending the call.

"What was that for?" Zemu asked.

"We were about to die!" Gides shouted. "I thought your idea was good but that was just…" the fox sighed. "Now what," he said, putting his face into his hands. "We had an excellent plan, and it is gone."

Growling, Terros thought desperately about what he could do. He just wanted to save his people, but had now made the situation significantly harder for himself. They needed a miniship and then everything would be good.

"What if we find one?" Gides asked. There had to be ships floating all over the jungle. Surely it would not have been too much effort to find and hijack one?

"We can certainly try that," Zemu said. "That could be a good idea."

"So, we are just going to walk up to the enemy," Gides sighed. "I guess at this point that is our only option."

There were trees over them, completely shielding them from the sun above. The beast knew that if he could climb to the top of them, then he could oversee everything and find a ship floating somewhere. He had enhanced vision, superior to humans and most other animals, so he could probably spot a ship.

Without warning, Terros jumped out of the truck, dashing to the nearest tree and then scaling it in seconds, digging his claws into the bark and propelling himself upwards. He did this rather quickly and in a matter of seconds had made his way to the thicket of leaves at the top. He pushed his head through some branches and thick leaves until the brightness of the sun glowed onto his face. *Wow,* he thought, marvelling at the beauty of the world from so high up. The jungle was a wonder of Guinthra and Terros would often be forced to marvel at its beauty.

The beast then glanced from left to right, looking at the pale blue sky and at the distant vegetation for the disease that was machinery, sucking the life out of his world. Very far off was the Pirate King's main ship, but apart from that, there was nothing else.

Look harder, Terros said to himself, trying to hone in on every detail, looking for anything out of place. *Come on,* he scowled at himself when he was unsuccessful. He then pondered how long he could have stayed up there before his teammates started to get worried about his disappearance.

So, with a heavy heart, Terros slipped back into the jungle, climbing down the great trunk of the tree. As he did so, a vague idea crept into his mind, slithering through a crack in his conscience. *What if we send a signal to the main ship? Then a smaller one could be sent.* There would most likely be a flare gun inside the truck that they had. They could easily use it to their advantage.

"Where did you go?" Gides asked as soon as Terros touched solid floor.

The beast ignored the fox, heading over to the back of the truck and tearing open the boot. There were a few small trinkets and gadgets as well as a nasty array of guns, laser-swords and more. There was a small canon gun of sorts, with a short handle and a round snout to shoot through. *Flare gun?* Terros thought. He knew that these were special weapons that humans used to communicate, firing coloured smoke into the sky. Terros wondered what colour the smoke would be – a random question, but still something that reeled into his mind.

"What are you doing?" the fox asked.

Terros ignored him, taking the gun and crawling up into the sky. He would have fired from the ground, but there could have been a chance that it would have set the vegetation alight. Fire would have added to his endless list of worries. He pressed the trigger, sending a gust of energy up as a hurtling ball of flame screamed skywards, exploding into crimson smoke.

When the deed was done, Terros returned to the ground. He could now hear the distant humming of a spaceship.

"I did not think of that!" Zemu laughed.

"But now what?" the fox replied. "A miniship will scout this location. How are we supposed to intercept it?"

Terros went back to the truck and pulled out another gun, this one much heavier and with a spiked claw on the end.

"A grappling gun?" Zemu asked.

The beast nodded.

"That is going to get you killed!" Gides insisted. "How are you going to…"

"He knows what he is doing," Zemu smiled.

The soaring got louder as the trees started to bristle and rumble. Out from beyond, a silver shape enlarged and left behind a streak of blue, almost camouflaged against the backdrop of the sky.

"Actually, we do not need that grappling gun," Zemu whispered. "Pretend to be captured – *both* of you. We will revert to the original plan."

Gides the Fox and Terros the Beast both sat down, putting their hands behind their head.

The silver object blaster through the trees and started to land – a sleek machine with soft edges and a shimmering surface. The thrusters slowed and the craft slowly swayed down, revealing its green cockpit glass and within it, a trio of pirates. One at the front with a visor on and two co-pilots behind.

"Zemu, reporting for duty!" the pirate said, pulling his hand up into a salute.

"We are pirates, not space-rangers!" hissed the leader, a bulky pirate with stubby wings, an eyepatch and large fangs. He then used the back of his wrist to wipe his nose, snorting while doing so.

"Yes, sir!" Zemu called back.

The leader shoved him backwards, a crooked grin forming on his face. "Quite pathetic," he snarled. "How did you bring in these two?" The fat pirate then pulled his hand out his pocket, revealing a rusty metal hand with fingers withered down to nuts and bolts and small whizzing levers. He then shouted to his two co-pilots. "Oi scum, get these two in the ship!"

The two other dragons then started walking over.

As they did this, the leader strode over to Terros and started speaking, his pungent breath repulsing the beast. "I cannot wait to hand you in!" he hissed, revealing his forked tongue. "The Pirate King will let me drink the Golden Rum for this." He then proceeded to touch Terros' mane.

The beast did not hesitate in retaliation, hugging his arms tightly around the other pirate, squeezing him for a few seconds as he was incapacitated. Terros then let go, before punching him in the face, instantly knocking him out.

As the fat leader was flung backwards, a golden tooth burst out from his mouth and zoomed through the air. He then smacked onto the ground and a pool of drool formed underneath.

Immediately, the other two pirates raised their arms in submission. "We surrender!" one squealed, then the other, delayed ever so slightly, most likely from brain damage.

Zemu laughed, walking over. The next two minutes were then spent using the rope from the grappling gun to tie the three pirates to a tree, so tight that they could not wiggle free.

"Let's get out of here," Gides smiled, slipping into the cockpit of the craft. He then wriggled around, adjusting his seat and moving around the steering wheel. "Just like a car," he added.

Terros then got into the back seat, sitting on the worn leather, strewn with tears. Zemu sat next to him.

The glass above started to slowly close over them, sealing the three inside.

"You sure you can do this?" Zemu asked.

"Yep!" Gides laughed. "Will be a piece of…"

"You did not even select a destination," Zemu said, standing up and walking over, swiping his card into the console machine.

"Where to?" Gides asked, seeing a list of destinations pop up, in digital writing. He then pressed a few buttons and a display of lights emerged, creating a holographic image of Planet Guinthra.

"Hello Zemu," came a female voice.

"Who said that?" the pirate asked, looking around.

"I am Delta-52, the entity of this ship. How may I be of service?"

Terros looked around, amazed by the technology. He could not see where the sound was coming from, as if she actually *were* the ship.

Seconds later, some light started to glow in the centre of the ship and a body formed. It was a woman, completely blue and translucent, but looking very much like an actual human, but was tiny, standing on a mini-holographic podium.

"Since when did my crew get technology this good?" Zemu asked, trying to touch the being and watching as his hand went through the light.

"The Paradise Haven," she said. "The penguins gave the pirates my technology in exchange for some Rotu."

"Paradise Haven?" Gides asked. "Do you know where that is?"

"Of course," she said. "That is where they made me."

"Good," Gides said. "Now take us there."

"My programming is not advanced enough to fly this ship," she said. "I am merely a string of coding and advanced technology, but my mind is limited. I…"

"Enough of that," Zemu sighed. "Can you at least *show* us the way?"

"Of course," she said.

Gides then looked around, wiggling his hands about as he pondered which of the many buttons would start the engine.

"This one," the voice said, as a button glowed blue.

"Huh, neat," Gides said, pressing it and causing the ship to roar to life, clattering the metal and shaking everything. "Hold on!" the fox called out as he started pressing other things and then the vehicle blasted off upwards.

The force was immense, pushing Terros greatly into his seat, hurting his chest and causing his stomach to squeal. His breathing fastened while he clutched the bars to the side of where he sat.

"Do not worry," the voice said. "Everybody finds their first take off hard."

There was a sudden drop and Terros' stomach squelched.

"Can you even fly?!" Zemu belted out as they hurtled downwards, their trajectory clumsy and inefficient.

"Better than you!" Gides snapped. He then yanked the throttle, gritting his teeth until the ship had flattened out once more.

"Excellent job, fox," the voice said. "Now, you need to aim at 067 degrees from North. Head that way and I will alert you what to do next."

"Some pilot," Zemu whispered to Terros. "Without his lady friend, he would not be able to fly," he said with a laugh.

Terros just shook his head and took in the vast sights – the immense clouds, pale sky, soaring birds and more.

Whenever Gides would turn and go at an angle, the beast would see his home jungle, a small green world far from where he flew. Despite the beauty of this, he still felt queasy with all the motion, wanting to lurch backwards.

"You look pale," Zemu said. "Paler than you usually are."

The beast tried to wipe off the look of disgust on his face as they kept hurtling and summersaulting through the air.

"Not to worry," the voice said; "we shall be there very soon."

They flew over an ocean, a great expanse of just water splashing and folding over. Terros watched this in awe, seeing the white froth and the explosive waves. He had seen the ocean once, on a trip, but seeing it from so high was something else.

"We are approaching our destination," the voice said.

"Delta-52," Gides said. "That is too long. I am going to call you Del."

"That sounds good," the voice said.

"Del, all I see is ocean and that small island over there. Where do I go?"

"Go to the island," Del said.

Terros looked at the island, a small enclave of sand with some palm trees and coconuts but nothing else. There was no sign of life. Terros knew that the penguins had hidden their world somewhere and unsurprisingly, they had done a stupendous job.

The ship blasted through the air, gliding across the sea, until they got close to the sandy beach. Gides then started to slow down and angled the nose of the metal vehicle downwards.

Once more, Terros crumpled backwards and felt his toes tingle as they went down. His heart felt uneasy and his lungs spasmed in his chest.

"Shaky landing, here we come," Gides said, trying to maintain solid control of the throttle.

"Here we go!" Zemu shouted as he threw his arms in the air.

The ship scraped across the sand, clanking as it skidded across the ground, interrupting the solemn peace of the beach and turning it into a shipwreck. They spun out of control until friction caught up and brought them to a halt.

The three of them were flung backwards from the sudden stop.

"Good job," Del said. "Now then, there should be a gate somewhere around here."

The mind of Terros was spinning uncontrollably. All his vision was blurred and he felt unending dizziness.

"Terros?" someone called to him. Who it was, was a mystery.

"Give him a minute," Del said.

Gides then pressed a button and the glass screen started to open, allowing fresh air in once again.

As time went on, Terros' mind started to straighten up. He gave a nod, undid his seatbelt and crawled into the open world, sinking his paws and feet into the hot sand.

"Did not realise Guinthra had such beautiful beaches," Zemu said, stretching out his wings.

"Back in a bit, Del," Gides said, getting out of the ship.

"Feel around for the gateway," Del called out. "It should be somewhere there."

Zemu put out his arms and started touching the air, hoping to find something. "I look ridiculous," he sighed.

"Yes, you do," Gides laughed, also feeling around for something. "This better not be a practical joke, Del," he called back to the ship.

"I am unable to humour," the device replied.

A second later, Terros felt something. In the air there was a structure of sorts. As he touched it, the cloaking disappeared and all of a sudden there was a large open doorway, with the entrance hidden.

"What is with these ominous gateways?" Zemu sighed.

"How do we get in?" Gides demanded, patting the gateway, but being met with a solid wall.

"There is no way back in," Del said. "You must wait for the gate to open to let someone out, then you can go in."

"How often do people go out?" Gides asked.

"Never," Del said. "Only when someone is banished, the harshest of prison sentences. This happens at most once a week."

"So, we have to wait a whole week to get in!" Gides shouted, storming over to the spaceship. "You did not think to tell us this sooner!"

Terros' eyes widened as the black wall disappeared and a blue shape started to swirl within. There were purple streaks of light and a faint humming sound could be heard.

"I am going to power you off!" Gides hissed. "You evil, narcissistic…"

"The door is open," Del said. "Go in before you lose the opportunity."

Zemu did not even hesitate, leaping into the blue abyss as his entire body faded away and he was absorbed into the endless nothingness.

"Zemu!" Gides yelled, seeing his friend be swallowed whole.

Terros then gestured for the fox to follow into the blend of colourful lights.

"I am *not* going in there!" Gides snapped. "I do not trust this computer one bit."

"I may not have humour, but I still have feelings," Del said.

Terros shook his head, walked over to the fox and picked him up.

"Unhand me, beast!" Gides cried.

Trudging over to the portal, Terros could not help but smile. When they were close enough to the blue energy, the beast threw the fox in.

"No!" Gides screamed as he was absorbed into oblivion.

"Good job, Terros," Del said. "I hope you find what you are looking for."

The beast nodded back to the computer before jumping into the gateway, disappearing for good.

Chapter 9: Shame and Glory

"Narthelus, you have brought great shame upon our people!" a mighty voice boomed.

"I apologise," the one known as Narthelus said in response. The chains on his arms were hard, pulling him to the ground, so even if he wanted to squirm free, he could not.

"You do not deserve to live in such a paradise!" bellowed another.

Narthelus, or Narth, as he requested his friends to call him, looked up. Surrounding him were twelve thrones – high seats that stood over him like giants, with small silhouettes sitting atop them. Above the thrones was a great mosaic glass of red and purple tint, so that the sun glowed through it and echoed a sunset of gloom on the area.

"Do you plead guilty?" one of the high-ups called.

Narth looked around. He was in chains, surrounded by the twelve most powerful people in his nation, within the

Dome of Judgement; potentially the most guarded place on the planet Guinthra. *How did I let this happen?* he asked himself.

"What say you Narthelus?" another asked.

I did nothing wrong, Narth said to himself.

"Look at the disrespect he shows us," one of the leaders said. "We should banish him from the Paradise Haven and send him to the Underworld!"

"You cannot banish me!" Narth called back. "I did nothing wrong!"

"We have seen the evidence! The footage distinctly shows you."

"Then I was framed!" Narth cried.

"Do you take the judicial system as a joke?" one said. "For assuming we are wrong is a major crime."

"Some might say blasphemous!" yelled another.

"Now then," said one. "Plead guilty and you will be frozen for ten years. If not, then you will be sent to the Underworld, where you will be as good as dead, living amongst the savages of this planet."

Narth tried to figure out what was worse. Being frozen for ten years was torture, having your entire body still for years, without being able to move, but still conscious through the whole process, seeing everything around. Narth had only seen a handful of people who had survived the freeze, but they were mentally broken after the experience – just shells of their former selves. The other option was being sent to the Underworld – a land full of great monsters and maniacal creatures. Narth pondered whether he could survive such a place.

Being banished meant he would never see his family again, nor his friends. At least if he were frozen, they could visit him in his chamber and then be reunited with him after the decade. However, Narth was young. He did not want to lose the prime of his days of ambition to the dogmatic empire.

"Speak, child!" screamed one of them. "Or we *will* incinerate you where you stand!"

"Banishment," Narth sighed. "I plead innocent, so will accept my banishment."

"So be it!" one of them called out. "Narthelus Pingo, you are sentenced to banishment from the Paradise Haven. You will be sent to the Underworld and will be denied access to our world ever again."

"Take him to the gate!" one called out.

Narth sighed, accepting the adventure he was going to go on. The stories of the Underworld were horrific, of giants, molten trolls and more. But he knew he could make it a fun time if he truly tried – assuming he was not eaten straight away.

Another person came up to him, wearing full robotic armour. He held a helmet which he hovered over Narth's head.

"Goodbye, Narthelus. Enjoy the world under!"

The helmet was brought over Narth's face, blackening his vision and then making him go unconscious as he slipped away.

Narth awoke in a small room, his eyes blurry and his head ringing with agony. The helmet was off and everything felt strange.

"You're awake," came a voice.

Narth turned to see a metal door slide open and in walked a woman. She had a black robotic suit on, covering her whole body, except her head and was wearing red goggles.

"So, prisoner, this is it," she said. "You are standing in the Gate. When I push the button, you will be sent downwards very fast and then will appear in the vile world below."

Thoughts were going through Narth's head. The Gate had always been so dreaded and feared, yet it was just a small room as he had just witnessed.

"I have prepared a small bag of essentials for you," she said. "Just so you do not die immediately when you arrive. There should be food for a few days – rations really, as well as a torch. They have this thing in the Underworld called 'night' where everything goes dark for half a day. Quite scary, really."

"Have you been down there?" Narth asked.

"I spent a few hours there," she replied, scratching her head. "I will let you make your own opinion of it."

Narth pondered what he was going to do down there. Would he make friends and try to settle down? Or would he be chased endlessly until he was killed? And how would he die, by gladiatorial arena, by drowning, roasted on a stove or more?

"Here we go then," she said, standing back. "Have a good life." As the doors opened so she could exit, she took one more look behind. "One more thing. When you are down there, do not try and return here. It will not work. Trust me – I have seen hundreds die trying to crawl back." As soon as she finished speaking, the doors shut, leaving Narth alone with his small bag.

"Here goes," Narth sighed, picking up his bag. "Time for a new life."

There was a humming sound in the room and the floor started to vibrate. Narth's heart quickened as his feet started to tingle. "Will the journey hurt?" he called out, hoping the woman would respond. The being's heart started to quicken as he felt more and more light-headed.

One of the walls of the small room then dissolved completely, revealing a blue void of yonder. It swirled and glittered and there were red and purple streaks dancing through it – a reality of great mystery, writhing and whirling into the infinite distance.

"The gate is beautiful," Narth smiled, feeling almost drawn to the kaleidoscope of reality. There was a cool breeze coming out of it, washing over his body in bliss.

"Step through," the woman said, through some speakers.

Narth strapped on his rucksack and got ready to leave his world. "Here goes," he said.

Before he could step through, he felt a violent shaking, making him almost lose his footing. The portal started screeching and humming loudly. A blast of cold air pushed back at Narth, stinging his skin.

"This is not right!" the woman shouted.

"What?" Narth asked as he heard intense growling from the void. From far within it, he could see faint shadows, three of them bulging through the abyss.

Narth started banging on the door that the woman had gone through. "Let me out!" he shouted. He could feel the freezing cold.

"This is something," he heard a cackle say in the distance, sounding like it was coming from miles away.

"I am never doing that again," said another, coming from within the portal.

Narth saw three silhouettes grow in size before being spat out of the portal and into the room where he stood.

The three of them were all very tall – one of them with purple scaly skin and a tattered hat. Another had orange fur and a long, wagging tail. The third frightened him the most – a wide creature with intense white fur and bulging muscles. Its face was still and its eyes pierced through his heart.

"Who are you?" the orange one said.

Narth's heart froze as he pondered what to say. There were three of them and only one of him. If he could create a distraction, then he might have been able to fetch the knife out of his bag.

"I don't think he speaks," the purple one said, revealing an array of crooked, yellow and spiked teeth.

"I do," Narth let out, his eyes wide in petrification.

"Get back through the portal!" shouted the woman. "Leave, you disgusting Underworld creatures!"

"Creatures?" the orange one laughed. "Us? If anyone is a creature it is you penguin people with your flippers and plump bellies. I did not think you lot were real but here we are."

"What's a penguin?" Narth asked, realising that his feet were much larger and fanned than the newcomers.

"*You* are a penguin," the purple one hissed. "Now how do we get out of here? The portal here gives me the creeps."

Narth pointed at the door where the woman had left through.

"Thanks," the orange one replied. "Open it, Terros."

The terrifying one finally moved, snarling as it took its monstrous claws and wrenched open the door.

"All of you stand back!" the woman cried, pointing a gun at the orange one.

"Nope," the purple one said, shooting a small bolt of something that made her stop moving and start rippling on the floor.

"No!" she cried, trying to move.

"I guess we made it to the penguin world," the orange one sighed. "You want to be our tour-guide?" he asked, looking at Narth.

"I'm a – a – a criminal," he let out.

"So are the rest of us," the purple one laughed.

"What do we do with her?" Narth asked, pointing at the woman. "As soon as she gets back up, she will sound the alarm."

The white beast then picked up the female penguin with ease. "Put me down!" she screamed. The beast then threw her into the portal.

As she disappeared into the distance, slipping away into nothing, Narth could not help but laugh.

"The name's Gides," the orange one with the bushy tail said. The scaly one is Zemu and the big scary one is Terros. He is actually very nice once you get to know him."

The white beast nodded.

"My name is Narth," the one known as a penguin said. He then pushed a button and the void started to close up, disappearing from sight. Narth had been given the second chance he always wanted.

Chapter 10: A Hefty Target

In the orbit of space was a ship. It was one of a diamond shape, with a narrow point on top and bottom and a wide mid-section. Within the cockpit a man named Kal sat, gazing at the stars in the distance. They somewhat amazed him with their sheer brilliance, lost amongst the vast blackness of space. He was wearing green, silk pyjamas and his feet were propped up onto the ship console. The boy had bright red hair – like that of a rose, falling down to his ears in straight layers, and his face was warmly pale with oceanic eyes.

Directly below him was a vast green planet filled with huge jungles and large oceans.

"Omicron, what is the name of this planet?" he asked.

"This is Planet Guinthra," said a digital voice. "Currently it is not under Federation control – for there are no people living here – just the odd race of animal."

"Well then it looks like the perfect destination for my holiday. Scan it for habitable beaches."

"Scanning…" said the voice.

Kal yawned, getting out of his seat and then stretched. "Still haven't recovered from that last job. Tracking down that smuggler was quite something."

"One hundred and eight beaches," the computer said, entirely emotionless.

The boy then walked down the passageway of the ship, the cool silver surface under his toes. "Guess we are going then."

"Would you like me to scan for tasks?" the computer asked.

"Erm…" Kal thought. He was certainly not in the mood for any bounty hunter work. "Anything of high importance?" he asked.

"No," the computer replied.

"Good," the boy said. "Now then, help me pick my outfit for this holiday."

"Yes, Master Kal," the computer replied.

He walked into a small room – that felt almost like an extended wardrobe with lilac lights on other side.

"I suggest the following apparel," the computer said, creating a hologram of a short-sleeved shirt with a flowery pattern.

"Looks good," Kal said. "What about sun exposure on this world? Will I need sunglasses?"

"Yes," the computer replied, adding a pair of glasses to the hologram. "Should I print?"

"Go ahead," Kal replied.

Some lasers got to work, together with some flashing of lights. A thread started rapidly weaving together the

The Beast Known as Terros

clothes, pattern included. Seconds later, the cotton top was ready and the boy replaced his pyjamas with the new printed outfit.

"This holiday is going to be so good," he said. "A whole week of no bounty hunter work." He then looked out the window. "How long is a week here?" he asked.

"The same as the Intergalactic Federation timing. Plus a few hours." the computer replied.

"An even longer holiday!" Kal smiled, putting on his sunglasses.

"Exactly," the computer replied.

"Now then, take me to the beach. I want to relax."

"Of course, Master Kal," the ship replied.

As he got into his seat to help with the flying, the computer spoke up once more.

"There is a bounty here," the console said. "Just showed up."

"Nope," Kal replied. "I am not taking part in any of that."

"The Pirate King has sent out a bounty to bring in a Gedrul known as Terros," the computer said.

"*The* Pirate King?" Kal asked. "What is he doing here?"

"Not sure," the computer replied. "But he has promised a handsome reward for a task. There is a side note saying that he is only outsourcing help due to the incompetence of his own squad. I am not sure what that is supposed to mean."

"What that means is we have ourselves a mission!" Kal said excited. "If I can get on the Pirate King's radar then who knows what trajectory this will have on my career."

"So, holiday cancelled?" the computer asked.

"Of course," Kal said, taking off his sunglasses and tossing them to the side. "Surely this job will not take too long, depending on what it is."

"Let us see," the computer said.

"Pirate King!" Kal shouted, getting excited. "I cannot believe this. I am about to work my way up the underworld. The likelihood of him being here while I am on my holiday is the perfect coincidence."

"Now then," the ship said. "Let me get your suit ready."

"Pirate King," the boy muttered. "I must look my best."

A hatch in the wall opened to reveal a pale blue suit of armour that was slender and bulky at the same time, with purple highlights throughout. The helmet was simple and round with a visor. However, this suit had multiple chips and scratches on it.

"This is not perfect," Kal said. "I cannot wear that in front of the Pirate King. I need to give a good first impression if I am to get a reference in the bounty hunter world."

"I thought you liked the rugged look," the computer said.

"Not today," Kal replied. "Fix the suit and make it look perfect."

"Yes, Master Kal," the ship said, closing the hatchet where the suit was.

"I need to look my absolute best."

Kal was grateful for his ship, having been given to him by his father. His last good memory of him.

After a few minutes, the ship had finished cleaning up his spacesuit.

"Commencing suit-up," Omicron said as the metal plates of his armour were strapped onto him, fitting perfectly. All apart from his waist which felt a little tight. "Apologies for any discomfort caused," the ship added.

"Don't worry," he said. "The suit is a bit tight though."

"That is because you have been putting on weight as of recent," the ship replied. "In the last one hundred hours, your mass has risen by…"

"Don't need to know," he said. "If I breathe in, it should be okay." He then pulled the helmet on. "It stinks in here," he said, his voice now transmitting as robotic through the mask.

"Spraying perfume," Omicron said from within the suit as a small squirt of strawberry scent was released, getting into his eyes.

"We are ready," Kal spluttered. "Plot course for the Pirate King. Let us see what he has in mind."

"Of course, Master Kal."

The Pirate King watched his favourite event occur. The hatching of the new eggs was a treasured event in his tradition. There were dozens of small eggs, all placed into a circular shape. When the time was right, he would roar and all the eggs would shatter, releasing the next generation into the world. Many dragons were there, watching eagerly – for these were the children of many of them. Since all the eggs were mixed together, nobody would know whose child was whose, resulting in the babies being brought up collectively as a herd of future pirates – assigned to random parents.

"Ready!" a pirate shouted.

The Pirate King then looked up at the sky, stretched out his wings and took in a huge breath, as if trying to suck in an entire cloud.

"RROAAAR!" he let out, his voice blowing the trees to the side and echoing into the sky.

There was the faint sound of scratching as the yellow eggs started to twinge and hair-thin cracks started to form in rivers and meandered around.

"Arise, my children!" the Pirate King yelled. Whilst not biologically his children, he treated all dragons as if they were his spawn.

There was a crack as all the eggs smashed, and out popped tiny, purple limbs with tiny wings that would never be exercised. They then started to crawl free – at least one hundred baby creatures, all with large, black and adorable eyes.

"So beautiful," the Pirate King sighed, leaning back into his seat. "Hopefully this next generation will not be as hopeless as all of you!" he said, hissing at his underlings.

"Sirrah!" one of them called out, using a megaphone, walking closer to the king.

"What do you want?" the Pirate King replied.

"You sent out a message for a bounty hunter! One has arrived for you," he cried.

"Thank you," the Pirate King responded. "Someone move the babies to somewhere safe while I meet with my new minion." He looked up at the sky as a ship passed into orbit, pulsing through the air above and tearing through clouds at immense speeds. "You know it shows how bad all of you are if I need to outsource assistance," he muttered. Yet when he spoke quietly, everyone could still hear what he had to say.

A diamond shaped ship hovered above the ground, blue thrust trailing behind it. As it slowed down and a door opened, a figure wearing blue armour flew out using a jetpack, before landing on the ground. The being removed the helmet to reveal a pale human face with bright, red hair. He had a rifle in one hand and his other wrist had a keypad on it.

"Pirate King!" he called out, bowing his head. "I am Kal, a bounty hunter. I received your signal and will gladly accept your challenge. What must I do?"

The Pirate King saw him as a tiny dot. And so he pulled a large magnifying glass strapped to the side of his throne and then zoomed in on the boy.

"There is this Gedrul beast called Terros. He has escaped my captivity and is leaving behind a trail of chaos wherever he goes. Bring me Terros' head and you will be paid handsomely."

"Yes, Your Highness," he said with a smile. "Any hints or leads you can give me before I…"

He did not finish speaking for there was a 'zip' sound. Kal looked down to see that a laser bolt had torn through his chest and left a small hole. "Oh," he mumbled before collapsing to the ground, his chest smoking.

There was a rustling from the nearby bushes as out emerged a being, with a metal helmet that was under a thick black hood. He had a long, tattered cape and strode over to Kal's dead body, his heavy boots digging into the ground.

"Who are you?" the Pirate King asked, puzzled. "And why did you just kill my associate?"

"I received your signal," the figure responded, his voice mechanical and static, very deep and almost inaudible if not for the Pirate King's large, fanned ears. "I am here for the bounty," he said, stealing Kal's rifle and slinging it onto his back. He then took the keypad from his wrist and put it on his own.

"Can you do a better job than him?" the Pirate King asked, raising an eyebrow. "Bring me Terros' head and you will be handsomely paid."

"I care not about payment," the bounty hunter said. "The glory of the hunt is good enough for me." The man then jumped onto the stairs of Kal's old ship, pressing a few buttons to cause the hatch to close behind him. And just like that, he had stolen the ship and seconds later he had blasted off into the sky to go and hunt down Terros.

"Wow!" the Pirate King said. "I was not expecting that." He paused for a moment. "Now where are my eggs? And someone please clean up this body!"

Chapter 11: The Resistance

"Welcome to my world," Narthelus Pingo smiled.

Terros looked at the penguin, a short being with black flappy arms, a white face with a baby nose and massive, soulless eyes. Narth did look relatively creepy, especially since he was wearing human clothing, with trousers and a vest.

Narth then opened a door, revealing an immense world, one filled with skyscrapers, flying ships, robots storming the streets and more.

"So much technology," Gides said, staring in awe at the fact that every last building made him feel like a pebble.

"Aren't we going to stand out?" Zemu asked. "I am a dragon after all."

"Dragon is a stretch," Gides laughed. "You are more of a lizard, since you cannot fly, nor can you breathe fire."

"You will *all* fit in," Narth said smiling. "We often have visitors from other worlds."

It appeared that even though they were so high up in the sky, they all felt very much grounded, as the floor felt solid beneath them.

"So why are you here?" the penguin asked at last. "It is not every day that you see a fox, a dragon and a… whatever he is, working together."

"We are here for a robot," Zemu said.

"A really big one," Gides added. "One large enough to take the Pirate King on in combat."

"Pirate King?" Narth asked. "Isn't he a giant?"

"Yes," Zemu said. "That is why we need your people to build us a massive robot to duel him. We know you have the resources to do that."

"Take us to your leader," Gides said. "He will understand that the Pirate King needs to go. It is for the betterment of Guinthra."

"Nope," Narth said. "I am a criminal, remember? The council of this world just sentenced me to banishment. If I am seen within a mile of the courtroom then they might just execute me," the penguin said in a whispered voice. "Not to mention that the Pirate King has signed a treaty with my people. In exchange for our technology, we have been supplied with Rotu."

"Del did mention this," Gides said. "Why would your leaders want hallucinogens?"

"So they can supply the criminals," Narth replied. "There is no crime in the Paradise Haven. Because of this, the rulers create crime to justify the existence of the police robots that patrol the place. It is a deep-rooted conspiracy."

"How would you know that?" Zemu asked, scratching his head.

"The same reason I was arrested," Narth replied. "I am part of the Penguin Alliance!" he whispered forcefully, putting a hand to his heart and bolting upright.

Zemu and Gides looked at each other for a second before erupting into howling laughter. "Penguin Alliance?" they laughed in unison.

Terros simply shook his head.

"Is that some kind of rock band?" Gides asked.

"No," Narth said with dead-seriousness. "It is the name of the rebellion. A team of penguins working to overthrow this totalitarian authority."

"Boring," Zemu sighed. "Do you know how many rebellions there have been across the galaxies? Such an unoriginal idea."

"Oh," Narth said, his mouth drooping into a frown.

"State your business!" a robot called, bursting out in front of them and taking them all by surprise. It was in the shape of a cuboid with wheels at the bottom. It had small slits for eyes and two basic, stiff arms.

"My name is Qualindorius," Narth said with dead seriousness. "These three are travellers and I am showing them the beauty of our world."

The machine stared Terros in the eyes for a second, not flinching or blinking, not that it could. It then beeped and turned around.

"Enjoy your stay," it said, rolling off into the distance.

"That was a close one," Gides sighed.

"Not really," Narth laughed. "The robot police here are dumb. The council have not yet made artificial intelligence widespread, so all the robots lack true sentience. There are a few demos of true intelligent machines, some of which we sold to the Pirate King and some were sold to…"

"You seem to know a lot about the government here," Gides said.

"We had a spy," Narth replied. "Sent to infiltrate the ranks of the top and learn what he could. When he was discovered, he gave away my location – hence my banishment."

"What a retard," Zemu said. "Giving you up like that. In my culture we say that snitches are glitches."

"I think you mean snitches get stitches," Gides replied.

"No," the dragon insisted. "It is…"

Once more, Terros gave the two of them a hard stare, causing them to back off.

"Anyway," Narth said. "I can take you to my people. They might be able to create a large robot out of some scraps."

"Scraps?" Gides asked. "We need something strong enough to fight a giant lizard."

"What is the biggest robot on this island?" Zemu asked. "We can just steal that."

"The Juggernaut Model H," Narth replied. "It is about four times the height of me. A truly *glorious* machine."

"Four times your height?" Zemu laughed. "So twice my height?"

"How will that be useful against the Pirate King?" Gides asked.

"You could maybe grab onto his toe?" Narth replied, raising an eyebrow.

"Just take us to the rebellion," the fox said. "Perhaps they know more."

"Sure thing," the penguin said.

As they were all walking, Terros could not help but be confused by his surroundings. There were penguins, wearing shirts and ties, going about their daily lives, flooding the streets. In addition, the box robots were wheeling around, looking clueless. On the roads there was no traffic, with cars hovering and zooming through the streets with no delay - a smooth system.

The vehicles were ultra sleek, with no edges and having only curves, making them as streamlined as possible. They had no sort of glass at the front, so it was impossible to see the drivers.

"This is a very strange place," Zemu said, looking around. "A bit *too* perfect."

"That is what they want you to think," Narth said. He then put out one of his flabby arms. "Taxi!" he yelled.

Taxi? Terros thought, unaware of the term.

As Narth did this, a bright yellow flying car pulled up beside them, with the word 'Taxi' glowing in red on the sides. As it stopped, the doors at the side opened like wings and some stairs folded out, landing on the pavement.

"Is there enough space for all of us?" Gides asked as Zemu stepped in.

"More than enough," Narth replied. "I shall sit in the front."

Terros sat in the back of the vehicle, on the metal seats, wedged between a fox and a dragon. Zemu's wings were pushing against his back, creating pain.

The driver was a penguin, like Narth, but wore sunglasses and had a blue cap on backwards.

"Greetings," the taxi driver said, pulling away from the side of the road and slowly speeding up. "Where to?" he asked.

"The Great Arch of Krius!" Narth said with a smile.

Zemu and Gides could not help but let out a small giggle at that name.

Between them, Terros was just shaking his head, looking completely unamused.

As the taxi started driving, a penguin was walking across the street, wearing a suit and tie, while holding a briefcase. In his mouth was a cigarette. The taxi would have hit him if not for the driver slamming the breaks.

Angry, the penguin slammed the bonnet of the taxi, spitting out his cigarette. "Hey!" he shouted. "I'm waddling here!"

"Sorry," the taxi driver replied, allowing the pedestrian to finish crossing the street.

They then continued driving off, towards the so-called 'Arch of Krius'. As they travelled, Terros kept looking out his window, observing the world around them. While it was impossible to see through the windows from the outside, on the inside it was just like normal glass.

They drove for a few minutes, almost entirely undisturbed, until they could make out a large arch in the distance, going over the road like a rainbow.

"This is it," the driver said, pulling up at the side. "Not sure why you lot want to visit this ancient thing, but oh well. Payment please."

Narth put a flappy arm out, putting the tip onto a console for a few seconds.

"Payment received," the driver said as the doors started to open. "Have a nice day."

"How did you pay?" Gides asked once they were back in the fresh air.

"My fingerprint allows him to transfer money from my digital currency account to his. A seamless transaction."

Terros looked at the penguin, confused, not understanding a word of what he had just said. Instead of saying anything, he just shrugged and waited for instructions.

"Where to now?" Gides asked, looking at the giant arch over them, reaching to the clouds and kissing the sky.

"The Great Arch of Krius was constructed after the civil war, where General Krius won and overthrew the monarchy. He then…" Narth stopped talking, turning around to see Gides and Zemu laughing.

"A penguin civil war!" Zemu laughed, rolling onto the floor.

"I thought I had seen everything," the fox squealed. "I am trying to imagine penguins sitting in tanks."

"This is not something to laugh about," Narth growled. "Many of my people gave their lives that day, sacrificing themselves for the greater good. This arch commemorates the sacrifices of…"

"Gides," Zemu chuckled. "Imagine a penguin dying in battle – lying on the floor and flapping his flippers as he breathes his last."

The fox burst out laughing, saliva spluttering everywhere.

In fact, even the beast known as Terros found himself grinning mildly at the idea. He was part of a warrior race and was built for battle, with large muscles, ferocious teeth and claws. A penguin would not survive ten minutes on the battlefield.

"Laugh it up!" Narth growled. "All of you are disgraces."

"Just show us where to go," Gides said, biting his tongue.

"Now there looks like there is nowhere to go right?" Narth said, getting excited. "But you are about to witness the heights of our technology."

"Secret lift?" Gides asked.

The penguin drooped his head. "How did you know?" he cried.

"Boring!" Zemu let out. "Now, where is the lever?" He put his hand on the side of the arch, feeling around until a plate moved under pressure. Then the ground opened up as two sheets slid, revealing a silver circular lift. "Not very discrete," he said.

"That is because penguins are dumb!" Gides laughed. "None of them would even suspect a hidden lift was here. And when they see us go down, they will be oblivious to what is going on."

Terros wanted to laugh at that statement.

"They told me creatures from the world below were cruel," Narth let out. "But you are worse than gnarly."

"If it was not for us, you would be out there," Gides said. "You would not last ten days in the fiery landscape of our world.

"Fiery?" Narth asked.

"Yes," Zemu said. "Filled with scary monsters the size of skyscrapers. You would be turned into penguin stew within ten seconds."

"I…" Narth gasped.

"We saved you from a fate worse than death," Gides exclaimed. "So, you *owe* us."

"Of course," Narth said, bowing his head. "Whatever you want, it is yours."

"Good," Gides said. "Now take us down there."

"Yes, sir," the penguin said, pulling a lever and causing the circular disk to go down.

"You sure nobody will suspect anything?" Zemu asked.

"No. It will be okay," the penguin replied as the four of them started descending into the darkness below. "I cannot wait for you to meet my brother," he said ecstatically. "General Marth will be glad to meet you."

"Who is that?" Gides asked.

"Our leader," Narth replied, as they all disappeared into the darkness. "Would you like me to recite a poem about him?"

"I would rather not," Gides replied.

"Here goes," the penguin said, taking in a large, deep breath, until his lungs were puffed up.

When the Paradise Haven was young,
And primitive was our nature,
There were two brothers by tongue,
But I will come back to that later.

Marth was a boy,
So fair, strong and wise.
Lest he would cry ahoy,
To when he faced demise.

And then there was I,
The fabled brother Narth,
As we do all say,
My love was sewn in my hearth.

"That's garbage," Zemu said, butting in. "It does not even make sense."

"Huh?" Gides pondered aloud. "Never thought I would hear a penguin recite poetry."

"Never mind that," Narth replied, annoyed he had been interrupted. "Feast your eyes upon my underground kingdom!"

Terros looked to see lights everywhere in the underground bunker. There was scaffolding all over the place and there were pipes riddled everywhere, meandering from one corner to the next. There was a rich smell of oil and metal combined with the ringing and clattering of iron.

They were in the underground of a world above their own. It was a strange concept to get their heads around.

"These are cool!" Zemu said, picking up some metal gloves and putting his hands inside them. "Perfect fit as well," he said with a smile, swinging them about.

"Put them down," Narth said.

"Who are these intruders!" boomed a voice.

From the other side of the hangar walked a very tall being, his heavy feet slapping the ground with each step. His shadow was immense, scaring Terros ever so slightly.

"Narthelus, you are back!" the monster said.

"Yes, brother," Narth laughed. "Good to see you too."

The being stepped into the light, revealing a normal sized penguin whose body was in the centre of a large robot with skeletal limbs.

"Like my new exoskeleton?" the penguin asked, jumping out. He looked like Narth, but his black skin was a dark grey, making Terros wonder if they were actually

The Beast Known as Terros

related. "I missed you brother!" he called out, hugging Narth. "I heard they banished you?"

"They tried, Marth," Narth said. "Luckily these people saved me from the dreaded gate."

"Wow," Marth said. "You three must be from the demonic Underworld. It is a miracle you have survived there so long."

"You have no idea," Zemu replied.

"Now then," Marth said. "What brings you three here? You saved my brother, so I owe you."

"They want a robot suit," Narth said.

"Of course," Marth replied. "Take your pickings, brave travellers. We might need to adjust the cockpit size so that you can fit in."

Terros looked at the robots – all penguin sized, with reasonably long legs that made them slightly larger than a human.

"These will not do," Gides said. "We need something big enough to fight the Pirate King."

"The Pirate King?" Marth replied. "No can do."

"Why not?" Zemu asked. "Just make it bigger."

"The Pirate King is taller than a skyscraper. The largest mech we have made is twice the size of a human and even that had stability issues. Not even the government has been able to make a machine that large. And if we somehow were able to do it, we could not power such a mechanical behemoth."

"It was worth a try," Narth said. "Let me show you the way back to the portal so you can go home."

"No!" Terros growled, standing over the two penguin brothers and glaring at them. "Make the machine!"

Gides looked at his buddy, unsure of what he was trying to do. Was he going to eat the penguins? That would be quite the sight to behold.

"I cannot," Marth said. "I am sorry."

"*You* cannot," Narth said, "But someone else can?"

"Who?" Marth replied.

"Exekus Imporius. He must know how to create such a machine."

"We cannot trust him. He is crazy!"

"Crazy is good enough," Gides said. "Where is this Exekus?"

"Banished," Marth replied. "He *was* the best scientist in the haven, being the one to have designed much of the machinery used by the government. But the more he invented, the more his desires took control of him. He became so obsessed with building Celestial robots that he was imprisoned."

"Celestial robots?" Zemu asked.

"In order to protect this kingdom, Exekus wanted to make giant robots that he would use to destroy the Underworld – to prevent them from ever attacking us," Marth spoke sombrely

"Exekus was banished for his heresy," Narth said. "He has not been seen in over a decade and we presume he is now dead. If he is alive and you can somehow find him, then we can provide him with the resources to make this machine."

"Guinthra is a large planet," Gides said. "How do we find one being? Someone so crazy that he could be anywhere, in an underground lair or in a submarine or even off-world."

"A bounty hunter," Zemu said. "We pirates have access to the bounty hunter database. We will need a professional."

"Let me put out an advert," the dragon said, walking up to a computer. He then started putting numbers in and suddenly the screen went black. "Huh," he said as some writing appeared on the page.

"What is it?" Gides asked.

"There is a hefty bounty on *your* head, Terros," the pirate said. "A hefty, hefty one, issued by the Pirate King."

"Ignore that," Narth said. "Put out a new bounty, under my name. For Exekus Imporius."

"How much do we ask for?" Zemu asked.

"One million Bonku," Marth said.

"What?" Gides asked. "How do you have so much money?"

"Family business," Marth smiled. "Our father owned a fish factory."

"Okay," Zemu said, typing. "What state do we want Exekus in? Dead or alive?"

"Zemu," Gides sighed. "If the penguin is dead, then how do we intend on building a robot?!"

"Good point," the dragon replied. "Alive it is." He pressed a few more buttons. "And sent."

"I guess we just wait now," Narth said.

"Not quite," Marth replied. "We still need to do some planning and must source some parts."

"Like what?" Gides asked.

"It needs a power core."

Sometime later, Terros was looking around the penguin facility, taking in all the strange sights and gadgets. There was a small hammer on a table, with a handle and metal parts hanging from it, including many wires. The beast picked up the light object. "I like this," he mumbled, throwing it in the air and catching it. It was much too small and needed to have more heft.

"You like that?" Narth asked. "It's unfinished at the moment. My brother calls it a vibro-hammer."

Terros dropped the object and gazed at the other penguin sized trinkets. There was one thing that caught his interest specifically, a pink flower, very bright in colour and almost mesmerising to look at as it danced. It was plucked straight out of his jungle – the dreaded Jyko Flower.

"My brother must be running experiments on it," Narth said, tapping the glass case that surrounded it. "Bit dangerous though, having it in its purest form. Could kill someone."

"Nonsense, it is just a flower," Zemu laughed, strolling in. "So, *this* is why my people came to this planet," he pondered, lifting up the dome and revealing the flower, propped up by a stand. "Such a delicate little thing that has called all this malarkey," the pirate said. "I wonder what one little whiff would do." The pirate's eyes widened as he looked at it in awe, his mouth starting to drool.

"Put it down!" Terros roared.

Zemu ignored his friend.

Gides was there, lurking around the corner. "What's that?" he asked, running over to see what was happening. "Team meeting without *me*?"

"This is the Jyko Flower," Zemu said. "My people travelled halfway across the galaxy for this dumb plant."

"You should probably put it down," Gides said. "Don't want to be inhaling that toxic stuff."

"One second," Zemu said, before breathing in heavily. "AACCHOO!" he let out, sneezing as smoke billowed out of his dragon mouth and struck the flower, tearing it apart and sending the petals everywhere, alongside a large pink cloud of dust. It spread through the air, an angry cloud of death, towards Narth.

"MOVE!" Terros shouted, pushing the penguin out the way and saving his life. But as he did this, he felt a twinge in his nostrils as something went in. A second later he was smothered by the substance and heard a heavy ringing.

"Terros?" Gides asked, his voice long and drawn. "Terroooooooooooos," he let out, rippling. "What did yoooou do, dummy?" the fox shouted, shoving Zemu back. The pirate seemed to look longer and taller, skinnier and stretched as colours filled Terros' eyes.

The beast tried to power through, but he kept hearing strange voices, and lots of cackling, hissing and more. Like quicksand, the ground beneath him started to morph, making him sink through as the world around him said goodbye and he was gone into a long black tunnel of darkness.

"Terros!" someone called out, shaking the beast awake.

Terros looked around, unable to see anything through the blurry fog of his eyes. "Who said that?"

"You are late," the same voice came again. "The Flunderfil has begun and you are *not* on time."

"The flunder-what?" Terros asked, scratching his eyes.

"The Flunderfil – when the Krazens have their yearly agreement with the Gooyoos under the tri-eclipse."

Terros could not understand what was being said. The gibberish that had just been spoken baffled him to the core. "What is this place?" he asked, gesturing to the purple river that was in front of him, the heavy thrust of the stream leading off into oblivion.

"No time to explain!" the speaker said, a short and fat mole, wearing a flowery shirt and sandals. He pulled his sunglasses on and jumped onto a small raft atop the purple rapids. "Come along!" he called out.

"What is your name?" the beast asked, maintaining his footing as he stood on the small plank of wood.

"Bimblim Blum," the mole said. "Well, that is just the shortened version. My actual name is Bimblimatus Blevenim Son of Blithiril, Blumatiarios. But that is quite a mouthful, don't you say Terros Tarthanian Mrilmus?"

"Quite the name," the beast said, sitting down and causing the boat to tilt. "So, tell me more about this Flunderfil."

"You okay if my friends come along?" Blum asked, ignoring his question. "We have Harvey Raptor and Ivan Neprios."

Terros looked at the mole, unsure of what to say. "There is not enough space on this raft for more people."

"Nonsense," the mole said as the raft changed size, turning into a large sailing boat.

It happened so quickly and so seamlessly that Terros was puzzled.

"I see you are Kwamfoodled," the mole laughed. "You Guinthrans always get surprised by the wonders of this world."

"This world?" Terros asked, still unsure of how he got to this place. "What is this world?"

"There is a time for everything. And that time is oh so unsuperiously now!" Bimblim Blum cried. "And here are my friends."

From the side of the bank were two people. One was a green dinosaur with scaly skin and a long tail. He had a long white beard and wore a monocle along with a human suit and tie.

"Greetings, gentlemen," the raptor said, hopping into the boat. "My name is Harvey Raptor. It is an honour to meet you." He put out a small, hanging hand to shake with Terros.

The beast shook it.

"I must apologise for my tardiness," Harvey said. "The Guild of Raptors and I were busy discussing the nature of an unidentified object floating through space. A glove the size of a planet is most peculiar."

"A glove the size of a …"

"I apologise for interrupting," the mole said. "Here we have Ivan Neprios, the greatest comedian of our time."

Terros looked to the riverbank, unable to see anyone there. "Where is he?"

"Look harder," Blum laughed.

The beast squinted, looking at the grass in detail. He noticed a small object leap up and into the boat.

"Ribbit! My name is Ivan Neprios," the small amphibian croaked, a frog with a baseball cap. "Sorry I am late. My wife just gave birth to centuplets."

"Centuplets?" Terros asked.

"Ribbit!" Ivan laughed. "One hundred identical children. Quite the achievement. Still doesn't quite beat my brother with his milliplets."

"How is Mrs Neprios?" the mole asked. "Must have been a painful birthing process."

"Nay," the frog said. "My wife is a great person. She endured the whole ordeal like it was nothing."

"My wife was the greatest astronomer of our time," Harvey Raptor said, wiping a tear from under his monocle.

"Do you have any family, Terros?" the mole asked, looking him dead in the eyes.

"Erm…" the beast said, starting to think.

"Forget about them," Blum chuckled. "We have more pressing matters – like this song I was writing. I need help composing the final verse."

"Sing it then, Ribbit!" Ivan Neprios croaked.

"Here goes!" the mole clamoured, taking in a deep breath.

A Twiddle dam Diddle,
And Deem Double Dip,
We all do like to row.
And even though we tend to giggle,
And seep in through in high and pip,
We all begin to know.

And a bing and a bong,
The growling lion squealed.
For if it was up to the daring eyes,
Of the Tuesday winter eerie cries,
Dim dabbled in the crispy fries.
On the Flunderfil afternoon.

"Why am I here?" Terros asked. Last he remembered, he was…

"Forget about all that!" Harvey Raptor smiled. "Join in with the song."

"Mind if I join in!" came a voice from underwater as a mass rose through the surface.

"Opera Croc!" the mole shouted to the crocodile.

"Greetings my beautiful friends," the reptile smiled as he rolled into the boat. "Are we going to the Flunderfil?" he asked.

"Yes," the frog croaked. "But we cannot go until Terros here joins in with our song."

"Don't be a party pooper," Opera Croc said. "Forget about your liiiiiiiife!" he sang. "Join in with us and you will be happy forever."

"Happy forever," Harvey said.

"Happy forever," Blum added.

"Happy ribbit forever," Ivan croaked.

"No," Terros said, with great strain. "This place is not real."

"If this place is not real, then explain the tri-eclipse," Blum said, pointing at the sky. "This is the real world. Your memories are fake – just an illusion created by the Fire King Ebelos, hallowed in his glory, revered in his intent and malevolent in his many ways."

"Not real," Terros said, jumping backwards and into the river. As he sunk into the purple haze, he knew that what he had done was right. He watched as the cracks in reality began to grow, glimmering with a shining bright light as the world faded into nothing.

"He's up!" Gides called out as Terros crawled back into reality.

The second he could see and breathe again, he leant to one side and vomited out intensely, as purple gook seeped out from his mouth, spluttering on the floor and smoking with hissing bubbles.

"Sorry about that," Zemu said, scratching his head.

Terros gave the pirate a hard glare.

Chapter 12: A New Mission

Elsewhere on Planet Guinthra, Kal awoke in the middle of a field. His eyelids snapped open and straight away he was overwhelmed by a revolting stench. The boy sat up and looked to see that he was caked in mud. Thick brown ooze was wrapped around him, smothering him by the second.

"My suit!" he called out, seeing that his state-of-the-art armour was gone. "How am I even alive?" he asked out loud, standing up and trying to source his pain. The last thing he remembered was a sharp hissing through his abdomen. And then…

It was all blank. The Pirate King was there, but now there was no sign of him. He truly was in a field in the middle of nowhere, filled with tall grass and trees. He only wore a, once white, vest and some underwear. And as for his vest, there was a hole through it, but his flesh looked perfectly intact.

Thinking that he was dead, the pirates must have ransacked him for his armour and ship. Now he was just a man, covered in mud, stuck on a desolate planet. "Maybe I should have stayed dead," he sighed, looking around for anyone who could help him. Unsurprisingly there was no-one. Kal then limped away, hoping to find some sort of salvation. "Being a bounty hunter is not as glamorous as they say," he grumbled, feeling his mud-soaked hair slither down his neck like a slug.

He picked a random direction and headed that way for the next few hours, slogging along, hoping to find something. In all his months of bounty hunting, he had never been marooned on a planet like that. After a while his feet became very sore. There were likely blisters and cuts forming, making him unable to walk much further. There was not even a river or a sea for him to wash in, so every few minutes he was wiping his eyes clean with his dirty hands, flicking off manure and mud. Soon his memories were back, for the most part. He had been shot while speaking to the Pirate King. By whom exactly, he was not sure. Then he had blacked out.

"Neigh!" he heard in the distance.

A horse? Kal wondered, unsure if the animal was native to Guinthra.

Fortunately it was, as he found one sipping some water from a small pond. Without even hesitating, he leapt into the water and cleansed himself of all the mud, subsequently turning the liquid brown. Climbing out, he awkwardly smiled at the horse which stared at him, unamused. The boy then washed his hair, now having returned to its red colour.

"Horse," he said. "Take me to your master."

The Beast Known as Terros

The horse continued looking at him, making him scared that it might bite. Then it nodded and turned around, allowing him to mount.

Horses don't nod? he thought, jumping onto its back.

The horse then bolted off, zooming through the countryside as darkness began to rise and the two moons made themselves present.

Kal looked at the night sky, gazing at the immense stars and wondered how far he was from home. Not his ship, his *true* home. Jindo Prime – the same one he could not return to due to his crimes against the Federation.

The horse slowed down, approaching a barn. As it walked closer, Kal thought through his plan. His ship was as good as gone now – potentially anywhere in the galaxy, so he needed another way of getting back to space. Guinthra was not on any intergalactic shuttle route, so he would need to either steal a ship or buy one. Stealing would get him killed, so he had to buy one. The boy had finances in an off the books bank, but only Omicron could access it – so whoever robbed him had probably taken all his funds. If he wanted to buy a new ship, he would have to make a large amount of money first – and a bounty would do that. He would not hunt Terros because now he did not trust the Pirate King one bit. He would have to find another.

"Is this your home?" Kal asked the horse.

The being nodded.

"Must be sentient," he muttered, walking up to the wooden door. He was about to knock, but then saw a reflection of himself in a window. The owner of the barn would be terrified seeing a boy with wild hair and wearing only a vest showing up in the middle of the night. Kal needed to rectify the situation. He looked left and then right, smiling as he noticed some clothes hanging on a wire. It would not be stealing if he was planning to return them. He then dressed himself into some overly large dungarees and as he did so, the horse looked at him, confused.

"I'm not stealing," he whispered to the animal. "I will give them back to your owner before I leave."

The horse nodded – still unsettling.

Kal took a deep breath, stood on the wooden porch and knocked three times. As he was waiting, he brushed over his hair and dusted his clothes.

"One minute!" a voice called out almost immediately.

Kal felt a sense of relief, knowing he had not just woken up the inhabitant.

The wooden door creaked open and out stepped a very tall man – which was unsurprising considering how baggy the clothes that the boy had found were.

The man stepped out of the shadows to reveal large furry hands with claws, dark fur and a gnarly head with sharp teeth.

A wolf, Kal thought, gulping.

Despite the being's ferocious appearance, he was wearing a night robe and was drinking a steaming liquid.

He's not a threat, the former bounty hunter thought.

"How can I help you?" the wolf-man asked.

"I crashed my ship here," Kal said in a sweet voice. "Any chance I could stay here for the night and then head back out in the morning? I know it is a tough ask since you do not know me but…"

"Sure," the wolf said.

"Just like that?" Kal asked, thinking that the animal might want to eat him.

"I just finished making dinner," the wolf said calmly. "I made a bit too much, so you might as well share some as well."

"Huh," Kal murmured, thinking about what a coincidence it was. He was also very hungry, having not eaten anything since spawning into the fields.

"Come on in then," the wolf said, taking a step back. "I see you are wearing my clothes. They are much too big for you," he chuckled. "Name is Wherul."

"Kal."

"Pleasure to meet you. Now come in and get out of the cold."

Kal smiled, stepping into the narrow hut and onto the creaky floorboards. The innards were very minimalistic with little to no furniture and no objects. "You wouldn't happen to have a computer here?" he asked. "I need one just to check the web."

"Yes," Wherul said. "First, you must eat."

"Thank you for your hospitality," Kal said.

"No, thank *you*," the wolf said. "Since my wife passed, I have been so lonely here. I never expected to have guests, especially from a human."

"I am sorry for your loss," Kal said sombrely.

"Don't be," the wolf smiled weakly. "She lived a good life."

"Are there humans on this world?" Kal asked, changing the subject.

The wolf picked up a pot of food and started pouring onto his plate. "I guess you are not from this world. We do get humans, but they are never made of organic flesh – usually grown in a lab."

Kal raised an eyebrow at that remark. He would have asked a further question, but then he saw what was one his plate. A pile of long, black worms that were thick and scaly; dead, but still grotesque looking.

"A local speciality," Wherul said, picking up one of the worms and sucking it in whole. "Delicious!"

The boy prodded one with his fork, checking if it was dead. "Is this edible for humans?" he asked.

"Yep," Wherul said. "Enjoy," he added, gulping down another.

You are a bounty hunter, Kal said to himself. *You have travelled exotic worlds. One worm is not going to kill you.* Gingerly he raised one up, looking into its dead eyes as he opened his mouth.

"Here goes," he said, gulping it down. At first it got stuck in his throat, giving off a nasty, rough taste. But once it was gone, there was an oddly sweet after-flavour. "Not half bad," he said, picking up another.

"So, what brings you to Guinthra?" Wherul asked, now having finished half his plate.

When Kal finished his second worm, he started speaking.

"Business," he said, unsure if he should mention being a bounty hunter. There was a stigma about his role and he imagined the Pirate King was also very unpopular amongst the common folk.

"Not going to ask," he said with a smile.

When the meal was done and every last worm was gone, Kal felt stuffed. He wanted to sleep there and then, but knew he had to check that computer.

"Thank you for the meal," he said.

"Computer?" Wherul asked. "Do you want to use it?"

Kal nodded and followed the wolf into another room where there was a small screen, no larger than the double spread of a book and there was a worn keyboard attached with rubbed off letters and a greasy shine.

"Would this old machine do it for you?" he asked.

"Perfect," Kal said, hoping it would work.

"Great. I shall get some rest. See you in the morning," the wolf said, yawning and walking away.

The boy then waited a while for the computer to boot up. Then he opened up a search engine, ignoring how dirty the keyboard was to the best of his ability. He typed in a special code that would take him onto the Intergalactic Bounty Hunter servers. Surprisingly it worked, as the screen went black and asked him for his username and password.

Kal filled it in and smiled as a list of jobs appeared on the page. He changed the filter to local jobs on Guinthra and saw what was available. The highest paid task, unsurprisingly, was to bring in Terros, as ordered by the Pirate King. For obvious reasons he ignored that. He gazed at the second task.

Find Exekus Imporius it read. The task was issued by one Narthelus Pingo. The prize for completing the job was one million Bonku – more than enough to buy himself a ship. He then opened the file and read more.

Exekus Imporius was one of the chief scientists at the Paradise Haven. He has designed great ships and intricate robots. For transgressions against his own kind, he was banished. Nobody has seen or heard from him in nine years.

"Sounds fun," Kal said, selecting the job. After doing that, he searched up a map of the area and started planning for the next day.

The boy spent the next few hours plotting and planning until it was deep into the night and he was beyond exhausted. He would have made one more search, but the screen went blank and the power went off, as did the lights for the room he was in, causing a wave of melancholy to wash over.

"What?" he asked, feeling around for some sort of torch or matchstick. Everything was pitch black.

Then there was a dull red light. It glared at him, then disappeared with a blink. Kal could make out a clear pupil in the middle of the light. "Wherul, is that you?" he asked. "Power has gone out."

"I have missed the taste of flesh," growled a voice.

"Wherul?" Kal asked, his heartrate rising.

"I am going to enjoy this midnight snack!" he yelled, pouncing at him.

Kal leapt to the side, almost screaming out in fear. The wolf stared at him, and he could see saliva drooling from its mouth.

"Wherul?" he asked again. "Are you okay?"

"Never been better!" the wolf shouted, jumping at him.

Kal burst through the door behind him and started sprinting for his life. He slammed through door after door until he was out in the open, under the night sky once more.

"Come back here!" the wolf shrieked, the visage of kindness completely gone, revealing a bloodthirsty monster.

The boy ran off into the night, panting. He had memorised the map and knew which way to go to get to the nearest town; but he had to be quick though, else the wolf would catch up.

The animal was slow luckily, getting further and further behind him.

"Must get away!" he called out, his feet getting scratched by the twigs below.

"AAAOOOOOOOOOOOO!" the wolf suddenly let out, howling into the night sky.

Did he just call his lackies? Kal thought, getting worried. One wolf was enough of an issue. A whole pack would be his demise.

The boy ran off into the distance and did not stop until he reached the local town – going until his feet were swollen and blistered while his hair was matted and filled with twigs. He never saw or heard from the wolf again.

The second his feet touched concrete, he collapsed to the ground – in uncharted territories, but at least somewhere he would be hopefully safe.

A period of strange dreaming later, Kal's eyes slowly opened. Immediately he noticed a roof above his head which was a good sign. He was in a large and warm bed. His feet were bandaged and were throbbing. *Who did that?* he wondered, sitting up.

"You're awake!" a soft voice called out.

Kal shuddered, terrified of who may be there.

"Don't be scared by my appearance," the voice said, stepping into the room.

Kal shuddered in terror. "No!" he cried. "Surely there must be someone on this planet who does not want me dead."

The wolf raised her hands. "I have no intention of hurting you," the animal said. She was wearing a bright pink dress, and her teeth and claws were blunt. "Not all wolves are evil," she said. "I take it you had a run in with old Wherul at the barn?"

The boy nodded, a tear streaming down his face.

"I heard terrifying stories of him when I was a cub. Him and his wicked horse need to be stopped."

Kal still felt off about everything. The last wolf pretended to be nice, until he was not. How could he know this wolf would not be the same? The bandages were a start. "I need to get out of here," Kal said, standing onto his bruised feet. "Wherever *here* is. I need to leave this planet as soon as I can."

"You are from space?" the wolf asked in awe.

"Yes," Kal said. "And I need to return there as soon as possible. Once I get this bounty sorted then I can buy a ship and be on my way."

"Bounty hunter!" the wolf exclaimed.

"Ssh!" Kal hissed. "I do not want anyone knowing my business."

"Can you take me to space?" the wolf asked.

"No," Kal snapped. "I don't trust anyone. First, I get kicked off my planet, disowned by my parents, got shot, then lost my ship, woke up naked in the middle of a field, then almost got eaten by a demonic wolf."

"Sounds awful," the wolf said.

"Yes it is!" Kal shouted. "Now if you do not know where Exekus Imporius is, then I suggest you get out of my way!" He suddenly felt bad for shouting. He would have apologised if not for the wolf speaking up.

"Exekus Imporius?" she gasped. "He is a legend."

"You know of him?" Kal asked.

"Of course," the wolf said. "I learnt about him at school."

"Tell me then," Kal replied.

"Only if you take me into space," the wolf replied.

"No," the boy said.

"Please!" the wolf cried. "I helped you. Now you have to get me out of this mundane town. I want to be your sidekick, hunting down aliens in awesome armour."

"No," Kal replied

"Well then you are getting no information on Exekus. I even know where he is…"

"Where?" Kal demanded.

"In the middle of the desert," the wolf said. "He is there, as the song states."

"Song?"

"A poem we used to say at school. I shall recite it for you later."

"I would rather not," Kal said, opening the door and leaving.

"So, you are bringing me with you?" the wolf asked.

"If you can get me to the desert then fine," Kal sighed. His feet ached with each step. "Where are we right now?"

"The town of Pogom," the wolf said. "I can get you a car and some suitable clothes and then we can go to the Kraim Desert."

"How far from here?" Kal asked, running a tap before washing his face. As the cold water splashed against his skin, he was bolted awake.

"Maybe a two-day drive?"

"Let's go then," he said, looking for a door to get outside. The insides of the house that he was in felt oddly normal. Apart from the wolf hair that had accumulated in all corners of the rooms.

"Wait!" the wolf said, dashing to the door. "I may have lied," she said, looking at the ground.

Kal raised an eyebrow.

Wolves are not nice people. Well, apart from me and my other dorky friends. But we are outcasts. If you go outside, they are going to eat you.

"What?" Kal asked. "I knew this was too good to be true."

"No no!" the wolf called out. "I am good. That is all that matters. Just *stay* in the house while I go and fetch you some clothes from the local store. Please trust me."

"Fine," Kal sighed.

"Great!" the wolf called out. "Now give me a minute. Make yourself at home and…"

The last time he had heard those words, disaster had struck.

"While I am gone, search up Exekus on my computer. Password is 'unicornlover' with a capital 'u'."

"Alright," Kal said as the wolf disappeared. His first priority was to get a weapon. Just in case someone could smell him from the streets and try to eat him. The boy went into the kitchen and looked around for a knife – but they were all blunt. After a few minutes of looking, the best weapon he could find was a belt. It was something.

He then went onto a computer and typed in the she-wolf's unique password. Then, on the web he did some digging. The world of Guinthra seemed to be quite interesting, far more going on than in the other worlds he had visited. There was the main jungle, where the Pirate King now ruled, with other territories such as one populated by foxes. After further research, he had learnt that the leader, 'The Elder' had been killed. A cyber kingdom existed, known as the Gigafactory, where apparently there was a group of humans – a sight for sore eyes for him. Perhaps if the bounty mission failed, then he would go and live with those humans.

Kal was now in Pogom, a small town in a large area of nothing, east of the jungle. If he went further east, then the wasteland would slowly evolve into a desert where his target resided.

Exekus Imporius was from the legendary Paradise Haven, a kingdom so advanced and technologically in the future that it was hidden completely. The world was ruled by super-intelligent penguins, which got a laugh out of Kal. Exekus had apparently been exiled from there, having served as a chief scientist and engineer. Rumour had it that he worked with the humans for a few years, creating a technical haven for them. Now he had built his own workshop in the middle of the desert to get away from everyone.

"I'm baaack!" the wolf called out, entering the house.

"There is a workshop. If I can print out a map of the desert then I think we can find it," Kal said.

"I got you some clothes for the desert," the wolf said. "And I bought us some snacks for the ride. If we are quick enough, we should be there and back in two days."

"Good," Kal said. "Then I can finally be off this world." He then walked over to the wolf who was holding two bags. "What did you get?"

"Goggles," she said, handing over some eyewear with a strap. "To stop the sand getting in your eyes." She then rummaged around some more. "Some binoculars, a scarf and some more clothes. When are we leaving?"

"Now," Kal said. "As soon as I get changed," he added, taking the clothes. "What vehicle do you have?"

"Great question," the wolf said. "You shall see in a second. The name's Lupera. I should have mentioned earlier."

"Kal Secant," Kal replied with a smile.

When Kal was changed, wearing a shirt and a leather jacket on top with some long brown boots, he looked in the mirror. "I look ridiculous," he sighed, missing his usual sleek armour.

"You look amazing," the wolf said, lurking from around the corner. "Now then, let's go get our car."

A heavy knock came at the door, thudding through the whole building.

"Who's that?" Kal whispered.

"You'll see," the she-wolf said, running over to the door and opening it. "This is Spyke." The door opened and on the other side was a wide figure, barely able to fit through the doorway. He had a large snout and was wearing a black leather jacket, tattered and torn with a few badges sewn on. His shoulders had spikes on them – most likely a reference to his name. The imposing figure entered the house, taking a large sniff. He then licked his sharp teeth and smiled. "Where is he?" he asked Lupera.

Kal's eyes widened in fear as he tried to hide from the menace.

"There he is!" Spyke let out, walking over to him with immense strides. Kal tried to get away, but the hulking beast picked him up by the jacket. "This the bounty hunter you told me about?"

"Let me go!" Kal called out, trying to wrench himself free.

"Some bounty hunter," Spyke said. "He looks more like a princess cosplaying as a hunter. You are going to suffer in the desert," Spyke sighed, putting Kal onto the ground.

The boy looked at him, confused. So he was not going to be eaten?

"Come on bounty hunter," Spyke said, gesturing for him to follow. "We have a penguin to catch."

"I should have mentioned," Lupera laughed nervously. "Spyke here will be taking us to the desert. He goes there frequently, taking travellers and doing odd jobs."

Kal scowled at the she-wolf, furious with her for concealing the truth.

"Hurry up!" Spyke shouted from outside. "Once night hits, the desert turns into a feasting ground."

Kal hurried outside in his overly tight boots, careful not to trip. When he saw the vehicle parked outside, he was shocked. It was a long black car, with a bonnet that had spiked thrusters. Inside there were two black leather seats.

"There are only two seats?" Lupera asked.

"Yep," Spyke said. "One for me and one for the 'bounty hunter'," he replied, creating quotations with his hands.

"But I want to come!" Lupera demanded.

"Nope," Spyke said. "Your dad would be furious. I ain't getting you killed out there."

"Kal?" Lupera asked.

He simply shrugged, getting into the passenger seat with Spyke. "Thanks for all the help," he said, feeling somewhat guilty for leaving his helper behind.

"Let the fun begin!" Spyke said, starting his engine as the whole vehicle shook violently and smoke burst out from the engine. "Let's go!" the wolf shouted as the two of them thrusted off onto their adventure.

Chapter 13: The Sniffer

The village was peaceful. As peaceful as it could have been, considering all that had happened.

"Big day today," said a voice, soft and soothing. Terros smiled, trying to hide the pain of his nerves.

"My little Terros, chief of this village," she said with a smile.

Terros looked at his mother, wearing a white outfit with a large, purple cape.

"I don't want to be chief," Terros said. "I am only twelve."

"By law of our people, you must take over from your father," Mella said. "Your Uncle Durren's time as chief regent has ended."

"I'm too young," Terros mumbled. "I barely have a mane."

"I will be by your side at all times," Mella smiled. "You have me, Uncle Durren, Aunt Tirra and even Ancient Nan to guide you. Your father was only fifteen when he took over from his father. Yet I remember his coronation day so vividly. Despite his mild mane, he looked so confident and majestic – like a true leader."

"I'm not my father," Terros grumbled. "If it wasn't for me, they never would have taken him."

"Your father died saving your life," Mella said sombrely, raising her son's head by the chin. "Now let's get you ready for the festivities."

Terros walked into the village hall a few hours later. The whole room was dead silent, watching him with great interest. The young Gedrul was wearing a large purple, oversized cloak.

"Introducing our new chief: Terros Tarthanian Mrilmus!" bellowed an old Gedrul wearing white robes with a tall black hat.

Everyone in the hall stood up and Mella prodded her son to start walking.

With great nerves and wanting to scrunch up into a ball, Terros walked across the aisle down the middle, feeling great pain from every pair of eyes that were staring at him. *Focus,* he said to himself as he held his chin high and walked. He could see Uncle Durren standing on the other side of the hall, holding his crown of leaves in his hands. There was a great big grin on his face which made Terros wonder if he actually wanted to step down as chief. Aunt Tirra smiled at him, her face gleaming with light. Her stomach was bulging slightly, from the new cubs that were to be born.

"Congratulations Terros," Uncle Durren said, bowing his head.

Congratulations for what? Terros wondered. *Letting my father die?*

"You look so good," Aunt Tirra charmed. "Like a real leader."

The old man with the royal robes, tall hat and sceptre – Archraes Trihm, took the crown from the former Chief Durren.

Terros took a seat on the large wooden throne, as rehearsed, leaving a large amount of space on either side due to his small size. His legs then dangled down, nowhere near long enough to touch the ground.

"Long live Chief Terros!" the Archraes called out as he slowly lowered the crown over Terros' head.

The cub looked to the audience to see Rufus, beaming with a great smile. He nodded at the new chief and that made him feel more comfortable. Terros waited for the crown to touch his head, but it never did.

The entire audience opened their eyes in amazement and shock. Quickly Terros turned around to see that the Archraes was lying on the floor, with red paint drooling from his chest.

There was a large hole in the wall and through the gap was a beast, large in stature, wearing a big black cloak. He had a long mane and stood very tall.

"Father!" Terros called out, running to Durros. He picked the crown off the floor and went to give it to the rightful ruler.

Durros' face remained still as he extended an arm and picked Terros up by the neck.

"Father?" Terros asked, feeling pressure around his windpipe and making him struggle to breathe. "Father, you are squeezing too tight."

"Brother, put him down!" Durren called out, brandishing a wooden spear.

Terros could not breathe and watched as everything started to go dark. "Father…" he mouthed.

Durren rushed forwards and knocked over Terros' father, freeing the cub. He tore the cloak off his brother and stepped back in fear. The sound of cogs whizzing could be heard as metal screeched and Durros got back onto his feet. His eyes glowed red and his metal body clanked into action.

"Brother, what have they done to you?" Durren called out.

"I…" Durros tried to say, his face remaining statue still, but he did not continue. Instead, he jumped at his brother and the two of them started to fight, slashing claws and roaring.

The Gedruls inside the hut started to get up, with a few of the larger males going to help Durren. They were a bit hesitant though, as Durros was their former chief and attacking him would be a form of treason.

"Everyone stop!" called out a voice. The walls of the hut were then smashed down as about a dozen or so humans walked in, all dressed in black, with goggles on and holding guns. "Capture *only* the males! Kill any females that get in your way!"

A ball was thrown in, which quickly erupted into thick smoke, blocking everything and making it hard for Terros to see. The cub looked around frantically, his eyes stinging and watering.

There was then the flashing of blue lights, followed by screams and shouts. Terros gulped hard and started to get worried. "Mama!" he called out.

Another scream sounded.

"Mama?" Terros let out. The young beast then remembered that he was going to be chief. He needed to be strong and act like a leader.

"Terros!" his mother cried out, jumping out from the smoke and picking up her cub.

"What's happening?" Terros asked.

"Humans," she said. "They…"

Terros stopped listening. He could see that his mother's cape was all tattered and torn and red juice was leaking from her stomach. She panted hard and ran with the cub as far as she could, out from the smoke-filled hut and back into the jungle.

"What happened to Father?" he asked.

"They…" she said, trailing off, water building in the corner of her eyes.

The smoke cleared, and Terros could see in the distance that many of the Gedruls were wrapped up in wires. Some were on the floor, sleeping, and others were crying in fear.

Terros watched as his friend, Rufus, was grabbed by the neck and slammed onto the floor. The humans then put a metal ring around his neck and tied his hands and feet together.

"Rufus!" Terros called out.

"Shhh!" his mother came.

"But Rufus. They got him," Terros cried.

"They've got everyone, my son," Mella whispered. "We lost this one."

"OI!" one of the humans shouted, pointing at the mother running away with her son. "Animal, chase them!"

Durros dropped the battered body of his brother and cranked his head to see what was going on. He then got onto all fours and zoomed over, moving swiftly and baring his teeth.

Terros watched from his mother's shoulder as his father got closer and closer. "Mama, watch out!" he shouted, hitting her on the back.

She tried to go even faster but was quickly outpaced as Durros jumped at them. At this point they were in the thicket of the jungle, surrounded by tall trees and away from everyone else, so that it was just them three.

Durros knocked his wife and son onto the ground and then roared at them, baring his metal teeth. He clanked them shut, giving off a ringing and grating sound.

"Father?" Terros cried, raising his arms in surrender.

"That's not your father," Mella replied, struggling back onto her feet. "Durros would never do something like this. Those humans clearly…"

She did not finish as Durros struck her across the face. He then bared his claws, revealing black, shiny daggers.

"Father, stop!" Terros tried calling out, but Durros was relentless, going full animalistic.

"Father!" Terros called out. "You are my father. We go hunting together. You are the chief!" the aged cub was trying to come up with as many things as possible, but his mind was running thin and he was clearly having no effect. "You saved me!" Terros cried. "From the nasty humans, remember? You told me to run but I got caught and then they took you. Remember?"

Durros froze in his motion and turned around, looking at his son. He stood there for a minute, breathing heavily and not moving whatsoever.

"It's me," Terros said with a smile.

"I don't know who you are," Durros growled, his voice deep and thunderous.

Mella jumped at him, slashing the beast over and over. But she was clearly dwarfed by his intensely large and muscular physique. Not to mention she had morals, and he did not. Mella was fighting her former husband while Durros was slaughtering his prey. So, Terros just stood there helplessly as his mother was thrashed.

"Must intervene," he whispered to himself. He had already lost one parent and would not make the same mistake again. "NO!" the cub screamed, embracing his position as chief. He bared his tiny teeth and jumped forwards, knocking Durros off Mella. He could feel the large mass of his father, combined with all the metal, so his push did very little. But he was enraged and would do whatever it took to keep his mother alive. She was the last thing he had.

Terros punched the mechanical creature, scratching his face with his tiny claws.

"Insect," Durros said, towering over his son as his eyes glowed even brighter. He extended his arm and picked up the skinny and squirmy cub before baring his metal teeth.

"No!" Terros howled, kicking the being in the face before jumping down and then grabbed his legs tightly. "You will hurt nobody!"

Durros tried walking, but struggled. He then took his large fist and punched Terros in the back.

The cub cried, feeling the great pain of being struck, shaking his bones. He powered on through.

Again.

Again.

And again.

The cub was not sure how much longer he could hold on for. "You won't hurt her anymore," he sobbed.

There was then the sound of a large crunch and a scratch followed by some spitting. He felt some metal sprinkle onto his fur. Terros looked up to see that a large branch was sticking out of Durros' chest, tearing through his metal interior as electricity sparkled.

Mella stood behind him, panting as she had done the impossible.

"No," the mechanical beast let out, collapsing to the ground, the red light in his eyes disappearing.

"We did it!" Terros called out, shaking the pain off himself and hugging his mother. "We did it," he said with a smile.

But she could not stand any longer and simply toppled to the ground, going limp.

"Mama?" Terros asked, as he tried to hold her body.

She weakly smiled back.

"Come on Mama, we need to go," Terros said. "The others need our help."

She put his hand onto his and said, "No. You need to survive."

Terros then noticed how faint Mella's voice was. His own hands started to feel wet and were coated in red. "Mama?" he asked. "Are you okay?"

"I am," she said. "You are a good boy Terros," she added, stroking his head. "A good boy."

"But," Terros said. "What about you?"

Her movements got weak as her hands lowered by her side.

"Mama? I don't want to lose you." He shook her, but her eyes started to close.

"Mama?" he called out.

She lay there, still, her body completely limp and her eyes shut. Terros noticed a small whisper of air leak from her lips and that was the last of them.

"Mama?" he called out again.

Terros sat, years later, at a desk, staring at a wall with his hands scrunched. While the others were littered around in bunks, he had not slept a wink.

"We have a bounty hunter!" Zemu called out, waking up everyone who was asleep. The sound of snoring ceased and one by one, the group started to crawl to action. "Well, we have about twenty people who claimed the target. So, I guess Exekus is coming in."

"Do we have a name?" Narth asked, yawning.

"Kal Secant," Zemu said. "He was the first to claim the offer. He says that he can have the penguin brought to us within three days."

"That's handy," Gides sighed. "Now we just need a power source."

"The human kingdom," Terros said bluntly.

"Great idea," Narth replied. "Their factories probably run on energy cores. If we can get one then we can power the robot that Exekus will build us."

"Everyone get up!" Marth called out. "We have got work to do. I will stay here and watch over the resistance. The rest of you go to the underworld and fetch that power core."

"I don't want to go out there!" Narth called out. "It is a scary place."

"You'll be fine," Zemu said. "Just don't look at anyone in the eyes for more than two seconds or you might turn into stone."

Gides giggled slightly, putting his hand in front of his mouth.

Terros nodded, picking up a long plasma rifle. He was eager to visit the humans – to exact revenge on the ones who had caused so much pain for him. Rett was hopefully still there, so he could provide assistance as well in stealing the energy core.

"Let's go then," Narth smiled.

Sometime later, Terros the Beast, Gides the Fox, Zemu the Pirate-Dragon and Narthelus the Penguin all stood in the hangar of the Great Gate. They had tied up the one operating it, hijacking it for themselves as the blue and purple whirlpool opened up.

"Ready for this?" Gides called out, his fur being pulled towards the gateway.

"No," the penguin squealed. Terros pushed him through, then his two friends jumped in as well. The beast then closed his eyes and hopped back into his own world.

A minute of frenzy movement later, he fell onto the beach, his face landing on the sand.

"Terros," he heard a mechanical voice say. The beast looked up to see all his friends were on the floor, completely knocked out and Zemu was snoring.

What? The beast thought, wondering what could have happened.

"Put this on?" a voice said, handing him a mask. Terros did not hesitate, putting it over his mouth before breathing normally. The air had to be toxic, with some sort of sleeping fumes.

"Now then," the voice said. "Your friends are down. Time for the two of us to dance."

Terros looked at who was talking - a cloaked being with a robotic face and a belt filled with an array of guns and weapons.

"Time for the glory of the hunt – just us two." The voice said, deep and pungent.

The beast assumed he was a bounty hunter – one sent by the Pirate King.

"The name's Dahk," he said. "And it will be the last one you hear."

Terros wondered why his enemy had put everyone to sleep except him. It was for the apparent 'glory of the hunt'. The beast then wondered if this man was crazy.

"Remove your mask now," Dahk growled. "The toxicity has passed."

For some reason, Terros trusted the man, doing as was asked. He then took a deep breath and thought through his battle plan. He had a pistol strapped to his waist. All he needed to do was draw and shoot and he would be victorious. That was presuming his enemy had no armour under his cloak.

Dahk raised a gloved hand, holding out his palm. As he did this, Terros felt a slight tingling on his side. Before he could even respond, his pistol flew through the air and into the gloved hand of his opposition.

"No guns," he growled. "Just good old-fashioned combat." He then jumped forward, his boots propelling himself with rocket fuel.

Terros let out a huge roar and leapt into the air, catching the bounty hunter and bringing him crashing to the ground.

Managing to squirm on top, the beast then started hurling punches at the man – aiming for the helmet.

"Glorious battle," Dahk said as the animal fist collided with his helmet. He then grabbed Terros' leg and sent an electric pulse through him.

The beast roared back in agony, giving the hunter the opportunity to run up and uppercut him through his chin and knocking his head upwards.

Saliva splattered from Terros' mouth as he felt the whiplash. Before he could even respond, the hunter was already on the ground, swinging his leg and knocking the animal over.

Terros landed face first, being dazed for a second. Dahk was then on his back. holding one end of string in either hand and bringing it to the beast's throat, pulling hard.

Struggling for breath, Terros acted quickly, jousting his elbow backwards and into the abdomen of the opposition.

Dahk let out a cough as Terros broke free of the string and picked up the man by the cloak, swinging him into a tree. The hunter's back collided with the bark and he crumpled to the ground.

Terros huffed intensely, knowing that that strike would have paralysed a normal man. But he knew better than to turn his back on an opponent. So, he pounced over and grabbed the helmet, tearing it off the being.

He did not get a chance to look, as a bright light flashed, hurting his brain and causing him to drop the helmet. The hunter then threw something that spun and twisted around Terros' legs, binding them with a metal wire that tightened and tripped him up.

"Impressive," Dahk said, audibly putting his helmet back on.

Terros lay on the floor, his head hurting and his vision starting to cloud. He would not lose to a random bounty hunter, so had to break free if he were to survive. In one gutsful move, he jumped up and clapped his hands on either side of the helmet.

Dahk screamed out, giving Terros the opportunity to snap his leg trap. He then swiped forwards for his opponent, but did not get very far when a thick billow of smoke separated them.

"I will return when you are strong enough to match me!" Dahk called out, his voice trailing off into the distance.

Terros looked around, confused, his eyes beginning to water from the irritation of the smoke. When the time was right, he picked up his unconscious friends and sat them at the back of the starship they had left parked a few days ago. Fortunately, it was still there.

"Good morning, Terros," Delta-52 said as the beast strapped his friends to their seats. There were only three chairs, so he put Gides on the floor.

"How do I fly this?" the beast grunted, sitting at the pilot's seat and getting intimidated by all the different buttons.

"I will show you the way," Del said, lighting up the relevant buttons. "Where to?" she asked.

"Human kingdom," Terros growled.

"Of course," the ship replied. "Estimated arrival is in four hours."

Terros got ready to work when he heard a voice.

"You trying to get us all killed?" Gides asked, his voice long and drawn. "I ain't ever letting you drive a car, let alone fly an aircraft."

The beast got up and nodded, happy to see that his friend was awake again.

"What happened to us?" Gides asked, gesturing to everyone else, still snoring like fat boars after a meal.

"Bounty hunter," Terros said, taking a seat.

"Figured," the fox said.

Chapter 14: Bounty Hunter War

"So, are you actually a bounty hunter?" Spyke asked, speaking for the first time since their journey had begun.

"Yes," Kal replied.

"You don't look like one," the wolf sighed.

They were now on the edge of the Kraim Desert – a great expanse of sand, filled with rolling hills and a pale blue sky that stretched on forever. The heat was intense, and Kal found himself sweating. Whether that was from the sun or the nerves of sitting next to a ferocious looking wolf, he was not sure.

"I am a bounty hunter," he said. "I just lost my ship and armour, that's all."

"The gadgets don't make you the hunter," Spyke replied. "It is the instinct, the combat skills and more."

"I can fight," Kal said.

"Ha!" the wolf spat. "No, you can't." He then slammed the breaks on the car, causing Kal to whip forwards and then back again. "Show me," he said.

"Show you what?" the boy asked.

"Show me that you, a princess from space, can actually fight." Spyke got out of the vehicle and stood on the sand.

Kal got out angrily, sinking his feet into the sand, careful not to trip. The baking sun was over him and it ached his skin.

"Strike me," the wolf said.

"We do not have time for this," the boy replied. "We need to…"

"Strike me!" the wolf growled, raising his fists into a defensive position.

Kal gulped, strode forward and threw a punch at the wolf's face.

Spyke slapped it to the side. "Harder!" he growled.

When Kal actually tried, Spyke dodged to the side, kicking the back of his left leg. As he was crumpling in stature, the wolf grabbed him and swung him to the side.

"I'm doubting if you are actually a bounty hunter," Spyke laughed.

The boy's face was now in the boiling sand and his body groaned with agony. Spitting out sand, he got up. "What was that for?"

"You are going to die on this mission, bounty hunter," Spyke sighed. "If not on this mission, then the next. If not the next, then the one after that." He then dusted his jacket. "You are on borrowed time, princess."

"Stop calling me princess!"

"Then stop acting like one!" the wolf shouted.

Kal's heart started to boil with rage and him breaths became heavy and loud. "Why do you care so much? Just get me to my destination and we can go our separate ways!"

"Just trying to help," the wolf shrugged.

That night, when the sun was gone and the two moons were visible in the sky, the two of them had set up camp. Spyke was fast asleep, and Kal was on watch for any sort of bandit or creature.

The boy was seated on the floor, holding a pocketknife and stabbing it into the sand, repeating the same phrase over and over. "I am not a princess," he hissed.

He started to delve over his past; how he grew up as the son of an aristocrat on Jindo Prime. His father, Klarence Secant, owned steel mines and was a close assailant to the Federation.

Kal's mother died when he was young, so both Kal and his sister Klara spent most of their childhood in boarding schools. Klara went to an academy on a different planet to him, so he only ever saw her once every few years.

Kal remembered how on his fifteenth birthday he was gifted a personal spaceship, with its own artificial intelligence and all. He started taking flying lessons, and after failing his test thrice, he finally passed.

On his sixteenth birthday, a member of the Federation walked past him; an officer. He tossed his gun over to him and pointed at another officer who had been shot. 'You killed him,' he said, before making the arrest. Since Kal had touched the gun, his fingerprints were all over it. Kal tried pleading innocence to his father, saying how he was framed, but his father ignored him. He said that the

Federation was a sound system, and its high-ups would never stoop to something as low as framing someone.

After his trial, he was taken to a space colony, where he was sentenced to reside for the next fifteen years. On his first day, his long, red locks were shaved off and he was put into an uncomfortable straitjacket, eating only mouldy vegetables and sloppy porridge. Every evening he was scrubbed by droids who used horse brushes until his skin was raw – as a precaution to prevent him from catching alien diseases.

Kal made friends with a gruff and mysterious individual, Darren Longbow. He was a veteran bounty hunter who had figured out a way off the prison colony. So, when he escaped, he took Kal with him, wanting to train a new protégé. Kal ended up only spending five weeks in his cell, but they were easily the worst days of his life.

On the escape, Darren was mortally wounded by a stray gunshot while trying to protect Kal. The boy was able to leave the prison, but he had lost his potential mentor. He then found his old ship – removed it of any tracker and then did his own thing, opting for a life of crime. Not because he wanted to – but because there was no other option for him. His name had already been blacklisted on every major system's database.

A year ago, he tried visiting his father, but he denied him access, instead calling troopers on him. He even tried reaching out to his sister, but she also showed no interest. Now he would just float through space, trying to fill the void in his heart with senseless missions and trying to become something.

Kal looked at his reflection through the glossy surface of the car. "I am a bounty hunter," he said with dead seriousness.

"So, you *do* want to be a bounty hunter?" the wolf yawned, having been woken from his nap. "I won't call you a princess no more," he said, slapping him on the back of the head. "Alright," the wolf said. "You want to rest or should we get going?"

"Let's go," Kal said. "This bounty is going to get stale soon."

"Don't tell me that's your catchphrase," Spyke sighed, hopping back into the car. The wolf then slammed the accelerator, and they blasted off into the desert.

There was sand slapping the bonnet while they ventured through endless fields of nothing. The boy was excited by all this, never having been in a desert before. The journey was bumpy – filled with lots of offroad sections as they went up and down, zooming over ramps of dune.

Even though he had travelled in space a lot, there was something about that car that made Kal uneasy with all the turbulence. He tried to stop his heart from popping out his chest, but the jerks in speed were not helping.

"So, tell me about yourself?" Spyke asked, running his right hand through his furry mane while his left one stuck to the steering wheel. "What happened to your ship? Lupera told me something, but I wasn't really payin' attention. I was too busy getting some meat out from between my teeth."

"Erm," Kal said, scratching his head. "I got ambushed. The Pirate King wanted something and…"

"The Pirate King!" Spyke laughed. "What are you doing mixing around with someone like that?"

"I was supposed to be here on holiday, but I got an alert telling me of some grand prize for bringing in a Gedrul known as Terros."

"Yeah, I saw the ad," Spyke sighed. "Never mix yourself with people like the Pirate King. He is scum, through and through. He might pay you handsomely, but then he will make you his slave or something dark."

"Oh," Kal said.

"Anyway," the wolf said in his usual deep voice, "continue your story."

"Erm, I was with the Pirate King. And then I got shot from behind. I got ambushed and…"

"You let yourself get ambushed?" Spyke demanded, shaking his head.

"I got sniped. There was nothing I could do," Kal pleaded.

"Kid," Spyke grinned. "There's *always* something you can do. You need to make sure there is someone watching your back, or you scan the perimeter or something." The wolf paused. "So, you got sniped. Then what?"

"Then I woke up in the middle of a field, no armour, no ship, no nothing."

The wolf laughed. "How did you survive?"

"No idea," Kal said.

"You are lucky they did not steal your kidneys, or worse, send you to the human kingdom."

"What's wrong with the…"

"The stories I have heard," Spyke said in a hushed voice. "Legend has it they replace humans with machines."

The boy did not know how to respond.

The Beast Known as Terros

A moment later, he felt a vibration – a small murmuring through the car on top of the engine noises. "What's that?" he asked.

"If I had to guess," Spyke said, "it is what I expected."

"Which is?" Kal asked.

"Put your hands on the wheel," he said, sticking his head out the window of the car.

"What?" the boy snapped, rapidly grabbing the steering wheel and trying to maintain it from a weird angle.

"Ha ha!" the wolf shouted from outside. "It is glorious!"

Kal was getting increasingly patient as he was struggling to steer the car, turning his head from the road to look at the wheel and then make adjustments, repeating the same process over and over.

The large wolf then got back into the car. "Here goes!" he said with a smile, pushing Kal's hands off the wheel.

"Here what goes?" the red-haired boy replied.

The vibration was getting stronger and now there was a great sound in the distance, a metal thrum becoming louder by the second.

"Kal," the wolf said with an immense grin. "You are about to witness a bounty hunter war."

"A what?" Kal asked, getting confused as his heart rate started rising uncontrollably.

"You have never had a big hit. But usually you will get a clash between multiple hunters over who gets the prize. We are about to witness one now." The wolf then viciously rummaged under the dashboard and pulled out a large glass bottle filled with brown liquid that could easily have been diarrhoea. While he kept one hand on the steering wheel, he used the other to wrench the cap off.

Kal then looked outside the car and his jaw dropped. His beating heart froze as if a hand had grabbed it still. His toes tingled and his eyes widened.

A ginormous, mechanical beast was trailing across the sand. It was an immense tank, with wheels the size of houses and treads that could wrap around a mountain. Every inch of it was spiked with sharp, rustic iron. The central fuselage of the machine was like a huge slug of metal, with multiple hatches for entrance, and on the top there were turrets throughout.

"A war machine!" Spyke laughed.

"I… I…" Kal tried saying.

The wolf then took a large glug from the bottle and his eyes immediately shot open. "AARGH!" he yelled. He then bit hard and smiled. "There we go!" he cackled.

The boy, looked at him, completely terrified by the metal machine.

Spyke shoved the bottle into his hands, the lip covered in thick saliva. "Drink some!" he shouted over the mechanical whirring.

"What is it?" Kal demanded.

"Pure FIRE!" the wolf howled, shaking his head in joy. "Dragon-chilis mixed with vinegar!"

The boy looked at it, confused. That sort of concoction could kill him. So he shook his head. "What about the tank?"

"Drink the liquid!" Spyke exclaimed. "It will help you!"

Kal ignored him, focusing on the massive behemoth headed their way. He saw that it was piloted by scaled beings with long mouths and fat teeth. *Crocodiles*? he wondered.

The boy then suddenly felt a strong hand grab his head. Spyke let go of the wheel entirely and picked up the bottle of death and forced some down Kal's throat.

He tried to fight back, but the wolf had a strong grip on his hair. The second the liquid touched his tongue, it felt like it had been stabbed. Daggers started to roll through his throat, stabbing every bit of flesh as it went down.

Spyke removed the bottle and grinned as Kal gasped for air, gagging and flailing his arms.

"I told you it would help!" the wolf laughed.

"AAAARGH!" Kal screamed, feeling every inch of his body light up, enflamed in agony. His scalp reeled in flames, and he felt like his hair could fall out at any moment. His blood gushed around his body and his eyes were seeing so many things at once. And then his heart went into overdrive, slamming into his chest over and over, like a deranged beast. "AARGH!" he let out again, seeing everything flash before his eyes.

"Maybe I gave you too much!" the wolf laughed. "OOPS!" he cackled, his saliva hitting the human's face.

Kal's mind snapped into focus. Everything was going on so fast and he seized the moment. There was a large truck heading towards them, and it no longer scared him. In fact, he was excited to battle it.

A third vehicle came into play – a large blue truck with the fin of a shark coming out the top. It had red lips and yellow teeth haphazardly spray-painted on the side. It did not get far before a large silver harpoon was shot out from the giga-tank and pierced the shark-vehicle.

Just like that, the blue truck was yanked across the sand and pulled into the giant slug, onto a conveyor belt that led to humungous metal, chomping teeth. A second later, the shark car, and its inhabitants were eaten, chomped into smithereens.

The display left Kal in awe as he smiled. "Here goes!" he shouted, pulling his goggles over his eyes and crawling out of the car and then stood on the roof.

The wind was in his face, trying to chuck him off. He stood strong, holding a plasma rifle. Kal looked through the scope at the pilot of the metal slug – another green skinned crocodile with a sleezy smile moulded in. He aimed and got ready to fire, steadying his weapon against the speed of the car and the strength of the wind. When he pulled the trigger, the bullet flew through the air, but simply grazed the windscreen.

"Hey!" Spyke shouted from within the truck.

Kal dunked his head upside down to see what he was saying.

"You need something much stronga!" he yelled. "Get the canon from the boot!"

Canon? Kal thought, lifting open the back of the car, careful not to fall off and into the sandy mists.

BANG!

He instantly dropped down, narrowly missing a silver harpoon that was shot at him. One hit from that and he would have been dead.

A gatling gun then started from the slug, shooting dozens of rounds per second.

Kal clung to the side of the car, using it as a shield while he held on for dear life.

"Ima get some distance!" Spyke clamoured, jolting the wheel to the left, causing the two of them to yaw away from the enemy truck.

They did not get very far before another car slammed into them from the left. A second before the collision, Kal had crawled onto the top, else he would have been flattened.

"Wolf scum!" the driver of this vehicle said – a fox looking person wearing an eyepatch and with golden teeth. "The bounty is mine!" he growled, steering his green truck to the right, pushing Spyke's vehicle towards the slug they had just escaped.

The red-haired boy looked to see that the crocodiles were reloading their gatling guns, which gave them some time. But from the size of the fox's truck, they only had a few seconds until they were going to be completely sandwiched and pulsed into the spikes of the metal behemoth.

The green truck had a fox pilot and two more at the back. So, Kal jumped onto the vehicle, firing one of them with his rifle, while using the butt of it to knock out the other. But the fox was strong, catching his gun and wrenching it free from his hands.

"Pathetic!" he spat, lurching forward and knocking him over.

A second later, Kal found his head being pushed into the moving tyres, mere inches away as the fox was trying to kill him. He tried fighting back but was much too weak. The blaring sound of the tyres was howling against his ears, and he could smell the rust and sand.

"Watch out!" Spyke shouted, pulling a shotgun from where he sat, firing at the fox and knocking him off the truck, which gave Kal an opportunity to climb back on.

Spyke looked right to see that the crocs had reloaded the harpoons and were preparing to fire again. "Here goes!" he clamoured audibly as he slammed his brake pedal. As he did this, the car screeched to a halt and when the harpoon gun was fired at them, it instead hit the green truck that was in its place.

Kal wobbled as his new vehicle was pierced by multiple spears, then dragged into the slug. He ran over and leapt off it, clambering onto the side of the enormous tank, while the fox and his truck were gobbled whole, reduced to scraps.

The boy lay on the high-speed vehicle, feeling the adrenaline and taking cover from all the shards and glass that were exploding out from the eaten vehicle. He wiped the dirt off his goggles and got back to work.

In the distance, Spyke was still stationary, having gotten out of his car and was rummaging through his boot. He was slowly getting smaller and smaller.

Kal had two options – to jump off the vehicle and take in the damage, before running back to Spyke or stay on the truck and get to Exekus. If he ran off, then a gatling gun or harpoon could hit him, so he was safer where he was.

"Oi!" a crocodile grouched, picking him up. "I got 'im!"

The boy's blood started boiling as the fire coursed through his veins. "I've got this," he muttered, kicking the crocodile in the stomach and knocking him back. "I've got this!" he called again, now having regained his footing.

"No you don't!" a raspy voice curdled as something hard hit the back of his head. He was on the floor a moment later, dazed.

"Fireworks time!" a croc shouted, picking him up by the jacket and dragging him across the top of the vehicle. A moment later he found himself stuck to the side of a large metal rocket, aimed at the sky. The crocs started wrapping rope around him, tightly digging into his stomach.

"What colour will the fireworks be?" a croc asked.

"Purple, methinks," another giggled.

Kal tried wiggling free, but someone was holding him in place.

A crocodile then took a fistful of the boy's hair, yanking his head back to the metal rocket while a rope was brought around his neck, tying him to the rocket.

Kal started to gag and his head was heating up.

"Get ready to light it up!" someone cackled as the sound of burning could be heard.

Pfft, came a sound and one of the crocs was knocked over. *Pfft* the sound came again, incapacitating another.

Kal looked in the distance to see that Spyke was sitting on top of his car, a large sniper in hand and was picking off the crocodilian crooks one by one. When the time was right, he broke free and took the weapon from one of the smoking crocs.

"Thank you," he mouthed, knowing that the wolf probably could not see from so far away.

The boy huffed and puffed, wiping the sweat from his brow as even more crocodiles crawled onto the top. He took out a few, kicking them into the sand where possible and dodging blaster shots. The only issue he had was that he was light when compared to how big and burly they all were. So, when one of them picked him up by the neck, there was nothing he could do as he squirmed, trying to break free while his lungs were reeling in a frenzy. *Not again,* he thought.

"Dinner is served!" one bellowed heartily.

How had he managed to lose again in under a minute? Spyke was gone now, so he was the only one in charge of his own fate.

Kick, Kal, he said to himself, trying to swing his leg forward. It was no use, as his core was not letting him do it. "Come on!" he hissed at himself, swinging his leg again and kicking the face of the crocodile holding him. When he was phased, he took the opportunity to pick up a blaster and fire at him.

"I wouldn't do that if I were you!" screeched another, grabbing onto the boy's foot and pulling him back. "We are going to get that bounty first and then we will be stinking rich!"

His leg was stinging as the reptile's claws dug into his flesh. In a desperate attempt, he wriggled his toes and yanked his foot out of the boot, which the croc was still holding. Then he had the chance to stretch forward, grabbing the blaster and firing at him.

Kal continued to pant, sweating more and more. "I can do this," he said, feeling very tired and heavy, but devoted to moving onwards.

"We gonna get that penguin!" a croc spat, climbing onto the deck. This one had a hooked hand, a cape, and a belly that was so bulbous, it looked like it had a horse inside. It was so large in fact that he had to lean back just to stand upright and not topple forwards.

The boy acted quickly, shooting the fuse of the massive firework before knocking it over so that it was pointed at the large croc.

The creature did not get a chance to waddle away, so he was hit by a massive rocket that pulsed off with him into the distance, only to explode into golden rain.

The Beast Known as Terros

"No way I just did that!" Kal smiled, taking a seat.

As he did so, a black car zoomed up to them, moving with immense speed as it left behind a blue trail from the exhaust. He could see Spyke wearing his goggles, his cheeks and fur being pulled back by the wind, since the windscreen had been smashed.

"Took your time," Kal cried, seeing even more crocodiles crawl onto the top. "How many of these brutes are there?" he whispered to the air.

"FUEL TANK!" Spyke shouted from the car, now neck and neck with the behemoth.

"What?" Kal asked, watching as the wolf hurled over a bag to him.

"Drop this in the fuel tank!" he shouted again.

The boy picked up the bag, realising how heavy it was, and seeing the ball shape at the bottom. *Bombs*, he realised. While fighting, he had seen that there were barrels of fuel in the centre of the truck. So he dropped the bag there, setting one of the spherical balls to detonate in ten seconds. He then dashed over, preparing to jump back onto Spyke's car when a croc grabbed his sleeve. As a result, with only seconds till detonation, he pulled himself out of his jacket and jumped. The moment he touched Spyke's car, he veered off to the left, going as fast as he could. And then it happened.

The massive truck was enveloped in a ball of flames as a shockwave of sound, metal and cinder spread out in all directions.

Kal smiled at his feat, amazed that he had come out of that unscathed – apart from the fact that he had lost a boot and his jacket that he had grown to like. Also his goggles had a crack in the left lens, so he could not really see through it anymore. Pulling them off, he sighed and went inside, collapsing onto the bullet-torn seat.

"Not sure if this bad boy can get us back in one piece," Spyke sighed, his breaths long and drawn. "But hey, at least it was a fun ride!"

"Yeah," Kal groaned, sinking further into his seat.

"You wanted to be a bounty hunter," Spyke laughed. "This is the life you will be living if you want to make the big buck!" He then pulled out his glass bottle. "One more for the ride," he smiled, glugging it down. "Absolute beauty!" he snarled afterwards, cackling out the heat as his eyes went red. "We'll be at the penguin's residence very soon. You might want something to drink," he said, handing over the bottle to Kal.

"I'm okay," the boy muttered, pushing the glass away.

The wolf then looked at him and his eyebrows raised. "My, what happened to you?"

"What do you mean?" he asked.

"Your head," the wolf said. "It is leaking."

"What?" Kal said, touching his forehead and feeling some moisture.

"That's not good," the wolf said. "We were so close as well," he added, pressing the breaks. "Let's get you patched up, then we can be on our way."

Kal started to feel very weak. To the point where Spyke had to pick him up, out of the car, and gently drag him. He lay him down, propping him against the edge of the vehicle.

"Rest here kid," he said, pulling out a white roll from his pocket. "Always keep this handy," he said, unravelling some and wrapping it around his head, soaking up his blood. "I should probably sterilize the wound or something, but there ain't much I can use. I could use my fire drink but that would probably unalive you." He then tightened the bandage.

His arms and legs were also grazed.

Despite the heat of the desert, Kal was actually shivering, rubbing his bare arms. Before he knew it, Spyke had taken off his own jacket and placed it atop him, warming him up. He tried to mutter 'thanks' but felt too weak to do so.

The great big wolf then collapsed next to him, sighing and looking up at the setting sun. "Quite the adventure we had today. The wolf looked to Kal, whose eyes were closed. "You fell asleep quick," he laughed. "You're a good kid," he smiled. "It's just a damn shame you've been dealt this life, because this next bit is going to hurt a lot."

In the morning, the bounty hunter awoke, feeling slightly better. He looked around, taking in the morning breeze and inhaled deeply. "Spyke?" he called out, sitting up, and realising he had been lying in the sand. There was no sign of the wolf. "Spyke?" he called out again and saw that the car was gone.

"No!" he growled, seeing that there were tyre marks through the sand, in the direction of where Exekus lay. "No, he did not!" he hissed, pulling his massive jacket onto him before dusting his hair of sand.

To the side, there was a motorbike, the rider nowhere to be seen. He jumped onto it, flicked the gears on, causing the vehicle to rumble, before zooming off after his so-called ally.

Wind slapped across his face as he tried to maintain control over the vehicle. His thoughts raced as he rode, wondering why Spyke had abandoned him. Did he want the bounty for himself? Was that his plan all along?

Minutes later, the tracks ended and the black car was seen parked. Next to it was a large hole in the sand. Kal pulled his bike to a halt and looked into the gaping abyss.

"You are coming with me!" Spyke growled, his large fists around the neck of a strange looking animal with black skin, a short and plump body, and a small beak.

"Leave me alone!" the penguin called out.

"There is a hefty amount of money for your head," Spyke growled. "You are going to come with me, or I am going to *break* your legs."

Kal pulled a gun from the motorbike, one that had been strapped on by its previous rider. He then jumped down, into the underground bunker.

"And so it begins," the penguin said.

"What?" Spyke asked, looking behind him to see Kal. Suddenly his aggressive, demonic looking expression faded. "Kal!" he smiled. "So good of you to make it. Help me restrain this penguin so we can get you your bounty."

"You left me!" the boy shouted, pulling the gun out and aiming it at Spyke. "I should shoot you where you stand. Now drop your weapon and hand over the penguin."

"I am not just a penguin!" the small creature yelled. "I am Exekus Imporius, the smartest being alive."

"Shut up!" Spyke spat, squeezing the squishy animal. "Kal, I left you behind for your safety. I was going to get this penguin and then return to you."

"Prove it," the boy said.

"I left you my jacket – my most prized possession. There was no way I was not coming back for it." A soft grin appeared on the wolf's face.

"He's lying," Exekus said. "He told me that he is taking the money all for himself and that he…"

"Ignore the penguin," Spyke said. "He is trying to form a wedge between us two. Come on Kal. Drop the gun and let's go."

"No," the boy said, taking a step closer. "Yesterday you abandoned me on that massive transport – as if you wanted me to get killed. You used me to get the location of this penguin and then you ditched me."

"I saved you," the wolf said. "If I did nothing, then you would have been torn apart."

Kal wanted to believe him, but why did he abandon him in the sand to potentially die or be killed in his sleep by a bandit?

"He's lying," the penguin said.

"Shut up!" Spyke shouted. "I helped you, Kal. Taught you about being an effective hunter. I…"

The wolf did not finish. A laser tore out of Kal's gun and shot the wolf in the chest, knocking him back, causing him to drop the penguin.

"You taught me well," Kal said. "You taught me to never trust anyone – and that includes you."

Spyke gagged for air, his arms flailing about. "I… I…"

Kal saw the penguin trying to run away, so he chased after him, jumping on his back and wrestling him to the ground. "You are going nowhere," he growled.

"Mercy!" the penguin cried. "Mercy!"

He tore a section of his shirt off, and pulled it into the bird's beak, stopping him from talking. "You should survive, Spyke," Kal said. "Just don't come chasing after us."

With that said, the boy left the wolf, holding his bounty firmly in hand. "Okay," he sighed, opening up a small data-pad. "Time to meet my client."

Chapter 15: The Mechanical Truth

Rett the Human travelled for some time alongside his wife Arnetta and the head known as Cornelius. After a while he got fed up of him, so wrapped him up in a bag and stuffed him in the boot. The man then drove in the front seat with Arnetta being in the passenger one. She woke up after about a day, but still thought she were evil, keeping the persona of General 83. For that reason, Rett had her strapped to a chair with a gag in her mouth. He would feel great sadness seeing her like this.

The journey went on for a while, until they reached the so-called Gigafactory - a large tower in the distance, surrounded by a mini city with a large red laser grid all over it. "Looks spooky," Rett said. He then ungagged Arnetta to allow her to speak. "I am taking you in there, so we can fix you."

"I cannot be fixed!" she shouted, spitting on him. "I have sat here for days, listening to you talk and waffle. Once I escape, I am going to…"

Rett put the gag back on and sighed. "I'll bring you back, Arnetta," he whispered. "Now how do I get in?" he asked himself, standing outside the vehicle and looking at the techno-nightmare.

He did not get very far as he felt a sharp pain in his neck. He looked to see that a dart had hit him, and now he felt oh so sleepy. "How did they know I was here?" he asked, sinking to the ground. "But…" he tried to say before blacking out.

Rett's eyes slowly opened, his ears ringing as he did so. The last thing he remembered was… He tried to scratch his eyes, but his arms would not move. Perplexed, he looked at them and saw that his wrists were chained and pinned to the ground. *Not again,* he thought, trying to pry himself free.

"Rett," sighed a voice – one oddly familiar.

A soft hand then grabbed his chin and made him look upwards.

Sitting on a chair opposite him was a woman in white uniform with golden shoulders.

"Arnetta?" Rett asked, finally being able to see clearly.

"Let me reintroduce myself. I am General 83," she replied gently. "I admit, this body was once that of your wife," she said, with a cold-hearted expression; "but since then, I have been factory reset and a new conscience has been implanted." She was now much calmer than when they were in the car together, but her aura was just as menacing

The Beast Known as Terros

Rett opened his mouth, but decided to let her finish speaking.

"Now I am Amelia Arkus, daughter of Admiral Graham Arkus of the 32nd Battalion. He died when I was a small girl, serving the Federation. I aced my studies and got sent to the Federation Academy at the age of thirteen and quickly became the best there, graduating with flying colours. After time served, I left there and now serve the Pale King, helping him build his empire.

"These memories of course are not real, simply put into me a few days ago when they captured us. But it is as if they all happened. I can see my father's face the night before he went to war and died. I remember piloting my first ship. I…"

"Enough!" Rett shouted. "They have brainwashed you. But I still remember who you are. You are Arnetta, my wife; the woman who I married and spent years travelling the road with. Before that, we lived in the same town, went to the same school. Our world was destroyed, and we gathered any survivors and travelled."

"I am sorry, Rett," she said. "But I hate to break the news to you. This was all some experiment," she cried. "They created the memories of our old life and then set us off into the wild to live out our lives and 'become human'. Our old home was never destroyed. It was just a factory where they made us and implanted memories of our childhood. Then they put us into the jungle and programmed us to think we had some 'promised land' to find. Then by going on an adventure, they would see how our minds would work and if we could truly survive, thinking we were humans. It clearly worked, so now they have wiped all our memories and have prepared new personalities for us all – as elite soldiers. But for some reason we cannot reset you. It is as if you built such resilience in your human life that we cannot delete it. But when we do reset you, we have the perfect backstory for you. General 84, my husband and a super smart leader. We can be together again, Rett. You and I."

"No!" the man snapped. "You are lying." While she was rabbiting on about her conspiracy, he thought about ways he could escape.

"Now Rett, I suggest you let us reset you, or we will have to dissect your entire body manually and take out your memories. You are the first of a new batch of artificial being, the latest robot and it would be a shame to have to destroy you."

"What about everyone else?" Rett asked, trying to distract her as he continued to think of a way out.

"They have all been reset," she said. "Rig is now Colonel 213, chief engineer on the warship Pluribus. Johnny is…"

"No!" Rett growled, hoping the woman would stop speaking.

"Are you ready?" she said with a smile. "Just give me the word and we can reset you. All the pain and suffering you have endured will be gone and we will give you a nostalgic and loving backstory. How does that sound?"

Rett then thought about his life. He had never once gotten sick and would rarely ever get hungry – but he did eat food, something a machine could not. His hair would grow, and his wisdom teeth had only finished coming through a year ago. "I am human," he said. "I have thoughts, feelings and emotions and can heal from injuries, eat food and more."

Arnetta shook her head. "You are not human – just a very advanced machine. An organic simulation. I can show you the trials and the chamber of your birth as well as your training in the lab and more. When they were done with us, they threw us into the depths of the jungle, and we woke, thinking we had some special mission."

"Who are they?" Rett scowled.

"Me," snarked a voice, as loud footsteps echoed. Into the room walked a well-dressed man, wearing a lavender purple suit. His face was beamed into a smile. "New body, same old me."

"Cornelius," Rett hissed. "So, they took your head and secured it onto another body?"

"Yes," the man replied. "But this time I have been upgraded." His hand suddenly disappeared and in its place was a long blade. The man walked forwards, resting the sharp and cool tip against Rett's cheek. "You subjected me to so much agony. If Amelia was not here, you would be dead, and your conscience re-uploaded into a cow!"

"My love, ignore him," Amelia said, putting her hand on Cornelius' shoulder.

"Love? Arnetta you can do much better than *that*!" Rett said, spitting a large globule of saliva at Cornelius' face.

"You!" Cornelius yelled, but composed himself and stepped back, wiping off the spit. "Apes!" he called suddenly.

As this was said, a dozen or so chimpanzees walked into the room, using their fists to help them march.

"Reset him," Amelia said. "We could have been together, but I guess Cornelius will be my new husband."

"Hehe," the suited man laughed. "The Pale King will be much impressed by our work here."

The monkeys in their lab coats then grabbed Rett, pulling him to the ground.

"Not again," the man growled, trying to squirm free. As the metal mask came over his face, he tried as best he could to have happy thoughts.

"The truth," growled an ape, as the screws tightened and everything he saw started to swirl.

That was the last thing Rett heard before he was pulled into a dream.

"Aargh!" Rett cried, waking up. He was covered in a slimy substance that was very cold to the touch. In front of him was a glass wall, completely surrounding him.

"Awaken, Subject R-8!" a voice boomed in.

The glass doors slid open and Rett tumbled onto the floor, the sticky liquid dispersing in all directions.

"How does the organic body feel, R-8?" an ape asked, standing opposite him with a clipboard in hand.

Rett closed his hands and opened them over and over, feeling the skin press against itself and heat up. With his other hand he felt over his head – smooth and free of hair. "This feels great," he said. "Much better than my metal, clanky self."

The monkey nodded, writing more notes.

"When will I be deployed?" Rett asked.

"Soon, R-8," the monkey said. "First I need to check your bodily functions." He took a light and shone it in Rett's eye, causing him to flinch. "Eye behaviour is normal," the ape said. "Stick out your tongue."

Rett did as was asked.

The monkey placed a drop of liquid onto the pink and squishy tongue.

The Beast Known as Terros

"EEURGH!" Rett spat. "So that is what flavour is like."

"Indeed," the monkey replied. "Now let us check your pain receptors," he said, pulling out a needle and pricking Rett's skin, drawing blood.

Rett flinched backwards, unable to describe what he had just felt. He did not like it one bit.

"Now, go through those doors and you will see Subject R-N-8. She is currently designing the backstory that will be implanted into her. The other apes and I believe that you and her should be 'married' in your new life. This way we can test the emotion receptors and it will give you both a reason to keep going."

"How so?" Rett replied.

"Humans have this thing where they will do what they can to help their loved ones," the ape stated. "When we drop you in the middle of the jungle, we want you to survive – no matter what comes your way."

"I understand," Rett said, putting his hand onto the doorknob and trying to open it.

"Stop!" the ape called out. "You are human now. That means that you must feel embarrassed when naked."

"Huh," Rett replied, looking down. "That is strange that humans do not embrace their natural look."

"Put on these clothes," the ape said, handing over a white shirt and trousers.

Once changed, Rett walked into the next room, where there was a large computer screen. Sitting in front of it was a bald girl, also wearing white, swiping through vast amounts of information.

"R-N-8 is that you?" Rett asked.

"Yes, it is," the girl replied. "R-8?" she asked.

"That's me!" Rett chuckled. "What backstory have you chosen?"

"I think my name should be Arnetta," the girl said. "Arnetta grew up in the human kingdom and loved to read books. She then…"

This went on for a while and Rett watched with great interest.

At the end, the girl said, "The higher-ups suggest that you and I be a couple, R-8," she said. "I should incorporate that into my backstory."

"Rett," he said. "I choose that to be my name. How about we both went to the same school? One day I forgot to bring in my textbook and the teacher told you and I to share. Then we became friends."

"That sounds good," Arnetta replied.

Months passed, and Rett was tested every day – running speeds, strength tests and more. Soon he had grown a full head of hair and was able to walk and talk like a human. While this was happening, the apes had been synthesizing his memories, trying to make them as realistic as possible. Potential memories were fed into him to test his receptors – such as the death of his mother. This made water leak from Rett's eye – a tear, they would tell him.

Sometime later, Rett was sitting in a room full of other beings like himself. They were all wearing tattered clothing and had been made to look rugged. To his right sat Arnetta, his future wife – her hair matted, and her face covered in mud, as had been chosen. In Rett's hand was a locket, with a picture that him and Arnetta had taken together the previous day. It had been printed in black and white as well as having been weathered and torn.

At the front of the room stood an ape, briefing them on what to do. There was a screen behind him displaying a map from above the jungle they were going to traverse.

"In a few hours the test will begin. You will have your memory as a robot removed and will be given fake human memories that you engineered. After that you will wake up in the middle of the jungle, with a few scrap cars. You will then think that it is your duty to find other humans. That will bring you here, after a few years of journeying. Then once you have returned, you will be given your robot memories back and we will deem this operation a success. Then you will be promoted within the ranks and some of you may even be exported to another planet. Understood?"

"Yes!" everyone called in unison.

"Well then," the ape said. "I wish you all the best of luck."

"I am nervous," Arnetta said to Rett.

"Don't be," he replied. "We will be together on the other side."

Next, Rett woke up, surrounded by trees and his head ringing. There was a campfire, and everyone was sleeping around it. "Wake up!" he called. "We need to keep travelling."

Arnetta then looked at him, getting up from her nap.

"We have to find our new home!" he exclaimed. His whole crew then nodded, getting up from their naps. They all knew there were other humans like them out there. They just needed to keep on travelling until they could be reunited.

"No!" Rett bellowed, waking up. "It was all a lie!" he screamed, feeling his whole body be drenched in sweat and his cheeks sodden with tears.

"It was a success," an ape said, typing away on a computer.

"All those fake memories – when I was just grown in a lab!" he growled.

"You genuinely believed you were human," an ape said. "We deem that as a success."

"My life. My parents. All a lie," he snapped.

"Yes," the ape said.

"Why?" Rett or, as he learned to believe, R-8, called out.

"Why what?" the ape said, not even looking at him as he continued analysing the numbers on screen.

"Why go through all this? What was this test for? Why are you breeding robots?"

"Orders of the Pale King," the ape said. "We need human robots to integrate into the Federation and start to take apart the Grand Conciliator's work from the inside."

"What?" Rett replied. "You put me through all this, just so I could help this so-called Pale King? Who even is that?"

"Enough questions," the ape said, pausing. "Now then, Amelia Arkus has suggested that you serve by her side. However, that is proving to be an issue."

"How so?" Rett demanded.

"You will not let go of the human memories. They have become so latched to your conscience that it is proving difficult to reset you. I did not account for this," the monkey said, continuing to rapidly type and swipe at numbers and graphs. "The good news is, by experimenting on you, we can improve our current model of humans. If you refuse to be machine, then we can use that part of your brain and implant it into our next batch, making them entirely human. You have actually made our work so much easier by being stubborn, R-8."

"Release me," the man said.

"No," the ape replied. As he said this, a metal strap came across Rett's face, stopping him from calling out.

Chapter 16: Rescue

"The human kingdom," Gides the Fox let out. "Never thought I would be coming here." He gazed out to the Gigafactory, billowing out smoke that covered the sky with a layer of darkness and fear.

All the buildings were very tall, filled with neon lights of aggregate purples and navy blues. Terros clenched his fists as he looked at the dark and demonic world – the very place where his father had been taken and transformed into the mechanical creature that killed his mother.

"All we need is the power core," Narth said, looking over the cyber-dystopian world. "Should be in the middle of that factory – the core powering everything."

"So just to defeat the Pirate King, we need to power off an entire kingdom?" Zemu asked.

"This is not a kingdom," Terros growled. "This is a torture site – a haven of the worst of the worst."

"He really hates humans," Zemu laughed, nudging the penguin, who just ignored him.

"How do we get in then?" Gides asked, pointing at the laser dome that came into view as they got closer. "This ship is not getting through – and if it does, then those thousands of canons are going to open fire."

"Easy," Terros said. "Take me in as prisoner."

"How though?" Narth asked. "They will be suspicious that a penguin like me is out of the Paradise Haven."

"Zemu will take me," Terros said. "The humans will think he is bringing me in as a prisoner of the Pirate King. Then once we are in, we will get to work."

"What about us two?" Narth asked. "Did you just bring us for nothing?"

"Gides will pilot the ship. He is our getaway driver once we get the core. Your job is to protect him at all cost. Not only that, but you need to hack into the base and turn off the lights once we are in. Understand?"

They all nodded, but also shared a look of similar confusion. This was the most Terros had spoken to them, to the point where he was now the one taking charge.

As they landed in the musty, dusty, techno-dystopian wasteland, they all took a deep breath.

"Here goes," Zemu said, stretching his back in an arc position. "I am so skinny," he sighed.

"Terros can help you with that," Gides said. "Just eat what he eats and train like he does and soon you will be the same size."

"So much effort," Zemu yawned, putting a pistol into his holster.

"Focus," Terros said, clicking the handcuffs around his wrist into place. They barely fit, which did not surprise him.

"Approaching location," Del the Computer said.

"Yeah, that is obvious," Gides replied.

When the landing gears collided with the ground, they all got ready. They had parked in some shrubbery a few dozen metres away from the large dome.

"Let's go," Zemu said, pointing the back of his gun to Terros' head, making him walk like a prisoner.

"This is going to convince no one," Gides sighed. "How could someone as skinny as Zemu cuff Terros realistically?"

"No worries," the pirate said. "I have created an epic story. You will hear it in due course."

"Make sure you both keep your earpieces in and don't take off your trackers," Narth said.

"Move!" Zemu spat at Terros when they were close to the dome. They walked for a minute until the great red wall was right up to the beast's face.

"How do we get in?" Zemu asked. "Hellooo?"

"State your business," a robotic voice responded.

The pirate took in a deep breath. "I am Zemu Zarillian, first lieutenant to the Pirate King. I have delivered one Terros to you."

"Drop the animal and leave," the voice replied.

"I want to come in?" Zemu asked.

"That cannot be arranged. Leave the beast, for you are not welcome here."

"The Pirate King wants you to have him. It is a token of his love that I come in as well. Now let me in or…"

The wall split and a human-sized gate appeared. Terros stepped in and Zemu assumed he had to do the same. Fortunately, nobody stopped him.

"This place sucks," the pirate said, looking at the tall buildings with large screens on them. There was the odd human here and there, but they lacked any sort of personality, walking only in perfectly straight lines and seeming completely uniform.

"Terros Tarthanian Mrilmus," the one known as Cornelius said, walking into the street and in front of them. "I see you got caught in the end," he laughed. "Where is your fox friend? I heard about your little stunt with the Elder."

"Where is Rett?" Terros asked, worried that Cornelius was free and in a new body while his human friend was missing.

"Oh him," Cornelius laughed. "Shame about that. He just learnt the truth and let's just say is having a little mid-life crisis."

"Serves him right," Zemu said. "I heard what he did to your head."

"So, you know about that," Cornelius grunted. "Oh well. Anyway, thank you for bringing me Terros. Send my regards to the Pirate King."

Two large animals strolled in – both gorillas with thick black skin and dense fur. Their hands were covered with bright red metal gloves that looked lethal.

"Say," Cornelius said. "How did you bring in Terros? Someone as scrawny as you."

"Well, here is the thing," the pirate said, getting excited. "I…"

"Actually, I do not care," Cornelius said, checking his watch. "It is time for you to leave."

"No," Zemu said. "I am not leaving that Gedrul until I see him in a cell. Pirate tradition."

"Is it now?" the man replied. "So be it." The gorillas then grabbed Terros roughly, taking one arm each.

It hurt the beast as their metal fingers sunk into his muscular flesh. They also lugged him hard, and walked fast, virtually dragging him along. He then pondered what exactly they were. Were they robots or actual flesh and blood gorillas?

They took him into a tall building, filled with screens and drones flying about. A techno-haven some might say. But to Terros, this was a metallic hell.

As he walked in, he was scanned by multiple machines, and the bright lights made him wince. "What a beast," Cornelius said. "An unruly, disgusting, malevolent…"

Taking the risk, Terros leaned forwards and bit hard, inches away from Cornelius' face.

"Hmm," the man squealed as the two gorillas tightened their grips on the animal.

"I look forward to experimenting on you," the man then sighed. "A legion of robots in your image could prove to be the perfect slaves. Anyway, it is time to arrest you both. I hope you look forward to sharing a cell."

"Both?" Zemu asked. "But you…"

"The bounty for Terros is still open, which means you do not work for the Pirate King," Cornelius spat, slamming a thick pair of heavy-duty cuffs around Zemu's hands. "You really thought I would fall for your little trick? Rett will be pleased to see the both of you in prison with him –

give him some company after his revelation. That is, if we have not mind-wiped him yet."

"What?" Terros asked.

"He is a robot," Cornelius laughed. "Like every human in this city. Yet we programmed him so well that he still thinks he is human!" the man cackled.

Come on Narth, Terros was thinking. He needed his penguin friend to switch off the lights so he could run away. But then, these beings were not human and most likely could see in the dark. But still, something was better than nothing.

As they walked, more and more people flocked around them, creating an entourage of humans with guns, all pointed at him. His chances of escape were getting less and less.

"Into the lift," Cornelius said, gesturing as two metal doors slid open, revealing a large, mirrored room with an array of buttons at the side.

"In you go," one of the gorillas mumbled, surprising Terros that they could actually speak. The former pirate and the beast did as was asked, stepping into the small room.

Don't turn off the lights now, Terros thought as Cornelius and a few others stepped in. If Narth did his job there and then, they would have been trapped between floors – a great inconvenience.

"Right up we go," Cornelius smiled, pressing a key and then the room revved into action, starting to speed upwards. Terros was almost happy that it was not another underground lair.

ZHEEOM, came a noise as the lights went out, leaving them in pitch black.

Curse you, penguin, Terros thought, getting to work. He wedged an elbow back, into one gorilla, before biting another in the shoulder.

Zemu also got to work, using the weight of his heavy cuffs to build momentum and smash into the robots around him. The sound of metal smashing and Cornelius screaming went on for a minute, until the doors opened and the two heroes burst out, covered in oil and metal scraps.

"Backup lighting operational," came a voice from within the walls as the whole corridor lit-up.

"You will not get far!" Cornelius shouted from the lift, now a smashed body – a sprawl of wires.

Terros and Zemu dashed through the polished hallways, running for their lives.

"Where are we going?" the pirate called out.

"Rett," Terros mumbled.

"Who?" the dragon responded.

"A friend," the beast roared, getting onto all fours and then quickening his pace into a frenzied gallop.

"Wait up!" Zemu called out, panting rapidly.

Terros then burst into a room, filled with small cubes – all covered with a red laser grid for a door. They were stacked upon one another – building blocks in the dozens. *Dozens?* Terros thought at first until he got closer and saw that they were in their hundreds, stretching on and on and on, stacked up by three and in the length of infinity, a truly horrific sight.

There was a thick stench of sweat, vomit and drool that filled the area. Terros' eyes widened as he saw species of all sorts being held captive – wolves, penguins, foxes. There were even a few pirate dragons sitting in cages, their faces buried in their hands.

"What are you two doing here?" Zemu asked, going up to the laser.

"A trade," one sighed, his voice groggy. "The Pirate King handed us over in exchange for some technology, cool guns and more." he paused. "You'll see."

Terros went through each cage, seeing the common denominator. The humans were collecting other species. For what exactly, it was not quite clear, but there were animals he never even knew existed. Like strange reptiles that had skin that could change colour, dinosaurs, crocodiles, apes and more.

"My people," Terros whispered, his heart starting to race. "Could they be here?" The males were all captured those years ago, but where had they been taken? With all the cells, perhaps there were a few survivors here.

The beast started eagerly looking, hoping to catch some. Just one would have made him happy. But it had been almost ten years; maybe they were all dead?

He came across one cell, where there were two people inside – a man and a woman. The man looked unhealthily pale, and the woman was wearing some sort of uniform.

"R-8," she said. "Do you know where you are? This is…"

Terros did not hesitate, grabbing the woman and tossing her to the side. "Rett," he said gruffly. "Let's go."

"I don't exist," the man mumbled.

The woman, Arnetta, got up from the ground, huffing and puffing. "How dare you toss me to the side?!" she shouted. "Do you know who I am? I am General Amelia Arkus…"

"I don't care," Terros said, picking her up by the shirt and throwing her into the laser grids of one of the cells.

She was shocked for a few seconds and then collapsed to the ground, her clothes singed and her body smoking.

"Rett, let's go," the beast said, picking him up.

"I..." he said stuttering. "I'm not human."

"Good," the beast said. "Who would want to be a human?"

Rett then composed himself. "When you put it like that," he said, standing up and dusting off his clothes. "Where are we going?"

"We need to steal the energy core of this facility or this kingdom. Something with real power."

"I think I know where to go," the man said, walking past Arkus, who was lying on the floor, semi-conscious.

"She's your wife," Terros said. "We bringing her?"

"My wife is dead," Rett sighed. "Her body has a new host now," he said, kicking Amelia in the face.

"Zemu!" Terros called out. "Let's go."

"Let me save my pirate friends," Zemu cried. "How do I unlock the gate?" he asked, pressing buttons.

"Hey!" Rett called out, picking Arkus up by her shirt. "How do we open these cells?"

"I'm not telling you," she said, spitting a fat globule at Rett's face.

"You have a pretty face," Rett said. "I know, because I was married to it. But it would be a shame for you to lose it," he added, dragging her to a laser grid. "If I push your face into this for a minute, I doubt there will be much flesh left."

"Please don't!" she cried.

"Then tell me the code!" Rett growled.

"88324!" she squealed.

The Beast Known as Terros

Zemu pressed those buttons and the laser grid stopped, releasing the two pirates.

At the end of the corridor, a legion of robots dressed in blue outfits stormed in, wearing heavy riot armour and holding large guns.

"How do we fight them all?" Zemu asked.

"You don't," one of the two new pirates said. "Time for our sacrificial moment," he added, taking in a deep breath.

"Our?" the other one asked. "We did not agree to this."

"We can hold them back until you get to the power core. Then once that is gone, all the other cells will open and we can defeat these mechanical monstrosities."

"Why are you doing this?" Zemu asked.

"Ha!" the pirate laughed. "You are going to fight the Pirate King, right? Kill him and make us proud."

"Power core is this way," Rett said, waving them all to follow him. "We just need to yank it from the console and this whole place will go dark."

"Including all the robots?" Zemu asked.

"No, they have their own power supply separate to this grid." The man then kept on running, pointing at a small hole in the ceiling – a grate. "The elevators will be guarded so we need to find another way." Rett then gestured for Terros to give him a leg up.

"How do you know all this?" Terros asked at last.

"They awakened my memories from when I was a simple Model 8 machine. Back then, I knew the whole blueprints to this place."

"Model 8?" Zemu asked as Rett pushed the square to the side and did a muscle-up, getting himself into the pipeline.

"Another time," Rett replied.

Next, Zemu put a foot on Terros' hand and jumped up, putting his hands onto the sides of the elevated platform. He tried pulling himself up, but his skinny limbs were failing him.

"Here," Rett said, putting his hand in front of the dragon.

"No," Zemu squealed. "I need to learn to be strong." His arms wobbled and shook while his stomach felt uneasy.

In the end Rett hurled him up. "No time to be a hero," the human said. "Now, how will Terros get up?"

The arc of a smile formed on the beast's face as he bent his knees and propelled off the ground, flying upwards and into the grate with immense speed and precision.

"Wish I was that strong," Zemu sighed.

"Why do you need this core?" Rett asked, crouching and gently walking through the vent.

"To power a robot to fight the Pirate King," Zemu replied, crouching as well and trying to keep his splintering wings as low as possible.

"Hear that?" Rett asked, placing his palms onto the rungs of a ladder.

Terros' ear pricked as the faint hum of something was apparent. "Yes," he murmured.

"That is the power core. One simple orb is pumping this whole facility with life," Rett grinned.

"But how can we hold it?" Zemu asked. "Surely if it has that much energy, it will incinerate us at the touch?"

"No," Rett replied. "Hopefully there will be some sort of case to contain it. If not, we may need to rethink our plans." Rett made his way up the long ladder, until the humming started to get louder and more dramatic, causing the ladder to rattle in its position. "Through these doors," the man said, breathing hard and sweating intensely.

"If you are a robot, then how comes you are out of breath?" Zemu asked, knocking on the tough metal wall in front of them.

"I am Model 18," Rett replied. "A fully organic human with no artificial parts."

"So, you're a human?" Zemu asked.

"Like I said, another time," Rett sighed, pointing at the heavy door then at Terros.

The beast clenched his fist and ran forwards, pulsing through the air and throwing a punch that tore through the metal like paper, creating a hand-sized hole. Using it as leverage, he grunted, tearing the doors open.

"There it is!" Rett clamoured, walking through and grinning at the large cylindrical fuselage that stretched up and up as well as down and down. It glowed a bright blue that could have blinded someone if they stared at it for too long.

"Where's the core?" Zemu asked.

"One second," Rett replied, pressing buttons on the nearby console. "The energy from the core is being stretched into the tube which powers this whole city. If I can just stop the elongation, then we can take this core and be out from here.

"Your sabotage ends now!" came a sharp voice. The sound of hard boots entered the room as Amelia Arkus waltzed in, holding a gun pointed at Rett's head. Her hair was dishevelled and her uniform was singed, while her face looked angrier than ever. Surrounding her were a dozen other machines, all wearing heavy gear and pointing weapons at the three heroes.

"Arkus!" Rett scowled, halting his pressing of the buttons and raising his hands above his head.

"I gave you chance after chance, R-8," she growled. "But your recklessness and dominion ends here." The wicked woman then pressed her trigger, firing a blast of laser into Rett's body, throwing him backwards into the abyss below. "Such a waste of a perfectly organic body," she sighed.

Chapter 17: The Cogs of Disaster

Terros clenched his fists hard. His breathing heavied and a look of pure rage crawled over his face. "I am going to kill all of you," he growled. He did not know Rett all that well, but he could trust him – something very few people had earnt the honour of. He now had two options: absorb a few shots and take out everyone, but that would mean Zemu's demise, or simply hand himself in.

"We finally have you, Terros," Amelia Arkus smiled, walking up to the beast. "Such magnificent fur," she said, touching his mane. "Shame I can't turn you into a coat, for the Pale King has specifically demanded you for testing, since the rest of you male Gedruls went missing."

"Your people took mine!" scowled Terros, smelling the evil in the woman.

"You have much to learn," she spat. "I must commend you for what you did to Cornelius. That disgusting man needed to go, and I guess that puts *me* in charge here. So, I suggest you…"

Terros could not be bothered to hear the rest. He grabbed the woman by the throat and threw her into the robot whose gun was at Zemu's head, knocking him out. "Fight!" he ordered the pirate, who picked up a blaster from the ground and got to work, silencing robot after robot.

The beast took a few hits, biting his teeth hard. But he knew that Zemu was not strong enough to take such damage, so he did the majority of the fighting, letting Zemu act more defensively.

"You stupid, pathetic beast!" Arkus screamed like a witch, spitting out a tooth. "I am going to…"

Terros picked her up once again and this time swung her around like a wrecking ball. When he let go, he hurled her into the tube of light in the centre, accidentally. He did not want to kill her, but the forces of nature ended up doing so.

"NOOO!" she screamed as her body withered into nothing upon touching the bright energy.

"You finally shut her up," Zemu laughed, shooting the last robot.

"How do we turn off the power?" Terros asked, looking at all the buttons. "It has to be one of these." There were dozens, if not hundreds of buttons, all of different shapes, colours and sizes. Some were switches, some were levers and there was even the odd joystick.

"A little help," murmured a faint voice from below.

Terros looked down and a large grin formed on his face. Below them, clinging from a platform using his last two fingers was none other than Rett the Human.

"Of course!" Terros said heartily, picking up the man and placing him on level ground.

"Hell of a shot," Rett said, putting his hand to his abdomen. "Well, I guess Arnetta could never aim properly," he laughed awkwardly. "Say, where is she?"

Zemu gulped and then looked at Terros.

"She is gone," the beast said with no remorse. "I threw her into the energy."

"Oh," Rett said quietly. "Did she scream?"

"Yes," Terros said bluntly. "Quite a lot actually."

"Good," Rett smiled. "She was an annoying witch."

Zemu sighed a sigh of relief as he wiped the imaginary sweat from his dry, reptilian brow.

"Now let me get that core," the man said, pushing a few more buttons until the humming stopped and the tube ended in its brightness. A second later, the whole place went dark, except the white core which lit up only that room as it hovered in place.

"How do we hold it?" Zemu asked, looking around for a case.

Terros saw that one of the dead robots was wearing large metal gloves that had thrusters built on the side. The beast picked them up and adjusted them to fit around his own hands. "Will this work?" he asked, grabbing the sphere of pure light and holding it. It did not hurt, but rather ached his muscles as the vibration was strong, repelling against him. Next Zemu pulled a large metal case from under the console and the beast put the core inside of it, sealing it up with many locks and mechanisms.

"That actually worked," Rett said. "Now, let's get out of here."

Dim lights started to appear all over the black city as the backup power took effect.

"Let me call Gides," Zemu said. "Tell him we are here."

The laser dome around the city had disappeared and the remainder of the crew was able to fly in. Terros, Zemu and Rett all ran outside, taking in the cold air and the blustery rain. "Here goes," the pirate said, looking up and waiting for his ship.

"Give back the core!" a voice shouted, raspy and electronic. "GIVE IT BACK!" it bellowed again, even louder.

Large footsteps echoed through the streets as a large silhouette spread across the road and a mechanical being came into view, walking powerfully. It had a large chainsaw for one hand, spinning rapidly and the other hand was a claw. The lights of the cockpit revealed its pilot – a man looking withered and wild with a face half burnt off and the other half a mechanical skeleton of dark silver.

"I will kill all of you!" Cornelius cried; his organic voice mixed with radio static. He pushed a lever and made his mech take another step forward.

Behind him emerged an entire army of humans, robots, apes, gorillas and more – all looking completely personality-free and devoid of emotion.

"Far too many of them," Zemu squealed.

"But there are many of us!" another quirky voice shouted from behind them.

Terros turned around and a large grin formed on his face.

"Freedom!" a pirate bellowed as a hundred or so animals appeared from the wreckage of the building, all looking bloodthirsty and ready for war.

"FREEDOM!" they all bellowed out.

"Get back in your cages!" Cornelius cried, pointing the turrets on his back at them. "You are all vermin!"

"Leave no man standing!" someone exclaimed and a second later, the two factions charged at one another – the sound of screaming and yelling stretching far and wide.

There was then a mechanical noise in Terros' ear.

"Terros, this is Gides. Where do we land the ship? There are people everywhere."

The beast ignored his fox friend, because from within the army he could see one person – one being that filled him with pure joy and excitement. Reverting to his animalistic nature, Terros burst through the animal army, pushing the odd person to the side as he squirmed through.

"HEY!" he shouted, enveloping the other in a hug.

"What?" the other person said. "Another like me?" he added, looking at Terros' white coat and big muscles. "HA! Is that you Terros?"

Terros nodded. "Rufus?" he asked, recognising his childhood friend. It was difficult having the reunion over the sound of all the fighting and metal being shred apart.

Rufus squeezed his old friend tightly. "I thought you died in the attack?"

"I live," Terros mumbled.

"You are so big and strong!" Rufus cried out. "Unlike me. I've just been trapped in this cage for the past ten years, eating scraps and growing skinny."

Rufus was a sorry sight, with a withered and patchy mane, while his limbs were skinny and barely able to hold him up. Even his eyes were narrow, and his skin was hanging loose from his body.

"Where are the others?" Terros asked, scared for what the answer might be.

Rufus let out a deep breath. "They left."

"Left?" Terros asked.

"A few years back we planned an escape – so we could get away from this wretched place and reunite with all the females." Rufus then moved to the side to allow the corpse of a robot to fly past. "There was a visitor here, who came in a spaceship. The other Gedruls broke free and stole that ship and flew off into space. They left me behind since I was… too slow."

"Where did they go?" Terros asked. "And why did they abandon the rest of us?"

"No idea," Rufus let out. "Durren, your uncle, took charge and said it was adamant that they fled to another planet."

"But what about the rest of us!" Terros growled. "Why did they abandon us?"

"I don't know," Rufus said. "They used to have meetings and make plans – but they said I was too young to listen in."

"No!" Terros growled. "All this time they have been alive? And were just having fun in space?"

"Terros!" called a voice.

The beast turned to see that Cornelius' mech was squeezing Zemu with his claw, holding him in the air. He was bringing the chainsaw closer and closer to his head.

"TERROS!" the pirate yelled.

"Survive," the beast told the skinny Gedrul. Then, he channelled his rage and paced forwards, through hoards of fighting animals and robots, slashing one after the other.

He bit through the wire of one and then jumped up, latching onto the glass cockpit of Cornelius' mech.

"RRRRRR!" the beast let out.

Cornelius dropped Zemu and tried to fight back, but Terros was unhinged. He tore at the glass and smashed his head through it. He then pushed an arm in and seized Cornelius by the neck, clutching him hard and leaving claw marks. With a heave, he threw the machine out and onto the ground, into the midst of the clashing armies.

The robot tumbled across the ground. Quickly, he got to work, turning his arms into canons before firing at Terros.

"No," the beast hummed, dodging shot after shot and then swiping his left paw across the man's face, gliding his claws through his metal visage like butter. He then put one hand on either side of the robot's head and started squeezing until nuts and bolts started flying out.

"STOP!" Cornelius roared as his metal skull was turned to a crushed can and his head was reduced to rubble. The voice of the machine then turned into a long beep and faded into nothing.

"Above you," Gides said in Terros' ear. The beast looked up to see his ship hovering high, with a rope dangling down.

"Zemu," Terros said, pointing at the rope. The dragon then jumped on and started slowly clambering up, slugging his skinny body to the top.

The beast then gestured to Rett, who did the same. Unfortunately, there would not be enough space for all the animals, so Terros had to pick wisely. "Rufus!" he called out.

"No," the other beast said. "I will fight alongside them. I have unfinished business with these machines."

"Just survive," Terros said, jumping onto the rope and getting inside, clambering up and leaving the battle a memory in the distance.

"Quite the stealth mission," Gides laughed as Terros got in and the hatch closed. "What happened to a quick in and out? It looks like you just started a war."

"Where to?" Zemu asked, catching his breath.

"Back to the Paradise Haven. We just need Exekus and then we can build that machine."

"Who's the newbie?" Narth asked, pointing at Rett.

"Rett," he smiled. "Pleased to meet you."

As they spoke, Terros was looking out the window at the war below. The animals would most certainly win, but that was not what filled his mind. "My people are out there," he mumbled.

Chapter 18: Convergence

"Thank you for saving me," Exekus Imporius said, sitting opposite to Kal in the boat they had hitched a ride on – a small fishing vessel piloted by bears.

"Save you from what?" Kal replied, enjoying the gentle breeze. The boat would take them to the island under the Paradise Haven and then his journey would finally be over.

"You saved me from that gnarly wolf," Exekus said. "He would have just stuffed me in a bag for the whole journey and probably eaten me if he got hungry."

"You're welcome," Kal replied. He then thought about Spyke. He should not have shot him. But then again, he did not want to risk failing his mission. One wolf had already tried to eat him.

"I can make you a new suit," the penguin said. "Would probably take me a few hours, but it would be my way of saying thank you."

"I could do with a new suit," Kal replied, running his hands through his hair. "But once I hand you over, I will never see you again."

"Fair play," Exekus replied. "You do realise my suit would be the best out there. It could transform into any weapon, create holographic objects and more. It could…"

"Just be quiet," Kal said. "We are almost here."

The boat pulled up by the beach – a large sandy, tropical expanse. "Thank you," Kal said to the bear captain as he got off. He then tugged the penguin with him. "Come on you," he said. "You are my ticket off this planet."

Kal and Exekus were left alone. They spent some time there, watching the sun set – for that was the agreed time to meet their client.

"You know," Exekus said. "There is a gate there. It opens and takes you to my world."

"There's nothing there," the boy replied, getting impatient. He had spent the whole time doodling in the sand and throwing rocks at the ocean.

"It's invisible," Exekus laughed. "Wait until you see it."

"Just be quiet," Kal replied.

"I would," the penguin said, sitting next to him. "But I am so smart that my mind will never stop – no matter how much I try. Since there is nothing here to invent, I have studied you in great depth and now know everything about you."

"No, you don't," Kal said.

"You are the son of an aristocrat," Exekus said. "When you drank from your water bottle, you stuck out your pinkie finger – something they only teach in schools for aristocrats."

"Just stop," Kal said.

"I would if I could," the penguin said. "But I know how much you hated that school."

"How would you know?" the boy sighed.

"On both your feet, your big toe has curled inwards. This is from you wearing shoes too tight. Since your foot size is a twelve, larger than most boys at your school, they forced you to wear shoes that were size eleven, since anything bigger than that is considered abhorrent."

"You can stop there," Kal said.

"Why stop?" the penguin laughed. "Your voice has clearly posh undertones to it as much as you try to hide it. Your dialect is one of old Feplim, a truly aristocratic planet. Either that or Jindo Prime – both share the same language.

"They bullied you at your school as well. Your hair colour is a one in a million, a recessive allele in your bloodline dating back centuries. I imagine the other boys laughed at you for looking different. You have clearly gained some chubbiness over the last few months, a testament to past trauma. Too much cake? On Reftum they have amazing cakes. Hey, is that planet still around or did the… "

"Shut up!" Kal exclaimed, giving a hard stare at the penguin. "Why can't you just be quiet and stop snooping around other people's business?" He then stopped. "Go and count the grains of sand or something."

"I already have," Exekus said bluntly. There are about one million, two hundred thousand and forty-six grains in this section of the island. If we were to consider the entire island, then that would bring us up to…"

"Just stop," Kal said, his voice shaking slightly. He then discreetly wiped away a tear from the corner of his right eye.

"I made you cry?" Exekus asked. "I really have spent ten years away from humans or any other being to be precise; apart from that one crocodile six years ago. He taught me how to make tea, which I am grateful for. As for you, you seem to be showing extra signs of emotion – maybe because I plucked a nerve."

"Say another word and I shoot you!" Kal growled, pointing a gun at the penguin's head.

"No, you will not," the penguin said, brushing it to the side. "You are too emotional now, because I struck a chord, as musicians would say. I am the smartest being alive, and if anyone can help you with your problems, it is me." He then took a flipper and touched his chin. "I know you hate life – that you have no one to talk to about anything, except the digital voice in your ship, but it hardly counts."

Kal said nothing.

"Your hair looks terrible by the way," the penguin said. "It looks like you were the cleaner after a massacre and took the blood-soaked mob and glued it to your head. Or that you saw a mushroom for the first time and then decided you wanted to look like one. When was the last time you used a hairbrush?" The penguin stopped. "In all honesty, you are a terrible bounty hunter. I could list all the many reasons why, but judging by your 'I hate you' eyes, I'm just going to cut to the chase. Forget being a bounty

The Beast Known as Terros

hunter. Why don't you consider doing something else with your life?"

"Like what?" Kal murmured.

"Just lay low," the penguin said. "Ninety two percent of farmers say they have no stress. But the source of that claim is a bit of a fishy guy. But forgetting that, go and be a farmer or plant trees. You don't need to pretend to be someone you are not."

Kal opened his mouth to talk.

"Kaloro Eramund Secant V," he sighed. "Don't ask me how I figured out your full name. You are a good person. Bounty hunters *aren't* good people. Just look at that wolf who tried popping my head off with his claws. I can still feel it," he laughed. "You are not a bad person. You might be for all I know, but based on my approximate, no *accurate* assumptions, I can say that…"

The boy started sobbing, more loudly this time.

"Hey. I didn't mean to make you cry. Actually I wanted you to rethink your life, which does result in tears for ninety-five percent of people, but that wasn't my intention. The stuff I said about your hair was a joke. It is very pretty in fact and accentuates your features. Okay, that is pushing it a bit."

"I just want to be happy," the boy cried. "I hate this planet. I hate you. I hate this job."

"You hate me? I am not entirely surprised by that fact. My own people hate me, which is why they banished me for no reason. In fact, I did try and wipe out the rest of the planet, which is most likely why they wanted me gone, but hey, I did it for good intentions. The penguin empire could have prospered."

Kal kept on crying.

"I'm not helping, am I?" the penguin sulked. "I could never have kids. Too much emotion. Just don't be emotional, that is what I say. It is a chemical in the head, not anything of actual substance, so you can just ignore it. How old are you, boy?"

"Seventeen," he mumbled.

"Huh?" the penguin gawped. "You are far too young to be doing what you are doing. And nowhere near mature enough. Do you want to be twenty-seven? I can give you an aging serum. Should mature you as well, and you can grow a proper beard. It's the same serum I use to stay young, just reverse the polarity."

"I don't want to be twenty-seven. I just want you to be…"

"To be quiet?" the penguin said. "Yes, you have told me that about eighteen hundred times – or one thousand eight hundred if you use that numbering convention; never really did understand the difference in…"

Kal picked up the small log he was sitting on and swung it through the air, smacking the head of the penguin. There was a large crack and smack noise and the animal plopped onto the floor, completely knocked out. "Did I just kill him?" he asked, grabbing the animal and shaking him. "No!" he shouted. "It was supposed to be a gentle hit!" Fortunately, he could just about hear the bird sparsely breathing.

Out of nowhere, from the thinness of reality a humming noise started and a blue wall appeared, rumbling as it did so, creating sparks of purple. Out from the hole spawned a black silhouette that grew by the second. It was a large animal that was white in colour, with a thick mane and muscular physique.

The Beast Known as Terros

"Oh, I..." Kal stuttered, rapidly wiping his tears away.

"Kal Secant?" the animal asked, his voice deep and rough.

"That's me," the boy said. "Here is the bounty. He may look dead, but he's just knocked out,"

The beast nodded and picked up the penguin with ease. As he was carrying away the animal into the colourful portal, he remembered to ask more questions. "Are you Narthelus? Just wanted to check that you aren't some random person after the bounty."

"I am Terros," the animal said. "I was sent here by Narth."

"Terros?" Kal asked, wondering where he had heard the name before. "Terros? As in..." he pulled out his gun and shot the animal. This was the Gedrul with the hefty bounty on his head. He could take him to the Pirate King and then...

The beast growled, mildly wounded by the attack. "What was that for?" he called out, baring his claws.

Kal then realised he had shot the person who was going to pay him one million Bonku for the penguin. Had he just lost out on making a bunch of money and getting off world? He did not find out the answer, for the hulking beast threw a punch at his face, potentially breaking his nose and putting him to sleep.

Chapter 19: Construction

"Which one is Exekus?" Zemu asked, pointing at the two beings that Terros held. One, a small looking penguin that was fast asleep. The other, a boy with bright red hair, that was also deeply dormant.

"Exekus is a penguin, dummy," Gides sighed.

"Another human?" Rett asked, standing up. "Is he flesh and blood," he asked, taking the boy from Terros and dragging him onto a table. "He's a heavy one," he let out.

"So, who is he?" Zemu asked. "Is he Exekus?"

"Does he look like a penguin?" Gides hissed.

"What's a penguin?" Zemu shrugged.

Rett then started looking at the boy, lifting open an eyelid. "He seems like a human, but so did I."

"How do we check?" Gides asked.

"The good old-fashioned way," Rett replied, taking a knife and walking over to him.

"Wait!" Narth shouted. "He brought us Exekus. So he must be Kal Secant. Please don't chop up our guest."

Rett dropped the knife allowing it to clatter on the ground.

"Secant?" Zemu asked. "As in House Secant?"

"What's that?" Gides asked.

"Klarence Secant was some aristocrat. Steel mill owner or something of the sort. An old guy who looked like he had never had fun in his life."

"How did you know him?" Gides inquired.

"Pirate King did some business with him once. I remember we parked the ship just outside his castle. From the quick look I got while cleaning the bathroom, I was in awe. There was… I'm not going to get into it. So, this must be Klarence's father."

"You mean son?" Gides replied. "He is younger than the 'old man' so cannot be his father."

"I thought humans reverse aged?" Zemu asked, shrugging.

Everyone looked at him blankly.

"I guess not then."

"Why was the Pirate King visiting a steel mill owner?" Gides asked.

"No idea," the dragon replied. "All I know is that it was one pretty house. I wonder if this boy will be able to take us there." He prodded him in the cheek with his index finger. "You alive?" he asked.

Kal's eyes slowly fluttered open as his breathing got louder. When he saw the dozen strange individuals, surrounding him, he jumped back in shock. There was a fox, a dragon, a penguin, another human and a big white beast. "A human?" he asked, looking back at the only one that looked anything like him.

"Robot," Rett said. "Well, I might as well be a human, but I was born in a lab."

"Clone?" Kal asked. "That's what we call it on my world. I swear artificial life is deemed illegal by the Federation." His surroundings came into focus and his memories came back to him.

"Long story," Rett said. "Why did you knock him out, Terros?" he asked.

"He tried to kill me," the hairy beast growled, staring at him with maniacal eyes.

Kal gulped, scratching his head. "I…" he let out. "I'm sorry. It's just that there is a big bounty on your head."

"Forget about that," Narth said. "You brought us *our* bounty, so take your one million Bonku and go."

"Why does he need that much money?" Zemu asked. "He is the son of Klarence Secant so surely…"

"How do you know that?" Kal snapped. "Did Exekus tell you?"

"Who is Exekus?" Zemu asked.

"Exekus is fast asleep," the fox replied.

"Is he dead?" the boy replied, remembering how he smacked his head with a log.

"He's okay," Narth said. "Now take your money and go. We can have it transferred to you or given in cash."

"Wait," the boy said. "How do you all know who I am? I tried to hide my identity."

"It literally says your name on your bounty form," Narth said. "Are you even a proper bounty hunter? Your hair-colour makes you stand out a mile away."

"Maybe I should dye it," he said, touching his tousled hair. "That way no one can find out."

"Do it purple," Zemu said.

The fox nudged him hard. "Do you ever have anything useful to say?"

"Just trying to lighten up the mood?" the purple reptile said, raising his hands in surrender. "Didn't realise making jokes was illegal now."

"Shut up, both of you!" scowled Rett. "How do you put up with such idiots?" he asked, looking sternly at Terros.

"I should be on my way," Kal said, standing up. "Need to get back to space."

"Wait!" boomed a voice, as a silhouette appeared on one of the walls. "Terros, I have given you time to prepare. Now we fight again!" A cloaked being stormed into the room, with a long black cape, robotic looking armour and a large gun. "Kal," he said, looking at the boy. "Fancy seeing you here, *alive*. Thanks for the ship, by the way."

Kal's heart stopped as he turned to look at the terrifying being – one he did not recognise. Was he the one who sniped him, the one responsible for him being stuck on this dreadful planet, the one who stole his ship, armour and money? "No!" he growled.

"I am here for Terros," the bounty hunter said. "The rest of you are just side quests."

"Who is he?" Gides asked, looking at Terros.

"The one who put you all to sleep," the beast grumbled, getting ready for round two. He took heavy damage the first time, but now he had the help of his entire team.

"How did you get into the Paradise Haven?" Narth asked.

The being did not answer, striding forward towards Terros.

Kal did not hesitate, jumping out of his seat and grabbing a gun. He shot Dahk seven times – all of which did nothing to him as his armour absorbed the shots. "You took everything," he screeched, jumping at him and throwing a punch.

"I don't care," the being replied, catching his fist. With his other arm he punched the boy in his round stomach, causing him to ripple on the floor in agony.

Dahk continued walking towards Terros.

Rett dashed towards the being, holding a large laser sword, swinging the heated blade at the being.

The bounty hunter raised an arm, absorbing the blow and then used his other hand to punch Rett in the chest, winding the human.

"Just us four left," Gides said. "We need to stick together."

Zemu ignored the fox, running forward.

"Zemu, get back!" Gides yelled, but the pirate was too far ahead.

"You think you can come here and take Terros?" Zemu asked, shooting at the being.

"I can do what I want," Dahk replied, gliding forwards and pushing the skinny pirate to the side with ease. He then continued towards Terros.

"Hey!" Zemu shouted, getting control of himself. "How dare you disregard me like that?!" the dragon jumped at the bounty hunter, but Dahk caught his arm, and held it tightly. "Wait," the pirate said.

A second later there was a loud crack, like thunder, and Zemu howled out, collapsing to the floor.

The Beast Known as Terros

"Minbots go!" Narth said, pressing a button on his wrist as a swarm of fly-sized drones flew in, buzzing around Dahk. The hunter then did something, and all the drones fell to the ground, instantly out of power.

The three remaining heroes pulled out guns and started firing.

Dahk raised a hand and pulled all three weapons towards him simultaneously.

"Magnetic technology?" Narth asked. "I have not seen that before."

"Stick together," Gides said. "Three of us should beat him."

"No," Dahk said. He held up a gun that made strange sounds, as the snout split into two, one pointed at Gides, and one pointed at Narth. Before they could do anything, the hunter pulled the trigger and two large balls of energy flew out, hitting them both and causing them to ripple on the floor. "Distractions are gone," he growled, looking at Terros.

"What do you want?" the beast exclaimed.

"The perfect hunt," Dahk hissed. "Now fight me again!"

Terros ran forwards, filled with rage, having witnessed all his friends be taken out like nothing. He threw his first punch which Dahk avoided, followed by a second. The beast then clenched his two hands together and smacked down the large ball of muscle at Dahk.

The hunter raised an arm and absorbed the entire hit.

"RRRR!!" Terros growled, his hands stinging from striking metal.

"Like my arm," Dahk said, raising his right fist which opened up to reveal a large blue canon. "Courtesy of your father, after he removed my real one." A large beam of shill blue energy burst out of the mechanical arm and hit Terros in the chest, causing him to cry out.

The beast refused to be pushed backwards.

The beam stopped a second later and Dahk's arm was smoking like a factory chimney.

"You knew my father?" Terros asked, curious and enraged.

"Yes. I knew him and I knew you. You were there when he did this to me."

The beast looked at the cloaked mechanical being in confusion.

"I was there when we captured him. I was young back then, but still craved the glory of the hunt. And that was the first hunt I lost; but I experienced a *true* battle. Too bad your father was long gone after I finished recovering, as was your entire village of adult males. So, when I learnt that there was still one alive, let alone the son of my nemesis, I made it my duty to hunt you. And it could not have been more disappointing."

Terros' mind darted back to when he was a cub, how the humans had tried taking him and his father had saved him. There was one with a helmet back then, who got cracked after his father beat him, and then there was the red paint.

"You!" the beast roared, pumping up his arms and biting hard.

"That's more like it," Dahk bellowed.

In a split-second Terros had leapt forwards and went for the bite, sinking his teeth into the man's robotic arm. He then extended his claws and started slashing at the man's chest, hoping to peel away at him until he was nothing.

Before he could land any real damage, he heard a high-pitched screech that rung. This dazed Terros, giving Dahk the opportunity to punch him hard a few times.

The Gedrul threw a strike and knocked into the man's robotic face, which was mostly intact, apart from a few new hair-line cracks. He then opened his jaw and bit into the man's helmet, sinking his teeth deep, until the cracking got louder, and shards of glass started to pop out.

This bounty hunter was a sick individual. Terros tensed his jaw hard as he brought his mouth closed. He did not care about killing this man one bit.

There was a hissing sound as Dahk pulled his head out from under the helmet, causing Terros to completely bite through it, crunching it into a mesh.

And there Dahk stood – his face finally revealed – a bulky head with pale skin and a big black beard.

"Impressive," the man said. "I finally brought the beast out of the beast. Now come at me again."

Terros swung arm after arm, but Dahk just moved through each attack. He then got his robotic arm and punched the beast across the face. "Part man, part machine," he said. "But also, part Kryx." He then pulled off his other glove to reveal a red, scaly hand with poignant claws. With minimal effort, he punched Terros with this arm, sending a flaming strike at him and knocking him onto the floor.

The beast looked up in terror as the insane hunter stood over him, his eyes blazing with actual fire. "You are still not ready," he let out. "Until next time," he said, walking off.

"No!" Terros growled, wanting to chase after him, but his body would not let him.

The aftermath of the battle was not a glamorous one. Zemu had his broken arm put into a sling. Terros sat on a chair, devoid of joy, holding an icepack to his stinging jaw. He had thought about his opponent. *Part Kryx*, was what Dahk had said. Terros had heard stories of the Kryx. They were a disgusting and terrifying race of bat-like monsters that served the Fire King Ebelos, ruler of Planet Glashu. So was Dahk part Kryx? How would that have worked?

Gides and Narth both sat aimlessly, feeling shame in being beaten so easily. And Kal, he walked around frantically.

"Why don't you leave?" Narth asked the boy.

"He has my ship. I can't just let him get away with that. The only reason I am on this stinking planet is because he shot me. I am going to quit being a bounty hunter, but before that, I need to get my revenge."

"I'd say leave now," the fox said gently. "Things are about to get messy on this planet."

"We can't let this minor defeat affect us," Narth said. "Building that robot is our priority. We have the core, the engineer and the parts. It is time to get to work. You staying or are you going?" the penguin asked Kal.

"Staying," the boy said. "I'll help you kill the Pirate King."

"What the ice happened here?" Marth called out, walking into the room filled with depressed looking individuals, debris and broken lights.

"Bounty hunter," Narth replied. "But it is dealt with."

"Alright. Exekus is awake. We are lucky Master Secant here didn't bash his brains to mush," he said, glaring at the boy.

"Good," Narth said, standing up.

"Now then, let's get to..." Marth then coughed hard, spluttering into his flipper. He coughed again, harder this time. "Sorry about that," he said, his voice raspy.

"I want to see Exekus," Kal said. "To apologise."

"There he is," the wise penguin smiled, taking off his breathing tube. "The boy who *almost* killed me."

"I'm sorry," Kal said. "I should not have..."

"Leave it," Exekus replied. "I went well over my boundaries."

"That you did," he smiled. "How are you feeling now?" he asked.

"Better than ever. Apparently, they want me to build a giant robot. They fished me out of my hole in the desert just to construct a basic mech? I could have just emailed the blueprints. Oh well. I should be able to do it in a day, then I can go back to inventing in my wasteland."

"Inventing?" Kal asked. "What have you been working on all these years?"

"Huh," the penguin let out. "Someone is finally showing interest about my work. Well, you see..." he then paused. "Actually, I'll let it be a surprise. Anyway, I assume this is the end of our little friendship. You know, for a penguin as smart as me; actually *hyperintelligent* is more fitting. Forget about that. What I want to say is that I might miss you, Kal. You are an interesting person and I have enjoyed mentally dissecting you. I hope you take joy in space and find something worth..."

"I'm staying," Kal said. "At least until we defeat the Pirate King. I found the hunter who stole my ship and I intend to take it back."

"Very well then," Exekus said. "I was going to give you a little present, but it can wait."

"Present?" Kal asked.

"Yes. While I have been lying here, I designed you a new suit – since I imagine your original one has been destroyed by a joyriding pirate. I got bored which is why I made it."

He handed a tablet over to him.

"It used to be my heartrate monitor, but I hacked it and installed a software and designed your suit. If you can get it to a 3D printer, you'll have it. Take a seat, I want to show you the schematics.

"Your last suit looked like bubble gum, according to some photos I found online, so I changed the colour scheme – going for a dark purple with black visor and blood red streaks. The helmet is of a cushioned design and there is a heads-up display on the inside. Furthermore, the weight is negligible and should not slow you down. Next are the in-built weapons which really excites me. I…"

"That's enough," Kal smiled. "That is very sweet of you, considering what I did to you. But I am giving up bounty hunting once I get my ship back. I thought about what you said, and I think the quiet life is for me."

"Huh, I did not expect that," the penguin said. "But I was expecting not to expect something about this encounter, so in a way I did predict it. Okay then, but you can still wear the armour to this final battle. Then you can just sell it on the black market and make some decent money. How does that sound?"

"Good. Do you need measurements?" he asked.

"Already taken them," the penguin replied. "Head circumference 42 inches, height 5 foot 10."

"So, I just need to take these schematics to a printer and it'll do all the work."

"Should do," Exekus said.

"Thank you," Kal said, leaving.

Zemu was sitting down, his arm uncomfortably in the sling. His whole body hurt, and he felt horrible. He had just wanted to help, and that bounty hunter had snapped his arm like paper. The others would always make fun of him for not being smart enough and he would constantly hold them back, being so skinny and pathetic. He could not even fly or flutter if he wanted, like most pirates.

The dragon then thought to his upbringing, popping out of his shell and then being taken in by a family. He was easily the slowest of his folks and the most disappointing. He would remember sitting in toilets, scrubbing the floors, working day and night, only to be belittled by his family. His siblings all made it to high ranks in the Pirate Guild, with his younger brother being a heavy soldier. And Zemu was stuck cleaning poo and peeling gum off cabin walls.

The dragon, using his left arm, opened his pager. He had removed the tracker, but still kept the device in case anything interesting came up. There was just the usual pirate notification about changes in ranking, food prices and more. But one message, hidden under the others, caught his eye. The sender, the Pirate King.

Zemu instantly opened it, seeing what his former leader had to say.

Dear Zemu,

You know I rarely ever message my pirates individually, but for you I made an exception. I know how you used to clean bathrooms as the ship janitor but have now converted to the opposition. In all honesty I would have done the same if I were you. It is my duty to oversee the wellbeing of all my children, so the fact that you were mistreated pains me. I will have your superiors punished for how you were spoken to.

As for you, my message is simple. Come back. You were a valued member of our team and your smile used to bring joy to those around you. I know you have sided with Terros and his band of misfits. Tell us where they are all residing and I will take you back with open arms, my child. You will be promoted to the rank of Enforcer and I will let you drink the Golden Rum, Just know that I care for you and those misfits would throw you under the starship whenever the chance may arise. Remember, they see you as a pirate, as scum of the world. I see you as my revered son and loyal follower. Whose side would you rather be on?

Zemu stopped reading and took a deep breath. "The Pirate King acknowledged me!" he cried out. "Me?!"

"All good?" a voice asked, stepping into the room.

The pirate quickly squeezed his teleprompter into his pocket, avoiding trouble. "Never better," he replied.

"How's the arm?" the fox asked, pointing at the sling. "He got you quite badly."

"I'm fine," the dragon laughed. "Like I said, never better."

"You need to be more careful," Gides sighed. "That monster could easily have torn your whole arm off."

"Well, he didn't."

"No, but in the battle, I told you not to advance. And still, you did. This injury is on you." he paused. "You know, if you did not ignore me, we could have actually won that fight. Now we are all battered and Terros has never looked more depressed."

"I heard about what happened to you," Zemu replied. "I heard you were taken out with a single shot! Now if anyone is pathetic; it's you."

"Now listen here, *pirate*," Gides hissed, leaning in. "I thought we could be friends, but based off your attitude that ain't happening. You don't listen to orders and that is something I cannot live with. You are in this group, so had better start acting like a team player. Understand? You were a nobody, a janitor, and we took you in - gave you a second chance. You were scum, working for that Pirate King, and as a token of our good will, Terros and I, well mainly me, took you in. If you want to be one of us, you had better start acting like it. So, join in, listen to orders and stop making dumb, stupid, stupid, *stupid* comments. Honestly, it is like you have the IQ of a two-year-old."

"What's IQ?" Zemu asked.

"You see!" Gides shouted, shoving the pirate back. "You are so blimming retarded. No wonder they kept you as a janitor for so many years. If I were the Pirate King, I would have just thrown you offboard to lighten up the ship." Gides started to walk away. "Annoy me again and I will personally throw you into orbit!"

When he was left alone, the pirate felt a twinge of sadness. *I thought he was my friend,* he wondered. Zemu took a deep breath and found a tear coming out from one of his eyes. *Do any of them like me?* he thought. Nobody had spoken to him or even consoled him after his arm was broken.

'You are nothing Zemu. Always have been and always will,' the words of his adopted father whispered in his ear on his first mission to space as janitor. The emotions came flooding back to him and his heart stiffened.

Terros is my friend, he thought, standing up and walking to the adjacent hallway. The beast was just sitting there, statue still and staring out into the distant sky, filled with immense clouds.

"Terros," Zemu chuckled. "You don't think I'm dumb? Do you?"

The beast remained in his statue position, not even moving.

"Do you?" the pirate asked again, his tongue feeling heavy.

Terros turned his head ever so slightly, looking at him directly for a moment before staring back out at the sky.

"Nice talk," the pirate mumbled, waddling off into the next room.

The whole team was in shambles. The one known as Rett was still coming to grips with his lack of humanity. Narth was busy walking around in circles. Marth was coughing every time Zemu saw him. Terros was having an existential crisis. The newbie Kal looked like he had never held a gun before in his life. And Gides was… Gides.

"This isn't going to work," the pirate mumbled, knowing that the team could not defeat the Pirate King if they even tried. So, he did the logical thing and went to the very person who treated him like he actually mattered. Zemu thought the decision was going to be hard, that he would have to think for ages, when in reality he barely thought about it. The Pirate King had his servitude.

And so Zemu made his way to his ship and got inside.

"Where to?" Delta asked as the pirate made himself comfortable.

"Take me to the jungle." the pirate said.

"I cannot fly you," Del replied.

"Then make yourself useful and help me fly this thing!" the dragon snapped.

"Bad day?" the computer asked. "Want to talk about it?"

"No," Zemu hissed. "Just take me home."

The flight took several hours. The pirate did not even speak once, just cycling through his thoughts and rekindling bad memories. Not once did he feel any sort of regret; for if he had stayed with the others, then they would have instantly lost to the Pirate King and died anyway. No robot could defeat such a powerful being. Zemu had heard the legends of the Pirate King when he was young – how he had bargained with and tricked the Fire King Ebelos, how he had destroyed an entire Federation warship with a single breath of fire, how he had stolen the Rune of Gratification from the ancient world of Kablirum. He was a legend through and through and Terros' crew of misfits had no chance against him.

Soon the scenery was filled with tall trees and Zemu smiled. He could see his old ship up above and could smell the rum of his pirate friends. The thought of the splendiferous Golden Rum then came to mind and his mouth started to water.

He landed the ship and stepped out into the open. "I can't believe I just did that!" he laughed, realising he had just done his first ever flight, with a broken arm at that. He was much more able and smart than his so-called friends gave him credit for.

"OI!" a pirate grouched, running at him with a gun. "Who are you?"

"Home sweet home," Zemu smiled. "I am here to see the Pirate King," he said, raising his chin.

"And I'm here to see the Grand Conciliator!" the pirate laughed. "Get lost."

Zemu pulled out his pager and showed them. "See," he said.

"Oh my," they said in unison, getting onto one knee. "We apologise for our transgression, oh great one."

"Just take me to the Pirate King," Zemu smiled.

Up and down and left and right,
They say I am always right,
That's cos I'm the Pirate King,
And I force my subjects thus to sing.
Now everyone join in!

Oh hey ho, merry ho,
We are pirates through and through.
We drink rum and we all know,
That singing is a what we do.

We all love the Pirate King,
He makes us so filthy rich.

That is why, we do sing,
Else we'll end up in a ditch!

We sing high, we sing low,
He shows us what to do and say,
For he roared us up from dough,
And we love him oh so every day.

Up and down and left and right,
We say that he is always right,
That is because he's the Pirate King,
And so we must a always sing.

"And stop!" the Pirate King chanted. "We have a visitor." The immense crowd of pirates then split in half, creating an aisle down the middle as Zemu was escorted to the Pirate King's throne.

Zemu's heart quickened, and his breaths fell short. He was now in the presence of the Pirate King and felt great awe and amazement, watching his mighty ruler sit upon his magnificent throne. Not to mention all the other pirates watched him in awe, actually looking at him for once and not disregarding his importance.

"Do my eyes deceive me?" the Pirate King bellowed. "Are you whom I see?"

"It is I, Zemu." The pirate said, kneeling down. "I betrayed you, and for that I am sorry."

The entire crowd gasped in unison, filling him with fear.

"But I return, and I bring intel on Terros' crew of… idiots."

"And for that you will be rewarded," the Pirate King said, leaning in. "What happened to your arm?" he asked. "What have they done to my precious child?"

"Erm," Zemu said. "It is my fault for being so skinny."

"No more," the Pirate King cried. "You shall be taken to the evolution chamber and will drink the Golden Rum!"

"Me?" Zemu asked.

"Yes, you. There is no one here half as brave and mighty as you, Zemu the courageous."

The pirate smiled. The next words spilled from his tongue with ease. "Terros and his friends are camping out in the Paradise Haven. They are building a giant robot to kill you."

"To kill me?" the Pirate King cried. "What heresy!"

"Please don't kill them though. They were nice to me, except the fox one. You can do what you want to him."

"Good," the Pirate King howled. "You shall be honoured for your service. Take him to the evolution chamber!"

Chapter 20: Epidemic

Kal's new suit felt perfect. It was just as Exekus had described – sleek, light and filled with weapons. Now he stood a fighting chance against that creature who stole his ship. He would have thanked Exekus for it, but the penguin was deep into the construction of the giant robot, having not slept for two days straight.

Kal removed his helmet and walked into the main hangar where the whole team was.

"Anyone seen Zemu?" Narth asked.

"Nope," Rett said. "Gides?"

"Erm…" the fox replied. "No."

"We plan without him then," Terros said.

"Nice suit," Rett said, nodding at Kal.

"Thanks," he replied. "Last ever mission. Time to go out with a bang."

"Where's Marth?" Rett then asked.

"In bed," Narthelus replied. "He said he's feeling under the weather today." Narth then spoke again. "Anyway, here's the plan. We get a ship and we fly over the jungle. Then Terros jumps down with Gides, and they challenge the Pirate King. If Zemu is correct, then the lizard will allow us the fight, which is when we deploy the mech from above. Exekus will pilot the robot and kill the Pirate King."

"How do we know we can trust him?" Gides asked.

"He is okay," Kal said. "Trust me."

"And how do we trust you?" Gides demanded.

"He is a good one," Rett said. "And you trust me, don't you…"

"Focus!" Terros growled.

Narth then spoke again. "Exekus will defeat the Pirate King in combat and become the new Pirate King. Then he will hand over the reins to Zemu and they can all go off world and do their own thing. Then Terros gets his people back and the Paradise Haven is rid of pirate interference. Then we can all enjoy life and hopefully never see one another again. Terros will be with his people, Exekus can go back to the desert, Marth and I will continue building the rebellion, Gides can return to stealing cars and Kal can enjoy space. No idea what you want to do with life, Rett. The rebellion could do with someone like you."

"Maybe," the man said. "But one step at a time. First, we need that robot."

"How's Exekus getting along with that machine?" Terros asked.

"It'll be done tomorrow morning," a voice said as a door opened. In walked the penguin, wearing goggles over his eyes. But I think I might need more workers."

"Why?" Narth asked.

"They all got sick," Exekus said.

Later, the group watched through a large glass window as there was a row of beds, all filled with penguins. They had oxygen masks strapped onto their faces and there was a lot of beeping.

"Very strange," Rett said. "Maybe there was some sort of radiation coming out of the core and it has made all the penguins working on the mech sick?"

"I told them to go to a *real* hospital," Exekus sighed. "They are using up unnecessary space here."

"That's a bit harsh," Gides replied. "And how do we know you aren't sick. You've been in that room the most."

"Because I am enhanced," Exekus replied. "No mere disease can harm me. Now, if you'll excuse me, I would like to get back to that machine. But since I am low on manpower, I will need a batch of droids."

"Droids?" Rett asked.

"A thousand drones ought to do," Exekus smiled. "Now if you'll excuse me, I need to..." Exekus stopped and coughed into the air.

Everyone darted back from him as quickly as possible.

"Ha!" the penguin laughed. "Surprised you fell for that one," he said, returning to his lab where he would continue construction on the robot.

The rebellion of penguins had all left the facility and went to proper hospitals in the Paradise Haven where they would be saved, hopefully. Narth was concerned about the life of his comrades and most importantly his brother. But in the moment, he needed to focus on the mission regarding the Pirate King.

Exekus had been hard at work, taking on the task of construction single handedly and refusing anyone else from stepping in.

Nobody had seen or heard from Zemu which got everyone worried. The ship they had was gone, so they assumed the dragon had taken it. Where to exactly, they were not sure.

Terros and Kal spent a lot of time training, with the grizzled beast teaching the bounty hunter the basics of combat – something he had never truly learnt.

"My shipment is here!" Exekus called out as the lift to their bunker roared into motion. As it opened, a thousand small boxes flew in, landing at Exekus' feet. They then started opening up to reveal small droids, that were light and skeletal. "Everyone, meet my construction team."

Terros looked in confusion as almost one thousand robots had arrived and were following Exekus, a mini army. The beast then wondered if they could be used in the fight against the Pirate King.

"We will be done by the morrow," Exekus said. "Get your team ready to drop in."

Terros nodded and a smile crossed his face. The time had come for war.

The crew suited up soon enough. They were all too big for penguin outfits, so Narth had to tailor make them. They all had black tactical outfits with masks and goggles that had utility belts with weapons, tasers and more. They got ready, leaving one suit on the floor, unused. One with holes in the back for wings.

"Should we just leave Zemu's suit here?" Narth asked. "What if he comes back?"

"He isn't," Gides mumbled. "He's gone for good."

In a flash of anger, Terros turned around and picked up the fox by his clothes and slammed him into the wall, bringing his teeth close to the slimy animal. "What did you do?" he growled.

Gides was not even phased. "I did nothing!" he spat back. "May have said a few things, but nothing he did not already know."

Terros tightened his grip. "What did you say?!"

"Stop!" Narth called out. "We are about to go to war! There is no time for your petty squabbles. Gides clearly stepped out of line and now we are a man down."

"We can adapt and evolve," Kal said.

"Exactly," Narth replied. "I got into contact with the new rulers of the human kingdom. The freed animals won the battle and took the land for themselves. They should be lending us a helping hand since we lost a lot of the penguin resistance."

Terros dropped Gides to the ground. "So, this is the end. Our final battle. And then we never see each other again. Good riddance."

The next morning, the group was in a spaceship, hovering over the jungle. They were all ready to act. Behind them was a much larger ship, piloted by Exekus and filled with the massive robot that he had been building. Terros had not seen it himself, but Narth had, and told the beast that it was most impressive.

"Remember the plan," Narth said, putting on his helmet that fit snuggly over his beak. "We land by the throne and then Terros challenges the Pirate King. The rest of us are just there to protect him."

Terros' heart was beating fast. The whole crew put on their helmets, but he refused to do so. Strapped to his back he had a vibro-hammer - a weapon he and Narth had both designed, a large hammer with in-built thrusters to make it swing faster and with a concussion blast that it would give off on impact. Hopefully he would not need to use it.

However, as much as the beast was thinking about this mission, and how he was going to rescue his people, he could not help but think back to the males of his tribe who had disappeared into the expanses of space. He still could not justify why they would make such a selfish decision as that. Would he tell Aunt Tirra that her husband was alive out there?

"Here goes!" Rett called out as the ground of the hangar opened up, revealing the harsh winds and the deep green below. The man was the first to jump, zooming off into the jungle.

"Me next," Kal called out, diving down and screaming as he fell.

Fear started to build in Terros' heart. Would he be too heavy for the parachute?

"See you down there, boys," Narth said, jumping off, and leaving just Terros and Gides.

"I'm sorry, Terros," Gides said. "I outspoke to Zemu and…"

"It's over," the beast grunted. "Just don't die out there."

The fox then jumped and disappeared.

"Here goes," Terros said, leaping down below, feeling the wind slap against his face as his mane was pushed back by the air. His heart was racing, and his stomach was tingling. Yet despite this, he had already adjusted after a few seconds, beginning to enjoy the ride as he dove down.

In the distance was the Pirate King, sitting upon his throne, with hundreds, if not thousands of pirates surrounding him, small purple dots.

"What are they all doing here?" Terros wondered aloud.

As they got closer to the ground, the Pirate King looked at him and did not even flinch. "Open fire!" he bellowed, as suddenly canons on the floor started spitting out ammunition, already aimed upwards.

Dozens of rounds were shot per second. Terros did what he could, trying to dodge as many as physically possible. In the distance, his crew was having the same issue, with a hole being shot through Narth's parachute, causing him to fall and land safely in a tree.

A shot hit Kal, but his suit absorbed the hit.

As for the others, they were frantically trying to dodge everything.

"SQWAWK!" came a harsh caw as shadowed beings flew at the diving heroes with flashing speeds. Winged birds dove at them and picked them off one by one, getting rid of the non-infected penguin backup they had within seconds, just leaving the core members of the group. These birds had great white wings, were wearing armour and held large guns.

"Not these guys again!" Rett called out, wrestling with one of the Tizi, mid-air.

One of them came for Terros, but the beast pulled his hammer free and swung it, smacking the winged creature to the ground below. Then he pulled at his parachute and landed on the ground, tumbling in the grass and standing before the Pirate King, and feeling the terror of his mighty flying throne. He took a split-second to appreciate the cleanliness of his landing.

"Kill him!" the Pirate King roared, almost ripping everyone's ears apart. They had all successfully landed but found themselves surrounded by hundreds and hundreds of bloodthirsty pirate dragons. They would not last more than ten seconds.

"Wait!" Terros called out.

The pirates did not stop, inching closer and closer.

"I challenge you, Pirate King to one-on-one combat!"

"Stop!" the dragon yelled at his subjects and they all halted in their steps. "He has challenged me," he said monotonically, sounding completely unsurprised. "All of you get back so I can face the opponent."

"I select Exekus Imporius to fight on my behalf," Terros said, pointing upwards.

Upon saying this, a large boulder fell from the sky, its edges gleaming in fire. The metal ball then unravelled, revealing itself, as it landed on the ground, slamming its knuckles into the mud and sent a shockwave outwards. The large mech then stood up, revealing how big it was – slightly shorter than the Pirate King. It was white and gold, with small accents of sand green littered throughout. Each and every limb was sleek and bulky, looking like it had taken years to build, when in reality, Exekus had spent no more than a few days on it. In one hand was a large golden sword, almost the length of the entire village where they stood. On the other arm, mounted, was a canon, a massive gatling gun.

The head was small with niche golden horns and within it was the cockpit where Exekus sat, through so-called 'unbreakable glass'. He was surrounded by buttons and lights and his flipper-hands were plugged into large gloves that controlled the limbs.

"Neat mech," the Pirate King said. "Will be a waste of metal once I annihilate it."

"Let's see," Exekus replied through a loudspeaker.

"All of you get back!" the Pirate King shouted again, breathing in heavily. He pushed forwards and planted his immense feet onto the soil and let out a massive roar, pushing everyone away.

"He walks!" someone shouted.

"He walks!" cheered another.

"What's going on?" Kal asked.

"The Pirate King never gets up," Narth said. "This is considered to be a momentous occasion."

"Terros, when I kill this mech, you and your friends die. Understand?"

The beast nodded. He trusted everything now to Exekus.

"Good!" the massive creature howled. "You all have immunity then. And all *my* men are immune until after this battle." The dragon paused. "General Zemu! Watch over these misfits!"

Terros' ears pricked at the mention of that name. He then watched as a large object flew over and soared through the air with majesty and landed on the floor gracefully. He then smiled and bared his teeth, while also pumping out his long and muscular arms.

"Like the upgrade," Zemu snarled, his voice deep and gravelly.

"What have you done?" Gides asked.

"Only made myself formidable," the tall purple reptile said, picking up the fox with ease. As he held him in the air, his long tail with a sharp spike, raised off the ground and glided against the fox's cheek. "You said I was a nobody!" he spat. "Now I am someone!"

"I…" Gides let out. "I did not mean…"

"*When* the mech gets destroyed, I will kill you myself," Zemu growled, throwing the fox along the floor.

Terros looked at his old friend, completely speechless. How had he let something so nasty happen to him? And that explained how the Pirate King knew to expect them; Zemu was the snitch.

"Huh," Zemu laughed. "I'm not so scared of you anymore Terros," he said, towering over the beast. "Maybe now you will actually pay attention to me."

The beast wanted to snarl back, but remained composed and put on his intimidating expression, not even blinking.

"Battle commencing in three!" called out a pirate holding a speaker.

"I look forward to killing you all!" Zemu hissed.

"Two!"

Exekus rolled the fingers of the robot one by one, into a solid, golden fist.

"One!" A horn then blared out and the robot hurled a right hook, connecting it with the dragon's head and smacking it to the side. The strike was hard and sent out a large shockwave billowing out in all directions with a ring of wind. The robot then took its left hand and grabbed the neck of the monster, tensing its fingers around its scaled flesh. A loud humming noise began as the ground began to shake. From the hand that was doing the choking, a canon shot out a beam of laser into the dragon's neck.

"AARGH!" the Pirate King called out.

The robot used his free hand to start punching the dragon's trapped head, thumping his face.

The Pirate King tried hitting the robot with his arms that were scrawny when relative to the rest of his body. Nothing was happening.

Exekus laughed through the speakers as he struck the dragon over and over until it was dazed. Then he unsheathed his mile-long sword from its holster and prepared to decapitate the beast.

Terros nodded. It had all come down to this. All the adventuring, all the new people he had met, all the foes he had faced off against: Frecto, Cornelius, Dahk, it all came down to this.

The Pirate King had a smile on his face as his eyes glowed a sharp orange. As he opened his mouth to laugh, a cackling of flames echoed from inside him as a funnel of pure heat blasted out in a beam and hammered at the robot's chest, gnawing away at the metal and reducing it to mush.

The mech was forced to release his grip and step back, shaking the ground. Exekus yanked at the controls and the robot raised an arm to deflect the energy as best as possible.

After a few seconds of sheer chaos, the energy died down and the flames stopped spurting out from the Pirate King's mouth. A long gust of smoke followed, clouding the sky with ash and gnarly soot.

The robot had taken heavy damage from that, as large drops of molten metal dripped from his body and splashed onto the ground, instantly singeing any grass. The being could only take one or two more hits like that before it would be fried.

"I've not had to use my breath in a while," the Pirate King gagged, taking his hand and thumping his own chest emphatically. "Nasty on the throat." He stepped forwards, vibrating the trees and jumped up, fanning out his enormous wings and pushing them back to create a wave of thrust.

The robot raised his hands to catch the dragon, but it was too fast – knocking it backwards with unrecordable amounts of momentum. The gears in its heals tried stabilising as best as they could, but the machine was knocked over and crashed onto the crowd.

As this happened, hundreds of pirates ran to the side to avoid being squashed. None were, but the shockwave did knock over a dozen or so.

"I am the Pirate King!" he screamed. "They sing my name now, and they shall sing it always!" he knelt on top of the robot and used his claws to start peeling away at the cockpit – first tearing the head off with ease before snapping the joining wires. Then he started punching the glass, with large amounts of force.

"Come on Exekus," Kal whispered into his comms.

"Get back," Exekus replied through static. "This next bit is going to be beautiful."

There was a loud sound as steam gushed from the robot's arm and then the fist shot off – a large meteor of metal that flew and smacked the Pirate King in the face and tore out a tooth that hurtled across the jungle and wedged into the ground – being the size of a small hill. Meanwhile the fist flew off into the sky.

Exekus took the opportunity to bring the metal behemoth back up, pushing the Pirate King off him. Now he had regained his footing, but was missing a hand – a worthy trade.

"Ha!" the Pirate King laughed, his spit raining down and causing a sticky shower over everyone. "That barely…"

He did not get a chance to respond as the robot aimed his gatling gun and started firing – shooting a dozen chunky bullets per second that pelted the Pirate King and started grazing him very quickly. When the spray finished and the dragon was dazed, Exekus formed another fist and sent a punch forwards.

The Pirate King smiled, his river-long mouth opening to show his gargantuan teeth and whale-like tongue. The creature ducked the punch and then surged forwards, biting the neck of the robot, where Exekus sat. His teeth sunk into the metal, and he started chewing away.

"No," Terros growled, tightening his fists and wishing from the bottom of his heart that somehow the penguin would be able to outsmart his opposition.

The dragon lurched his head backwards, tearing off metal and glass and spraying it everywhere, along with squirts of purple power juice.

The beast known as Terros could see that Exekus was still there, piloting the machine, but exposed now and sweat dribbled down his silky flabber.

"Crunchy!" the Pirate King gnarled, taking steps to the side.

The robot raised his arms to defend himself, but that did not do much.

The Pirate King used his tail and wrapped it around a tree, plucking it from the ground and tearing its roots up. Mud was showered over all the spectators. "Ha!" he laughed, holding the bark with his lizardy hands and then snapping it in half. "You did good," he smiled. "But not good *enough*."

The being threw one trunk into the knee of the mech, tearing through it. This caused the tower-like machine to wobble, which gave the Pirate King his next opportunity. He threw the other half directly at the cockpit, hurtling it through the air.

The robot was far too slow to block, and the trunk snapped through the fuselage, drilling through the cockpit.

"No!" Terros roared.

"EXEKUS!" Kal cried out.

The robot then started to wobble immensely.

"Boop," the Pirate King said, gently tapping the machine with the very tip of a claw and causing it to fall backwards.

The pirates all ran to the side, trying to avoid the collapsing titan. Some were not so lucky.

"And so it ends!" the Pirate King laughed. "Kill them all."

As his tongue was still moving, Zemu did not hesitate. He jumped forwards and grabbed Gides, flying across the ground and grinding the fox into the soil as he flew.

Kal pulled on his helmet and started zapping at the pirates. But they were in their thousands and showed no signs of stopping.

Zemu was tearing away at his former fox friend, landing blow after blow. "SKRRT!" he shrieked into the sky as he continued battering him.

Terros ran over, pulling the hammer off his back and swinging it into Zemu. A large shockwave blasted out as he was hit.

The Beast Known as Terros

"A fair fight," the pirate laughed, spitting onto the corpse of Gides. "Bring it on Terros," he cackled.

The beast knew this was once his friend. But that did not hold him back. He treated this pirate just like any other one.

While the two former friends were duelling, Narth and Rett were back-to-back, firing at dragons and trying to survive. Rett wielded a machine gun and Narthelus was using a plasma chain gun, firing hundreds of energy balls per minute.

Kal meanwhile had taken out a few enemies, but quickly became aware of the Pirate King-themed threat. Using his jetpack, he flew over to the cockpit of the dilapidated mech.

"Hurry up and kill them!" roared the Pirate King. "Else I will breathe fire and melt everyone!"

Kal still had a minor distaste for the smart penguin, but he still felt sad seeing him pass away like that. He had gone out in a senseless manner.

"Kal," came a faint voice.

His eyes widened as he saw that the penguin was still strapped in but had been hit by the side of the thrown tree and was slowly dying.

"Exekus!" he called out. "You must have a healing serum or something."

"I wish," he mumbled. "But this wound is far too great for that…" his voice trailed off, becoming increasingly croaky and hoarse.

The bounty hunter then unstrapped the penguin and gently picked him up and propped him against some metal. His hands became wet and sticky.

"Please don't die," he said.

"Ha!" the penguin laughed, but then instantly winced. "I cannot die," he groaned. "Well maybe this version of me will." The penguin then bit hard. "I have built a new body in the desert – he will take over. He has all my memories, except that of recent, for I have not been able to back them up since I were last there."

"So…"

"He, or should I say I, will not remember you. I will wake up in the vat, thinking it were a few days ago, with no memory of our current adventure."

"No," he sighed.

"Hehe," he let out. "I can never die. I have sent myself some notes, so he can continue where I left off. Now then, time to die…"

Kal looked at the penguin sombrely.

"I have done this five times before," the penguin smiled. "Relax…" he closed his eyes. "Wait, before I go. Get in the cockpit and finish off this fight."

"What?" Kal asked.

"It's penguin sized – but if you press the green button, it should adjust to your height."

"My height. Why mine?"

"Because I planned my death, silly…" the penguin said, taking his last breath. With a smile, he faded off.

Was he just blagging? Did the penguin know he was going to die? Did he purposely lose to the Pirate King? That was besides the point. The boy pressed the green button as was instructed and the insides started to morph. Even though there was a giant tree sticking out, it looked like no major parts were damaged. The boy then got into the cockpit and strapped himself in. He inserted his hands into the controlling gloves and then noticed some wires insert themselves into his suit, which made him realise that Exekus had designed his outfit to be compatible with the mech. "How bad can this be?" he laughed.

A few metres away, Terros and Zemu continued their duel. The beast would swing his large hammer and smack the pirate, but he would barely flinch from each attack.

"I told you," Zemu snapped. "I evolved. I drank the Golden Rum and now I am *perfect*!" He then swung his spiked tail, shooting it forwards like an arrow.

Without blinking, Terros caught his tail and then used it to swing Zemu to the side.

As this was happening, the whole jungle started to rumble. The sound of mechanical whirring was prevalent as metal grated against metal. Terros looked to see that the giant robot was slowly getting up, standing on its own two feet again. The being then grabbed the tree trunk and tore it out, giving a view of the one inside – Kal.

"More fish for the slaughter," the Pirate King laughed.

The mech looked a complete mess, cracked all over, missing a head and a hand, while also lacking any protective casing for the cockpit. One fire blast and Kal would have died. But the good news was, they still had a fighting chance against the Pirate King. For now, Terros had to focus on defeating Zemu.

"No!" the pirate spat, flying towards the Gedrul.

He was stopped by laser shots hitting him in the back. They did not wound him, but most certainly angered him.

"Zemu, I am sorry," Gides said, barely standing. "What I said to you was wrong."

The dragon flew over and prepared to stab him with his tail.

"I only hurt you because I saw too much of myself in you," the fox let out.

Zemu halted his attack, inches away from Gides' face.

"I know what it's like to be a failure. When my sister got into the Federation and I didn't, my whole world collapsed."

"I don't care," Zemu spat, raising his arm to make the kill.

"Nobody dies on my watch," Terros growled, grabbing Zemu by the neck and holding him in place. "Listen to him," he hissed, tightening his grip, but not hard enough to knock him out.

Up above, Kal was doing what he could. This was his first time piloting a robot of any sort and there was so much going on. It required a surprising amount of strength just to keep his hands steady. Fortunately, the controls were self-explanatory.

The Pirate King leapt forward, trying to bite him, but he dodged to the side, his feet feeling queasy from the sudden jolt.

Down below, the confrontation continued.

"I am sorry, Zemu," Gides said. "You really were my friend for those days we travelled together. When I grow old, I will remember this journey."

"That's *if* you grow old!" Zemu called out, his neck instantly heating up and his throat glowed orange.

As much as Terros squeezed, he could not stop what was coming next.

"Kill me," Gides let out. "At least that way you will be ending my turmoil."

There was a silence amidst the battle.

"What?" Zemu let out.

"I am so lonely," the fox said. "I have nothing to live for anymore. Just hurry up and end it."

At that moment, Zemu's eyes opened wide. "What have I done?" he let out. "I… I… NO!"

Slowly, Terros let go of the dragon, knowing it was now safe.

Zemu started taking steps backwards. "No," he said. "NO!" His eyes glowed red and he stared at his two oppositions. "IT IS TOO LATE!" he screamed.

Terros watched as the mech continued fighting the dragon. Now the Pirate King was stepping backwards, getting close to them.

"Zemu, watch out!" Gides called out.

"SHUT UP FOX!" the pirate yelled. "One more word and I'll slit your throat."

"Move!" Terros called out, seeing the Pirate King step back, with heavy thumping steps.

"All of you can…"

Zemu did not finish. The giant foot of the Pirate King went down, crushing him instantly.

Terros scrunched his face, feeling disgusted and grief-stricken simultaneously. Gides looked just as shocked.

"EURGH!" the Pirate King hissed. "I stepped on something squishy."

Kal pushed a lever and the mech went running forwards. With his only robot hand, he punched the dragon in the head.

"I admire your bravery!" the Pirate King snarled. "But it is time for you to die."

A humming noise began, starting off low and then picking up into a high, screeching pitch,

"Zemu," Gides sighed. "He's dead."

"He died the second he betrayed us," Terros said. "Now focus on the battle at hand."

"I can't," the fox said, wincing. "My leg is busted up."

"Then grab a gun and hop onto my back," the beast replied.

The fox nodded and jumped onto Terros, wielding one gun in each hand. Then when the Gedrul charged forward at pirates, he sat there, firing like a turret.

They both then stopped as they heard a great growling, frivolous sound. The veins on the Pirate King's neck were glowing brightly.

"Oh no!" Kal cried from within the mech. "This is how he kills me."

The Pirate King's mouth opened wide, and a pool of flames started to erupt out.

Kal Secant thought he could dodge out the way, but he did not want to risk it. And so, he unstrapped himself and used the mech's hand to grab himself and drop him to the floor. Then the beam of flames hit and melted away at the robot, incinerating its outer core until it was left as a pile of mechanical rubble.

Terros looked in dismay as the one chance they had at winning was completely obliterated.

The Pirate King then stormed over. "Poor misfits," he said. "I have waited for my pirates to kill you all, but they have taken oh so far too long. Lest I must smite you all with one fair blow." The villain then looked to the scraps that was the mech, and noticed a glowing orb, shimmering brightly. "Looks tasty," he said, picking it up, and not even being phased by the sheer amount of energy coming out of it. "Time for an upgrade, hehe!" he let out, grabbing the energy core and slamming it into his chest, causing him to howl out as his veins glowed gold. "AARGH!" the Pirate King shrieked as golden spikes ripped through his skin and covered his back and tail. His head then started to glow with energy. "Time to kill you all!" he screamed.

"Oh no," Terros cried.

Chapter 21: A Final Duel

"Sit still, Master Secant!" came a sharp voice.

"Must I?" the boy responded, looking into the mirror and seeing how ridiculous he was with all the white powder on his face and the black spot added to his chin. His hair had been pulled back, very tightly, into a ponytail and it was rock-hard and shiny from whatever goop had been poured over it. It was most uncomfortable. He looked across the ornate hall, filled with hundreds of books and a large chandelier that lay above, glistening with infinite crystals. Opposite him was a painter, an old and withered man, staring at him intensely as he captured every last detail onto his immense canvas.

Kal was so hungry, having barely eaten the past week – all in preparation for that painting. His nose was itchy and every time he tried to move, his tutor, the wicked Mrs Athtula, would snap.

The Beast Known as Terros

"Your father is getting an award tomorrow," the woman hissed, her voice high, mighty and lacking kindness. "This painting *must* be ready for then. It will be the most important day in your family's history, the most important day of *your* life."

"My life?" Kal asked.

"Yes," the woman exclaimed. "You are never going to do anything quite as extraordinary as your father has."

"Yes, Madam," Kal sighed as he continued to sit still.

Kal's eyes opened. He was covered in mud and could hear intense ringing. There were loud noises everywhere as purple dragons were in the thousands, buzzing through the sky like insects.

The boy crawled onto his knees, his matted hair falling in front of his eyes. He could smell burning everywhere and the bright light of lasers flooded the atmosphere.

The very ground was quaking, and he saw that the dragon known as the Pirate King was now glowing gold, white light bursting from his limbs as his eyes were now pale. He then looked into the distance and saw something coming closer, making him squint to get a better view. It got larger and the shape was more apparent – a flying diamond.

"Is that my ship?" Kal asked, struggling to see.

The ship that once belonged to Kal slowed to a halt, hovering over the ground. To the side, a hatch opened and out dropped a cloaked figure, his armour clanking as he hit the ground.

"Terros!" the being called out, pulling off his hood to reveal his helmet. "You are now ready for the next duel."

Kal was confused. What was the bounty hunter doing here and now? The Pirate King already had Terros, so the bounty was no longer available for claiming.

Terros looked over at Dahk who was staring down at him menacingly. The beast put the fox onto the ground and strode towards his enemy.

It was a moment of double trouble as the Pirate King stared at the ground, his spikes glowing sharply as the back of his open mouth starting to illuminate. He would kill everyone with a single breath.

"Stop!" Dahk called out to the Pirate King.

The dragon did not stop, getting ready to blow out pure energy.

Terros could do nothing, for no matter what cover he took, he would still die.

"STOP!" the bounty hunter yelled out, and this time the glowing ceased. "Let me kill Terros myself. That way you do not need to destroy your entire army."

"AND WHAT IF YOU FAIL?" the Pirate King boomed, his voice now frivolous with golden energy.

"I will not," Dahk replied. "And if I do, feel free to burn this place to the ground. But in the meantime, get your people out of the danger."

"HMMM!" the dragon wondered. "FINE! EVERYBODY STOP FIGHTING!" he called out, causing all the pirates to stop in their movements and look at their king, confused.

"NO MORE OF YOU NEED TO DIE!" His voice then soothed down. "All of you get back. This hunter here will kill the group." He paused to allow a wicked grin to creep onto his face. "And one more thing. Bring out *all* the Gedruls! Should Terros lose, I will incinerate his people as well." The dragon then took two steps backwards and sat on his hovering throne, causing the floating device to dip ever so slightly. "Kill away," he sighed.

Sweat dripped down Terros' face. He witnessed all the pirates depart, taking away their dead and leaving the field spotless. Then out from a hut, all the Gedruls were rounded up, all heavily chained and gagged. The sight of Aunt Tirra and her children looking skinny and withered filled Terros with rage. He could see the fear in her eyes, the desperation. And the cubs as well… The Pirate King had gone too far.

"Have fun," the Pirate King said to Dahk.

Terros looked around. Narth, Rett, Kal and Gides were all wounded, barely able to fight anymore.

"Stand aside," Dahk said to them. "I *just* want Terros."

The beast clenched his fists tightly and raised them in front of his face.

"May the best being win," Dahk nodded, pulling off his cloak. His armour was much shinier than their last fight, and he had gotten a new helmet.

Rather than be rampant as per his usual approach, Terros decided to play it safely and methodically. His friends and family's lives were at stake so he needed to be smart.

Dahk dashed forwards, swinging a knife at Terros' face.

This was an easy dodge, in which Terros simply tilted his head back.

"Smooth," Dahk said. He then went for the same attack again, faster this time, with a knife in either hand.

Left, right, left, down, up, Terros was saying in his head as he was morphing past slice after slice. His beast instinct was kicking in, monitoring his prey with absolute precision. He did this over and over until an opening was wide enough for him to strike. *Now,* he thought pulsing his right arm forwards and smacking Dahk in the chest. He then quickly retracted his arm and put up his defensive stance once more.

Dahk gagged, gliding backwards to catch his breath. Now he was weak.

The beast jumped forwards, bearing his claws and slashed the hunter across the face, leaving marks across his new helmet as small sparks of voltage spat out. Maximising his advantage, Terros pulled the hammer off his back and flicked a switch at the side, causing a pulse of sound to erupt, hitting Dahk and concussing him further. Then Terros, with a heave, swung the weapon into the side of the hunter's helmet, smashing him as there was a crunch.

Defensive again, he told himself, putting his hammer onto his back and raising his hands for protection.

Dahk, on the floor, peeled off his helmet, the side of his face cut from shards of metal. "Most impressive," he said as the lips of his wound closed and blood seeped no more. He stood up and ran his hands through his hair. "Round two," he said with a smile as his robotic arm started to morph. Metal spun and gears clanked until a canon had formed.

A spray of shots came towards Terros, who started running towards his enemy, ducking and rolling, avoiding every hit. One blast zoomed past his right eye and singed some of his mane, but that was the worst of the attacks. When he was close, he pounced onto Dahk, pushing him onto the ground with his strength. The hunter did resist, using his own power, but Terros was now unhinged, stopping at nothing to save his family.

The hunter aimed his canon at Terros, growling above him. The gun glowed bright as it was about to shoot.

But the beast was relentless, grabbing the metal and squeezing it tight, before pulling off the same move as his father, yanking the robotic arm off and tossing it to the side. The beast then went for the killing blow, but he felt heat as a large puff of energy knocked him up into the sky. He tumbled through mud and looked up, getting his bearings right once more.

The skin of Dahk's face had gone a dark red, monstrous and villainous, while his eyes glowed a sinister yellow. Red smoke started to fill where his missing arm was, and soon there was a new one in place, a bulky, monstrous limb with uneven spikes and skin of rock. His body lit aflame, and his glove melted off, revealing his other red arm. His then bit his teeth hard as large protrusions grew out of his back like trees. They then unveiled themselves and stretched out – enormous bat-like wings that fanned over him.

"What have you done to yourself?" Terros asked, looking in fear and terror.

"I hunt," Dahk said, his mouth spewing out flames and his organic wings started to ripple and flap, bringing him into the air. "Now give me the hunt I deserve, Terros Tarthanian Mrilmus!" the creature hissed, firing two beams of scorching fire at Terros.

There was no more playing defensive. Now Terros was running just to stay alive as fire blasts came and went, burning the grass and gnawing at his clothes.

"Now this is interesting!" the Pirate King bellowed from his seat.

The beast danced through the air, bending around blasts of fire, sweat accumulating in his fur and mane. There was not much more he could do of this.

Gides stood at the side, shaking. He was watching his friend be tortured alive and knew this could not go on for much longer. He was told not to interfere, which was better for him as his legs were shaking and his breaths got short and sharp.

"AARGH!" Terros growled as fire hit him in the chest. Dahk flew over and punched him across the face with his demonic hand.

Terros, Gides thought. *He's my friend. I have to intervene.* But he was so terrified that he could not move. "I…" he murmured. *I am no hero. I led Zemu to his demise and have never accumulated to anything. They rejected me from the Federation Academy. My sister disowned me. But…* Gides took a step forwards. He was not so sure why, but he did it.

Now step back, the voice in his head said as he wanted to be safe.

"No," he whispered, stepping forward again. "I will not be…" he said trembling; "a coward." The fox then unstrapped a gun from his back and opened fire on Dahk, blasting the creature multiple times.

The winged man lurched his neck to the side. "Who has the audacity to strike me!" he scowled.

While his neck was turned, Terros used the opportunity to strike him, smacking his face with his vibro-hammer.

"Stay back, Gides!" Terros called out, swinging his hammer back down again onto the creature.

"FOOLS!" he hissed, blasting out heat in all directions, knocking down Terros and Gides.

I can't do this, Gides said to himself as he lay on the floor, his shoulders shaking. *I can't.*

"Yes I can!" he screamed, peeling himself out of his cocoon and picking up a gun. "Die, fell creature!" he called out, firing at Dahk.

"You're not alone!" Rett bellowed, running onto the battlefield and firing at Dahk with his rifle.

"RRGH!" Dahk called out, getting up and flying towards them, with a large spike growing out of him that he would use to slice them all. But he did not get far as electric bolts travelled through him.

"Bingo!" Narth cried, pressing a button that activated the disc he had just stuck onto the monster.

Kal then started charging up his plasma canon, holding the trigger button until the blast got bigger and bigger until it would grow no further – an orb of pure energy.

The beast known as Terros stood up and punched Dahk into the air and then swung him down onto the ground, smacking his back onto the hard soil.

Kal let go and his blast zoomed through the air, the size of a large ball, disintegrating grass as it went.

"No," Dahk let out as the sphere of blue light hit him and he disappeared under a cloud of dust and energy.

The ground shook and the group of misfits looked at one another in joy.

"WHAT?" the Pirate King yelled. "You actually beat him? Oh well, it is time for me to finish off the job." The dragon then opened his mouth and got ready to incinerate them all with a single breath.

"WAIT!" clamoured out a voice. Uncrumpling himself, Dahk spread out his wings once more. "I am not yet done." His body was smoking, but his resolve remained true. The monster flapped his wings and flew over to Terros, picking him up by the chest, and then soared into the air, taking him high above everyone else.

When they were so high up into the clouds that the Pirate King was just a dot, Dahk started speaking in his gravelly voice. "All I need to do is drop you and you die."

"Do it then," Terros said, not daring to look down as his toes tingled. The wind was strong up there and he shivered from the cold. His heart felt weak in his chest and the beast came to terms with the fact that there was no surviving this.

"There is no honour in that," Dahk replied. "I brought you up here just to show you how much I have been holding back."

The beast's heart was thumping in his chest and he swallowed hard.

"I enjoyed this fight," Dahk said. "But know this – you still have *much* more training to do until we can have our perfect fight."

Terros was getting increasingly worried.

"Now then," Dahk said. "Let me fly you away from this dreaded place. That way the Pirate King will not kill you."

"What?" Terros asked.

"Your species has the potential to be the most powerful in the entire galaxy. I am not going to let you die this early on in your training arc."

"But…" Terros tried to say.

"The legends of old tell of the greatness of your species. I saw them carved into the walls of Ebelos' dungeons. You have all become too domestic as of recent millennia. For me to have the perfect hunt, I need to let you train. Now, where do I take you?"

"Back down," Terros said simply, an idea forming in his mind. "I will not abandon my people and friends."

"But the Pirate King will kill you?" Dahk responded.

"So be it. Then I will die by my people. And even if you take me away, I will return here and die trying to avenge my people. As long as the Pirate King lives, I die. Then you do not get your battle."

"Hmm," Dahk growled. "So, if the Pirate King is dead, then you are alive." The being blinked hard.

"Yes. And if I am alive, I will train relentlessly for our next fight, day and night until I am a warrior of true glory. Then we can fight again in a year. Where I will *beat* you."

"Beat me?" Dahk asked. "Impossible." He paused for a few seconds. "I would like to see that though." He then held on tightly to Terros and zoomed down towards the ground, before dropping him onto the grass, rather roughly.

"Terros!" Gides called out, rushing to his friend. "He didn't kill you?" he wondered.

"What is the meaning of this?" the Pirate King growled.

"Pirate King!" Dahk called out. "You are to spare Terros, his friends and his people."

"NEVER!" the Pirate King roared, the glowing core on his chest shrilling brightly as he opened his mouth to make the kill.

Dahk shut his eyes and flapped his wings, zooming forwards and tearing through flesh and blood, popping out the other side. The blood burnt off him as he did the deed.

The Pirate King's eyes were open in shock as his body plopped to the floor, off the throne, with a massive thud.

"Metatus is not going to be pleased," Dahk said, landing before Terros.

"Kill him!" the pirates shouted, running at Dahk.

"I killed your leader," the bounty hunter said. "Now I control all of you!"

They stopped running and looked at one another, confused.

"You will all get back onto your ship and leave this planet. Then you can find a new leader. That is my order!"

"Yes, Pirate King," they all said in unison, before scurrying off.

Terros could not comprehend what was going on.

"You have a lot of training to do, young Gedrul," Dahk replied, his skin returning to its normal colour and his monster arm fading away, returning to a stump. His wings folded in and disappeared, leaving the man to be just a man, naked apart from his torn shorts. "Good job today, all of you. I got the most thrilling battle of my life."

Kal looked at the being, remembering that it was his fault this had all happened to him.

"Oh, and Secant," Dahk added. "You can have your ship back," The man then sighed and limped off into the jungle, disappearing into the wildness.

Terros watched him vanish. How had a mortal man become so powerful and killed the Pirate King with such ease? He would not find out for a while.

Chapter 22: Sanctuary

The beast known as Terros did not hesitate to run over and cut his people free. First, he attended to the poor cubs and then he helped the elderly.

"Terros," Aunt Tirra smiled, enveloping her nephew in a hug. "I am so proud of you."

Terros squirmed free, not wanting to seem weak in front of his friends. Seeing her reminded him of Uncle Durren, all the way up in space. *Should I tell her?* He wondered.

The cubs were all jumping up and down in joy. By now all the pirates had scrammed from the jungle, standing atop the Pirate King's flying throne and then hovering up to their mothership.

The corpse of the giant dragon lay there, making Terros feel uncomfortable – as if he could awake at any second. There was no chance of that happening obviously, but the dragon still looked terrifying in death, with his eyes wide open. And what would they do with such a giant body?

They could not move it, and once it started decaying, it would leave a nasty smell, not to mention the millions of flies that would be feeding on it.

There was also the giant mech, smashed into pieces and scattered everywhere. The village was destroyed, trampled and the grass scorched. As much as Terros hated to admit it, his people needed somewhere else to live.

"Quite the fight," Rett laughed, wiping goo from his face. "Now then, where do we go from here?"

"My ship is here," Kal said, walking over to the diamond-shaped shuttle. "I will help you lot out, but then I am off."

"I appreciate the help," Terros said.

"Wait!" Aunt Tirra called out, walking over to the beast. "Since when did you start talking again?"

"You have missed a lot here, Mrs Tirra," Gides laughed. "Your nephew has gone on *quite* the adventure."

"Is that right?" Tirra asked, looking at Terros. "Well, you will have to tell me all about it. It's time someone told a new story to the kids."

"How do we repair this place?" Narth asked. "It looks…"

"We don't," Terros said. "The damage is too much."

"What do you suggest?" Tirra asked.

"We need to move," Terros replied. They needed somewhere safe for the cubs to grow up.

A horn blared in the distance. The engines of vehicles howled into the air. Out from the thicket of the jungle emerged a whole legion of trucks, all black and uniform in shape. From the front one emerged a Gedrul, tall, white and skinny, with eyes wide in joy.

"Rufus!" Terros called out.

His friend ran over, ecstatic to see all the Gedruls, his species he had not seen in almost a decade. From within the vehicles, dozens of other animals came out, all rescued from the human kingdom.

"We won the war," Rufus smiled. "We would have come earlier, but we only just finished the fight. The humans are long gone."

Terros smiled. "Then who rules that area?"

"I guess we do?" Rufus replied.

"Then we can all move there," Terros said with a smile. There would be defences and good facilities. If they put the core back in place, then it would be a haven for all the Gedruls and other displaced species.

"Rufus?" croaked an old voice from within the Gedruls.

"Mother?" Rufus called out, seeing the Ancient Nan slowly come forwards, leaning heavily on her stick.

The beast then ran towards her, giving her a hug.

"My son," she smiled, hugging him back. She then took a long look at him. "You have not been eating enough," she chuckled.

"Rufus was imprisoned there all this time?" Tirra asked.

"That is what I need to discuss with you," Terros said.

"Save it for later then," she replied. "Too much has happened this one day."

Two days later, the Gedruls had relocated to the human kingdom, populating the Gigafactory. The cubs were all enamoured by the vast structures, the lights and more. There was no sign of any human – for they had all been decommissioned or incinerated.

Rett never found the rest of his crew. He assumed they had all died in the war, after being brainwashed like Arnetta.

The group of misfits were sitting around a table, all enjoying a feast cooked for them by the Gedruls. It was their way of saying thank you for their hard work. A 'beast feast' was something spectacular, with long tables of food, meats of all different kinds, hundreds of fruits, vegetables and more. Aunt Tirra had used an electric oven for the first time in her life and it impressed her. Gone were the days of living in the wilderness. Now they could actually live civilised lives.

"This beats the fish in the Paradise Haven," Narthelus grinned, biting a salmon.

"And it beats the tinned food I had on the road," Rett laughed.

When Terros had finished eating, he got up and took his plate to the kitchen. He was most stuffed and felt great joy. When he saw Aunt Tirra there, his breath froze. *I need to tell her.*

"Did you like the food?" she asked.

"Yes," Terros replied. "It is time I told you that thing."

"Go ahead."

"They are alive. *All* of them."

"All of whom?" Tirra asked.

"Our people. Uncle Durren and the rest."

"What?" Tirra gasped, her eyes wide open. "How do you know?"

"Rufus told me that they all left. They fled to space."

"Space?" Tirra asked. "Why?"

"They abandoned us for some reason," Terros sighed. "But my uncle, your husband is alive, out there in the stars." He then noticed her eyes start to water. "I need to bring them back."

"Back?" Tirra asked. "How will…"

"Kal Secant," Terros said. "He is going back to space. I am going to go with him." The beast had only come up with this plan a day ago.

"But," Tirra replied. "It is dangerous out there."

"Our people are my priority," Terros said. "They would not have abandoned us without a good reason."

"But…"

"The cubs need their father. You are lonely without Uncle Durren." That was not the only thing. They needed the males to procreate. This meant that Terros' mission was to prevent the extinction of the Gedruls.

"Who will rule in your place?" Tirra asked.

"I would barely call myself a ruler. But in my leave, Rufus will take over." Rufus was of chief blood, since the Ancient Nan was the cousin of Terros' grandfather. And as for defences, the Gedruls had the finest human guns and technology to keep them safe. "Gides will help as well."

"Is the fox not going with you?" she asked.

"He wants to stay."

"Is this it?" Tirra asked. "You are going to leave?"

"I *will* return," Terros said.

"Does Kal know you are going with him?" Tirra asked. "He might not want your company."

"He does not know yet."

Kal was sitting in his ship, later that evening, playing around with the settings. In one hand he had a bag of crisps, something he had dearly missed. "Omicron are you there?" he asked. There was no response. Dahk had most likely uninstalled the artificial intelligence. He then analysed the hub screen, readjusting his settings.

Secant found himself writing a letter. To whom exactly, he was not sure. But he essentially spoke about the horrors of his time on that planet and warned nobody to ever go to Guinthra. He had been shot, stripped, almost eaten, abandoned in a desert, piloted a mech, and fought hundreds of dragons. That was more than enough to give him nightmares for the foreseeable future. He never truly did understand how he had survived being shot by Dahk. A bullet hole that big should have killed him.

"Boy," came a deep voice as Terros marched onto the ship, ducking on entry.

"Yes," Kal replied, spinning in his chair, wiping the crumbs from his face.

"I am going with you to space," Terros replied.

"What?" he asked, confused by what he was saying.

"I am going on an adventure – a hunt across the galaxy to find my people. Would you like to accompany me?"

Kal raised an eyebrow. "You are asking me, when it is my ship?"

"Yes or no," the beast said bluntly "Would you like to go on a voyage?"

"I…" Kal said, wondering what to say. He was done with bounty hunting and had not come up with what else to do with his life. He supposed that this adventure could be quite fun. And with Omicron gone, he needed someone else to keep him company. "Let's do it," he smiled.

"When are we leaving?" the beast demanded.

"In an hour?" the boy replied.

"Ok," Terros said. "Let me say goodbye to everyone." The Gedrul then took a step forward and snatched the bag of crisps, crunching it in his paws and reducing it to nothing but crumbs.

"Hey!" Kal protested.

"You are weak and fat," Terros said. "I am going to train you on this trip – turn you into a beast."

"But…"

"No buts. You will be a formidable fighter, starting now." With that said, he walked back outside and left the boy to himself.

"What have I just agreed to?" he asked himself. He then saw on his data pad that there was a red dot on it, a notification. *Who could this be from?*

A second later, he clicked on it. *From Klarence Secant,* it read. "Father?" he said aloud. "What's he..." he did not let himself think any further, deleting the message before he could even open it. "I'm done with that life," he sighed. "And besides, I'm going on an adventure," he said with a smile.

"I am leaving," Terros bluntly said to Narth, Rett and Gides.

"Where to?" Gides asked.

"Space. Going with Kal to find my people."

"Oh," Narth said. "That is quite unexpected."

"Yes," Terros replied. "Good luck with the Paradise Haven."

Terros did feel a twinge of sadness saying goodbye to his friends, but he tried very hard to hide it.

"I'm going to miss you, big fellow," Gides said, giving him a hug.

Terros then squeezed back, and the fox gagged.

"Try and get some muscles before I get back," Terros chuckled. "As for you two; be safe."

"We will," they said.

An hour later, Terros sat in a seat, next to Kal. They both wore space suits and were ready to go up into orbit. The beast was worried that his stomach would not be able to handle it.

"If it makes you feel better," the boy said, putting on his helmet. "The first jump to space is always the worst."

Chapter 23: A Protoplasmic Endeavour

Ever since he had been shot in the shoulder, Spyke saw no importance in leaving the desert and returning to his town. He was not surprised that Kal had shot him. In fact, he himself would have done the same thing.

The wolf succumbed to a lot of pain, but he had gotten up and explored the hole where Exekus Imporius resided. He had found a door that took him lower, and that led him to an elevator that went down and transported him to a workshop. Gone was the intense heat of the desert and sand, and instead there was cool fans blaring out and the wolf loved it. There were tables and on them were many ornate gadgets and colourful vials. One of them read 'healing liquid' so he took it. He did not know whether to drink it or pour it onto the wound, so he tried both. And then the blaster wound evaporated.

"Neat trick," the wolf grunted.

Spyke then spent some more time down there, going through everything he could find – drones, guns, colourful liquids and more. There were goggles that when he put them on allowed him to see through things, so he could gaze through walls and more.

The wolf knew there had to be more to the facility, so he started feeling for hollow walls, and soon discovered something underneath him – a place where the elevator would not go. When Spyke found a keypad, he tried a few combinations and failed. Annoyed, he used brute force to break through.

"Rabbits and bones!" he laughed as he fell through – into a large space that went on for ages. An entire hangar with tendrils, metal parts and more. There was a computer there and the wolf soon figured out that this was a car building station – evident from the racks of tyres, metal parts and more.

"Awesome!" he smiled, starting to press buttons on a computer and design his dream car. "How'd that small penguin get all this down here?" The wolf then went over and beyond, fussing over every small detail, trying to add as much of his own personal flavour as possible, putting spikes on the steering wheel, bumper and more.

Losing complete track of time, he went to sleep and returned to work some hours later. When he got hungry, he discovered a fridge filled with small tablets. Each one was enough to fill him up. He would eat five per meal.

"The Mean Machine!" Spyke cackled when he was done. The car was immensely large, making him climb up just to get to the door. There were spikes everywhere as expected and his name was embroidered into the gearstick. After spending time choosing the tyres, Spyke went for the ones with gold brimmed alloys.

The car was painted black with a grey wolf spayed onto the bonnet. Spyke was happy with his creation, but there was one thing missing. It was too perfect. He needed to weather it down, and the best way to do that was to give it a spin.

"Now how do I get this bad boy up there?" he wondered, stroking the fur on his chin.

He had finished building his car and now had been designing guns – rocket launchers with custom grips, snipers and more. He was going to become the best wanderer out there as well as the most stylish. The wolf had lost track of time and was not sure if he had been underground for a few days or a few weeks.

Walking around and exploring the facility further, the wolf's ears pricked up. The place was strange, but there had been no one else present – not even a robot. So, when he heard movement, he knew something was not right. A faint rustling came from behind a rocky wall. Spyke being Spyke, forced his fingers into the crevices and tore it open, walking through.

"What the…" he let out as he saw a row of tubes, filled with water and bubbling. They were all active and were flashing lights. Spyke walked up to them and peeked in, causing his eyes to widen. "No," he let out, looking left and right as fear started to cloud his mind.

Each and every tube was filled with a penguin – all different. They were breathing through tubes and were fast asleep, lying dormant in the bubbling water.

"What is this place?" he cried.

The penguin had boasted that he was the smartest being alive, but this facility was something else, a nightmarish one.

"Initiating Protocol Sapling!" came a robotic voice, infused into the rocky walls.

The glass of one of the pods then smashed and there was water and shards all over the place. Spyke jumped back, wanting to growl out in terror. He told himself he was not scared, but seeing a random penguin flutter on the ground did mess with his head.

"Evening, Spyke," the penguin said with a deep voice. "Huh, my new voice is kind of deep." The being then wriggled around. "New body, same old me," he added.

"Who the bone are you?" Spyke snapped, towering over the penguin.

"Me, Exekus. I know I look a bit different, but I did die after all, and a painful one at that. I have no memories of my final few days of life, but my previous self *did* send me some notes. He said the virus was a success and now we can move on to phase nine."

"Phase nine?" the wolf asked, not even bothering to ask how the penguin had built himself a new body.

"Come with me," the penguin said. "I could do with some muscle like yours." Exekus then touched his abdomen. "This body is quite fat. That's a shame."

"Where are we going?" Spyke asked.

"The Paradise Haven of course," Exekus laughed. "I need to pay the Parliament a visit."

"Parliament?"

"You'll see. If my calculations are correct, which they always are; seventy percent of the penguin population should be infected by now. Which means it is prime time for me to strike. Actually, yesterday was prime time, but my matters with Kal took a bit longer than expected.

"I never met Kal, you see, for my previous self never backed up his memories after leaving this place. So, all I know about the bounty hunter is a few notes. They say: red hair, fat, terrible bounty hunter, built him a new suit, smacked me in the head with a log. And there are a few notes about you."

"What does it say about me?" Spyke asked.

"I knew you were snooping around here this whole time. You built a cool car did you not? The thing is, that is stealing, so I will not permit you to leave with it – unless you do me a favour."

"I don't do favours for no-one," Spyke growled.

"Which means you do favours for everyone," Exekus laughed. "That's the thing about double negatives. Anyway, I need you to be my bodyguard when we go to the Paradise Haven."

"How are we getting there?" the wolf asked.

"Let's take your new truck for a spin."

A day later, they stood on the beach where the entrance to the Paradise Haven lay. The boat that took them across the sea was parked alongside them.

On the sand was a log and next to it was a drop of dried blood.

"This must be where Kal smacked my previous self!" Exekus laughed. He then rummaged around the sand and picked up a long strand of red hair, holding it up to the sky. "Brighter than I was expecting."

"Why am I even trusting you?" the wolf asked, folding his arms.

"Cool weapons. Actually, scrap that. The coolest!" he chuckled. "You want me as your friend, wolf. Trust me."

"So, this is the Paradise Haven?" Spyke replied, looking at the mediocre beach and occasional tree. "Isn't there supposed to be a portal?" he asked.

"Easy," Exekus said. "The rebellion has the codes to hack into this portal and open it from the outside. When I was working there, I snatched them for myself."

On the inside, Spyke gazed at the tall buildings, their tops disappearing in the clouds. Yet he could not help but notice that there were no lights on. The streets were filled with large bags of garbage, sprawled about. The stink was the worst – a mixture of vomit and sewage throughout. "This place ain't no haven."

"*Again* with the double negatives," Exekus sighed. "But yes, I see your point. This is what happens when a whole city gets hit with a non-curable virus."

"Virus?" Spyke asked. "How did that happen?"

"Me," Exekus laughed. "I knew it would be only a matter of time before I was recaptured and taken back to this awful place. So I injected myself with a deadly disease that spreads like wildfire and infects only penguins. My guess is that I infected 70% of my kind by now. Let's see what the Parliament has to say."

Spyke followed the insane penguin as they darted through streets, filled with coughing penguins and flooded water. They then went into a colossal building with many steps to get to the entrance. It had large pillars holding it up and there were statues of multiple penguins, all wearing long cloaks and armour – something that humoured the grizzled wolf.

Inside was deserted, with a handful of robots hovering about and that was it. But they were barely androids, being just boxes on wheels with two stiff arms.

"Welcome, my wolf friend, to the most heavily guarded location in the Paradise Haven!" Exekus called out, pointing at the empty hallway. "Now let's go and have a chat to the Parliament, or whatever is left of them."

Exekus then pushed open a large red and heavy door and walked into a vast room with tall seats that stretched into the infinite ceiling. The floor was mosaiced and the walls were all perfectly shined.

"Parliament!" Exekus exclaimed. He then smiled. "I see there are only five of you left," he said, craning his head up to see them.

"Kill he intruder!" someone shouted.

Two heavy armoured robots surrounded them, brandishing large swords that gleamed with red lightning.

"Boring," Exekus said, pressing a button on his wrist as the two robots lost any light in their eyes and failed to move any further, collapsing to the ground. "They forgot I designed these machines," he scoffed, gazing at the many empty thrones. "Gentlemen!" Exekus came again. "You may know me as your lead scientist. That is assuming you still remember me after my banishment."

"Exekus?" one of them asked, his seat lowering so that he was now in view – a penguin whose head looked so small when compared to his giant cloak that trapsed the whole way down his pillar-like throne.

"Exekus is dead," another said. "I had him killed five years ago."

"It was quite the painful death, I heard," Exekus replied. "But you forgot to check my facility for more bodies."

"What do you want?" another asked.

"Isn't it obvious? I crippled your entire kingdom in a few days with just a simple chemical."

"The virus was you?" one of them exclaimed, his voice long, drawn and old.

"Yessir," the scientist laughed. "I wanted to help build you robots to take over the world below – which, by the way, is *much* nicer than what you've brainwashed everyone into thinking it is. Regardless, I wanted to help you, and you *banished* me? Then you sent someone to kill me? Not cool."

"I am going to…" one tried saying.

"Do what?" Exekus laughed. "I am the smartest being alive and there is nothing you can do which I have not yet prepared for. Now then, the virus I made has a fifteen-day mortality effect. Which means there is only a matter of days before this entire kingdom drops dead. So, if you want to save your precious people, you will first have to hand over the reins of this world to me. Then I will cure everyone."

"Never!" one shouted. "This is utter blasphemy; a mere exiled commoner like yourself making pleas with us."

"You lot are the rulers," Exekus said. "The safety of these people are your concern. Have you seen the ruckus outside? There is nobody working for the electricity, water or garbage companies. Even if you find a cure within the next week, which you won't, then your society will have reached irreparable damage. Your currency is going to plummet in value and…"

"Shut up you *insolent* creature!" a being called out. "Say another word and I press this button and you fall – all the way down into the underworld."

"One big trapdoor," Exekus smiled. "You cheeky old politicians," he added with a pause. "Hand over the kingdom or you all…"

Exekus did not get a chance to finish as the ground opened up beneath him, a large white abyss of nothing. Exekus did not fall though and simply levitated where he stood.

"Jetpack," the scientist laughed. "That's the second time you've tried to kill me. I let you off the first time. Now you are not so lucky."

One of the council members reached to his side to grab a gun, but he did not finish. Spyke pulled his trigger and shot the penguin, ending him and knocking him off his podium to an audible 'clunk'.

"None of you care about your own people," Exekus sighed. "I told you that only I can save them, and you *still* want me dead? None of you deserve to be a ruler then." He turned to Spyke. "Kill them all. This is my kingdom now."

"Wait!" one squealed after the others had been killed, leaving just a solo penguin who was raising his hands and begging for mercy. "I'll give you everything you want. Whatever you desire – it's yours. Just please, spare me!"

Exekus smiled. "I can work with that."

Epilogue: The Core

Elsewhere in space, far from Planet Guinthra, was the warship known as the 'Pluribus', a ship so large that it put the Pirate King's mothership to shame. It was an immense vessel, capable of covering an entire continent in shadow.

A small vessel approached it, looking like a tadpole next to a giant shark. As the hangar doors at the side slid open, the small ship flew in through the airlock, before being sealed in by the metal gates. When the coast was clear and the vacuum of space was no longer a threat, the doors to this small ship opened and out walked a few beings.

Leading them was a reptilian general with harsh green skin and a long, teethed mouth. He wore black uniform that had been ironed to perfection and had an array of medals pinned by his breast. To either side of him were robots, with silver skin and wearing dark-blue militaristic uniform.

As he marched through the hallway, his black coattails dragged along the perfectly polished ground. He did not have to get too far before a floating metal orb appeared next to his head with a bright red eye, scanning him.

"He's alive," the crocodile general said to the flying droid. "Inform the Pale King."

"Arise!" someone shouted, and an electric volt boomed through his brain.

The being awoke, taking in his surroundings. Gone was the vast jungle and fields with tall trees and breezy air. Now he stood in a vast room with a throne in front of him. Behind that was a great window, showing the expanse of space, the never-ending void filled with sparkling dots.

"*KNEEL!*" a voice sounded in his head, so intense, heavy and sharp that he had no option but to follow, getting onto one knee and bowing his head. He could not remember his own name as he stared at the floor, watching as a drop of sweat trickled down his head and splashed to the ground. *Who am I?* he asked himself, unable to feel his legs, for they were fully metallic.

"So it actually worked," said a voice, rich and smooth, whole also echoing through the hall. "They brought you back from the brink of death. Now, raise your head."

As he said this, a cold metal touched the nameless one's chin, raising it up. He looked to see that a long metallic tentacle had stretched out and its origin was from the throne, shrouded in shadow. He could make out a long red, crimson cape that trickled down the stone chair like blood.

"Who are you?" he said, his voice trailing off. It sounded strange, with a mechanical hint to it, rustic and nasty.

"The Pale King," the man replied, standing up and out of the shadows, allowing his immense cloak to trapse the floor and cover his feet. He retracted his tentacle back from him and stepped down, until he was level with the nameless one. "You are Zemu, are you not?"

"I…" the nameless one replied, looking at his scaly and reptilian hands, now with sharp metal fingers. He tried to remember, but all he could see was that jungle. That dreaded jungle where… "I do not know."

"You are," the Pale King replied. "Your memories shall return in due course."

Now in the light, Zemu could make out the being – one of colourless skin that seemed almost translucent, with long white hair that flowed down his shoulders. He had a wide jaw and his eyes were a deep, glowing red. His body was one of cyber-metallic armour, dark grey in colour, sleekly designed with prominent pointed shoulders and a deep, blood red rumbling through.

"My true name is Metatus," the man said. "And you have had the honour of meeting me."

Zemu wanted to speak but his mind felt off – as if he were in some sort of dream state. *Who am I?* His thoughts then darted back to the jungle, amidst a battlefield with hundreds of flying creatures, and a large machine that touched the sky with its head.

"What are you?" the cyber-dragon asked.

"You will see," the giant man replied, standing at least two human feet taller than him.

"Why am I alive? Why do I exist?" Zemu gasped, his metal fingers trembling and his heart rate rapidly rising. More memories came into his head – one of a Pirate King, a large and glorious creature that was a fair and just ruler. Another vision was of a dire and disgusting beast with a white mane and large fangs.

Zemu's eyes widened as the painful memories came of lying helplessly in the grass, reaching out to his former friends. They left him for dead, celebrating after everything was over. They had forgotten him to rot as a corpse.

"Terros, Gides, I am sorry," he had said while bleeding out, stretching out a claw to them. But they turned their backs, laughing and jumping up and down in joy. Nobody even checked if he were alive. His mind then recalled being found by robots and scooped up, whisked away into space, where they put him on an operating table as a new jaw was given to him. His tattered and torn wings were replaced and his tail was fixed. No physical pain was remembered, just the emotional trauma of abandonment and betrayal.

"Ferux, or the Pirate King as you knew him, had an unforeseen death," the great being said. "Now there is a gaping hole in my empire and a struggle for power over the pirates has begun."

"Your empire?" Zemu asked.

"I control crime in this sector of the galaxy," Metatus spoke briskly. "I am the actual Pirate King. But silly names and titles have never appealed to me, so I rule from the shadows. The Grand Conciliator is corrupt, allowing me to worm in through the cracks of his authority. But while I have ambition and vast knowledge of the universe, I lack subordinates and smart underlings – hence why I resort to hiring doofus lackeys like Ferux and Cornelius Dalrethian, an artificial intelligence whom I prided myself in designing. Now they are both dead and I am most displeased. My control over Guintha is gone."

"What will you do now?" Zemu asked.

"I need you," Metatus said. "The pirates are travelling through space without a ruler, not knowing of my existence. You need to take over and become the new Pirate King."

Zemu felt strange as he started to hover in the air. He looked to see that a purple cloud of energy was around him, holding him tightly, before pulling him over to where Metatus stood. The dragon winced when he was so close, scared as to what the being might do.

A tentacle reached out from within the Pale King's cloak, a robotic arm with four claws on the end. It shot forwards and then clamped onto the side of Zemu's head.

"What are you doing?" the robot-dragon asked, now getting scared as a metal device was being inserted into him.

"I am uploading terabytes worth of knowledge into you – history of the cosmos, the lineage of the Conciliator, vast mathematical knowledge, fighting techniques from eight planets, fluency in sixteen different languages and most important of all; a part of me, so I can hear what you think at all times, and *if* you try to disobey me, I will *permanently* shut you down. Understood?"

Zemu wanted to respond, but his brain was whizzing. Information and numbers were filling in front of his eyes, flooding his vision and causing his ears to ring.

"Terros!" he called out from all the noise within his head. "I must have my revenge! He did this to me!"

"No," Metatus growled. "I have something much more exciting planned for him. Now, do as I say."

"Yes, Your Highness," Zemu replied, bowing down.

"Good," the grand being boomed. "Now go forth and rule, my Pirate King!"

Zemu then spread out his large and fanned wings, mechanical and deadly. He stood tall and embraced his robotic features, feeling pride before letting out a large shrill and epic roar. He had gotten what he had always wanted – importance.

Printed in Great Britain
by Amazon